Praise for the novels of Maureen McKade

"A very well-written book that will appeal to readers of romantic suspense." —*The Romance Readers Connection*

"An edge-of-your-seat romantic suspense, *Convictions* is a fantastic, fast-paced read. Maureen McKade has done a superior job in providing twists and turns that keep you on edge, until the end. A true romantic suspense with a blend of contemporary Western that will appeal to readers of all genres. Don't miss this one!" —*The Best Reviews*

"A fascinating romantic suspense thriller. . . . Fans will appreciate Maureen McKade's marvelous tale."

—*Midwest Book Review*

"Forgiveness and trust are key themes in this new tense and suspenseful story. McKade's characters are real, vibrant, and filled with contradictions. This is pure human drama."

—*Romantic Times* (four stars)

"Exciting, sexy, humorous, and a real page-turner are just a few of the words that describe this terrific story. Her characters are real and strong; the story moves along at a quick pace. Congratulations to Ms. McKade on writing a wonderful book." —*Romance Junkies*

"Exceptional romance certain to touch your heart . . . Absolutely wonderful . . . Warning: Keep a hanky handy."

—*New York Times* bestselling author Lorraine Heath

continued . . .

"Maureen McKade creates characters who step off the page and into hearts. I couldn't put down *A Reason to Live*. From the first page McKade's characters made me care for them. McKade shows the mark of a master storyteller by creating a world I've never been to and making me feel like I'm coming home as I turn the pages."

—*New York Times* bestselling author Jodi Thomas

"A story that will tear at your heart . . . Heated passion, fast pace, sizzling sexual tension."

—*Rendezvous*

"Watch out when sparks start to fly!"

—*Affaire de Coeur*

"Well done, uplifting, and enjoyable."

—*Rocky Mountain News*

"One of the must-read romances of the year!"

—*The Literary Times*

Berkley Sensation Titles by Maureen McKade

TO FIND YOU AGAIN
AROUSE SUSPICION
CONVICTIONS
A REASON TO LIVE
A REASON TO BELIEVE
A REASON TO SIN
WHERE THERE'S FIRE

Anthologies

HOW TO LASSO A COWBOY
(with Jodie Thomas, Patricia Potter, and Emily Carmichael)

WHERE THERE'S FIRE

MAUREEN McKADE

BERKLEY SENSATION, NEW YORK

THE BERKLEY PUBLISHING GROUP
Published by the Penguin Group
Penguin Group (USA) Inc.
375 Hudson Street, New York, New York 10014, USA
Penguin Group (Canada), 90 Eglinton Avenue East, Suite 700, Toronto, Ontario M4P 2Y3, Canada
(a division of Pearson Penguin Canada Inc.)
Penguin Books Ltd., 80 Strand, London WC2R 0RL, England
Penguin Group Ireland, 25 St. Stephen's Green, Dublin 2, Ireland (a division of Penguin Books Ltd.)
Penguin Group (Australia), 250 Camberwell Road, Camberwell, Victoria 3124, Australia
(a division of Pearson Australia Group Pty. Ltd.)
Penguin Books India Pvt. Ltd., 11 Community Centre, Panchsheel Park, New Delhi—110 017, India
Penguin Group (NZ), 67 Apollo Drive, Rosedale, North Shore 0632, New Zealand
(a division of Pearson New Zealand Ltd.)
Penguin Books (South Africa) (Pty.) Ltd., 24 Sturdee Avenue, Rosebank, Johannesburg 2196,
South Africa

Penguin Books Ltd., Registered Offices: 80 Strand, London WC2R 0RL, England

WHERE THERE'S FIRE

A Berkley Sensation Book / published by arrangement with the author

Cover photo of "Woman's Eyes" by Pando Hall/Getty Images; "Smoke" by PhotoLink/Getty Images; "Dockyard with Cranes at Dusk" by Ingolf Pompe/Getty Images.
Cover design by Annette Defex.

For information, address: The Berkley Publishing Group,
a division of Penguin Group (USA) Inc.,
375 Hudson Street, New York, New York 10014.

ISBN: 978-1-60751-114-4

BERKLEY® SENSATION
Berkley Sensation Books are published by The Berkley Publishing Group,
a division of Penguin Group (USA) Inc.,
375 Hudson Street, New York, New York 10014.
Berkley Sensation and the "B" design are trademarks of Penguin Group (USA) Inc.

PRINTED IN THE UNITED STATES OF AMERICA

Prologue

Night had fallen. Except for the occasional barking of a dog, stillness filled the neighborhood. A crescent moon hung in the sky, barely discernible through the city lights.

Years ago, as a child, she'd gone camping with her parents. She'd been frightened by the darkness, and her mother and father had sat on either side of her with their arms around her and each other. Surrounded by their love, she'd lost her fear.

Now the fear was of the darkness within, and there was no one to take it away. Not anymore.

No curtains hindered her view of the living room. A woman sat on the sofa, only her shoulders and head visible. Occasionally the woman laughed at something on the television. Normal, ordinary, done in houses all over the country every night.

Then *he* came into view. He walked past the window . . . with a bottle of beer dangling from his hand.

The watcher stiffened, and her hand crept to the revolver lying on the passenger seat beside her. Her fingers curled around the butt, the feel familiar yet not. She'd bought it on the street, from some kid in some back alley.

He sat down beside his wife. Her lips moved and she gestured toward the bottle. He scowled and said something back to her.

The watcher wished she could hear their words.

The woman crossed her arms and stared at the television, her body stiff, tense. He lifted the bottle to his lips and gulped. His Adam's apple bobbed up and down as he drank.

She'd seen a man shot in the throat once. Point-blank range. Blood spatter everywhere. Messy way to die. Fast, though. Too fast for a killer.

Her cell phone vibrated against her thigh, and she released the revolver. The phone vibrated again, and she blinked her macabre musings aside.

She flipped it open. "Detective Alexander."

Chapter One

Two weeks later

SHONI Alexander rubbed her gritty eyes as she trudged into the controlled chaos of the Norfolk Violent Crimes Unit. Fellow detectives tapped at computer keyboards, phones plastered to their ears, and scribbled notes on paper the old-fashioned way. One was taking a statement from a witness while a few others talked among themselves, gesturing and laughing.

It was no different than any other day, except this time Shoni's head pounded with every testosterone-charged grunt and every obnoxious phone trill. Cheap cologne and sour body odors overlaid the acrid scent of coffee, making her stomach roll, and she gulped back a rising tide of bile. For a moment, all she wanted was to turn around and stalk back out.

Moving on autopilot, she went to the big industrial-sized coffeemaker that reigned like a king overlooking his subjects. She filled a cup with sludgy black liquid and lifted it to her lips, ignoring the colorful oily residue on the surface. One swallow was one too many, and she barely managed to keep from spitting it out. She drew the back of her hand across her lips, trying to rid them of the lingering poison.

"Not strong enough?"

She glanced up to see Rafferty, immaculately dressed in a dark blue pinstripe suit and Italian loafers. Her casual hip-hugging brown jeans, knit shirt, and comfortable Timberland boots were at the opposite end of the fashion spectrum. "This crap been here since last night?" she asked.

"Nah. It was Delon's turn to make coffee."

Shoni tossed her cup, coffee and all, into the lined trash can. "Warn a girl next time."

"You look like hell."

She brushed a hand across her tied-back frizzy hair, then scowled at her vain reaction. "Not everyone can look like they stepped off a fashion runway."

She spun away, suddenly eager to get to her desk, her island among the raging currents of the busy room. She navigated between chairs, desks, and detectives on the way to her goal, managing to mumble fairly civilized greetings along the route. Rafferty followed.

"Get your eyes off my ass," she said without looking. She dropped into her chair.

Rafferty leaned against his desk, across from hers. His hazel eyes twinkled, but behind the playboy facade, Raff had a steel-trap mind when it came to pulling clues together. "Someone woke up on the wrong side of the bed." He waggled his eyebrows. "Or maybe in the wrong bed."

She propped her elbows on the desk and rubbed her throbbing brow. "Don't you have bad guys to catch, or is Delon doing all your work again?"

Lieutenant Bob Tyler, head of the Homicide Section of the Violent Crimes Unit, stepped into his office doorway. "Alexander! My office."

Shoni banged her forehead against her desktop. "Argh! This day just keeps getting better and better." She took a deep breath and shoved to her feet, the motion taking too much energy from her caffeine-depleted body.

"Maybe he's going to give you a day off," Delon Smith said as he came up behind Rafferty.

Shoni squinted at Delon's fashion statement of the day—an impossibly bright yellow shirt with glaring red hibiscus blossoms. He looked like a refugee from *Magnum P.I.* "Yeah, and maybe John Gotti here will start buying suits off the rack."

"Hey!" Rafferty smoothed his lapels. "Someone's gotta give this department a little class."

"Today, Alexander," Tyler boomed impatiently.

Geezus, was she ever going to get a break?

Shoni crossed the room and paused to sniff deeply of the ambrosial scent that wafted from her CO's office. She knocked on the door frame once, then slipped inside. The provocative aroma, more potent here, caressed and tempted her, more than any man had in a long time. Too long.

"Close the door," Tyler ordered.

She did so, then stood with her hands jammed in the pockets of her jeans to keep from snatching his personal coffeepot and risking a run for it. "Yes, sir?"

"Sit down, Shoni."

Shoni, not Alexander. Ooookay.

She eased into the chair in front of his desk.

As Tyler poured two cups of coffee, Shoni breathed a silent *amen* and *hallelujah*. He passed her one. "Tanzanian peaberry. Lemony aftertaste. A little acidic, just enough to dance across the palate."

Shoni doubted she'd ever get used to the tough, bullet-headed lieutenant waxing poetic about his coffee, but if it got her a cup of java fit for the gods, she wasn't about to complain. She curled her hands around the cup and breathed in the scent, prolonging the pleasure. She took a sip and closed her eyes in ecstasy.

"Wanna get a room?" Tyler asked.

She caught a glint of tolerant amusement in her boss's usually stern expression. "Closest I've come to an orgasm in months," she said with a smirk.

Shaking his head, he leaned back in his chair and drank some Tanzanian peaberry. A look of pure bliss crossed his face as he lowered his coffee cup. "So, how're you doing?"

Shoni glanced to the side, out the window to the threatening gray underbellies of the clouds. She should've known he hadn't invited her in simply to share his latest coffee blend with someone who appreciated it. Forcing a smile, she turned back to her boss. "A little tired, but eighteen-hour days'll do that to a person."

Guilt flicked across his face, but he knew her too well to let her sidetrack him. "That wasn't what I meant."

Grief abruptly welled, but she managed to bite it back. "I'm fine."

"Save it for the counselor."

The characteristic don't-give-me-crap tone made Shoni smile, but it quickly faded. She kept her gaze on a coffee stain on his narrow tie. "What do you want me to say, Bob? That I'm not going to have another meltdown? That I've forgiven the stupid asshole who didn't read the Miranda to my mom's killer?" Despite her vow to keep her cool, her tone sharpened with each syllable.

Bob narrowed his eyes, making him resemble a pissed-off pro wrestler, except his aggravation was genuine. "That'd be a start."

"Not going to happen."

The lieutenant leaned forward, setting his clasped hands on the desk. "I signed off on your paperwork because you dotted all the i's and crossed all the t's. But that doesn't mean I can't take you out of the game again."

Desperation clawed at Shoni's belly, and she bit the inside of her cheek to keep her expression blank. The last thing she wanted was to be chained to a desk again . . . and spilling her guts to a shrink. "With the overload of cases and shortage of personnel, you need all the people you can get."

"True. But I can't afford to have you go postal on me again."

She forced her jaw to relax. "I won't." *At least not at the station.*

He studied her, his keen eyes too perceptive, and she suddenly had an inkling of the type of interrogator he'd been. "I should've made someone else primary on the arson case."

Her heart missed a beat. "No, sir, I want this one. The arsonist stepped over the line with murder." She paused, then added with razor-sharp sarcasm, "Even if that person might only be one of the homeless."

A dark flush infused his face and spread to his smooth-shaven head. "It doesn't matter who the victim was. Each one deserves our best efforts to find his or her killer."

Although it sounded like the company line, Shoni knew her boss meant every word. His fairness and integrity were two of the reasons she'd requested a transfer to the unit a couple of years ago.

She let out a gust of air and her shoulders sagged. "I know that, Bob. It's not you. It's the whole damned system."

Bob heaved a long sigh, his defensiveness draining away. "I'm sorry, too." He aimed a crooked forefinger at Shoni. "Don't you ever let me get caught up in the political bullshit. And that's an order, Alexander."

Shoni gave her boss and friend a sloppy salute. "Yes, sir, Lieutenant."

Bob rolled his eyes, but he got right back down to business. "Was the fire last night started by the same perp?"

"Preliminary report says yes." She rose, too restless to remain still, and crossed to the window that gave her a bird's-eye view of the busy street below. Her interlaced fingers wrapped tightly around her coffee cup. "Another old warehouse down on the waterfront. Ian said it had the same burn pattern as the previous two."

Ian Convers, an arson inspector and twenty-year veteran with the Norfolk Fire Department, was working hand-in-hand with Shoni on the case. With a manpower shortage, Shoni didn't have a regular partner but worked with whoever was available. In this case, because of the nature of the crime, Ian took that position.

"Accelerant?"

"Should get the results back in a couple of days, although Ian thinks it was gasoline, too."

"Have you found any connection between the warehouses?"

Frustration was like alcohol poured on an open wound, and her muscles, already tight, grew taut as a bowstring. "Not between the first two. I'll be searching for a connection between last night's fire and the previous ones."

"And you've searched the database for similar cases?"

Although she knew Bob was only being thorough, she resented the implication she was incompetent. She turned away from the window and leveled a hard gaze on him. "SOP," she said, her jaw locked tight. "Nothing, Lieutenant."

He either didn't recognize her resentment or simply ignored it. She tended to believe the latter.

"Have there been any theories on motive?"

A sinking feeling settled in her gut. "No."

"Then maybe we should request some profiling help from the FBI."

Although she suspected it was inevitable, she didn't want some stick-up-the-ass Fed muddling around in *her* case. "You don't think I can handle it, sir?"

Impatience sharpened his tone. "I wouldn't have assigned you the case if I didn't think you could handle it."

She raked a hand through her hair, her fingers dislodging some strands from her ponytail. "Then why bring in the Feds? We have no evidence this is a serial arsonist. For all we know, it's a kid getting off on fire."

"Which still makes him a serial arsonist . . . and a possible murderer." The lieutenant kept his expression calm, contrasting sharply with Shoni's desperation.

Shoni slammed her empty coffee cup down on his desk and bit the inside of her cheek. She tasted metallic blood on her tongue. She was afraid she'd say something that, despite their friendship, would plant her butt right back behind a desk.

Her superior held her stare for a few moments then shook his head. "Fine. I'll give you a little more time. But if you don't come up with anything before there's another fire, I'm making the call. Is that clear, Detective?"

It was a temporary victory, but Shoni wisely accepted it. "Crystal, Lieutenant."

"Do you need any more help? Jackson is coming off of medical leave and she'll be at a desk for a week or two." Bob offered her an olive branch.

Jackson had good instincts, but no organizational abilities. "Give her to someone else. I already have Raff and Delon helping with interviews and following up on any leads. We're going to meet at ten to get started with this latest fire."

The silence that followed eased the high-strung tension between them.

"Did you get your mother's condo cleaned out yet?" Bob asked.

Shoni forced herself to lean against the window in a casual pose and lifted a corner of her lips in a rueful smile. "Can't seem to find the time." The funeral had been nearly two months ago, but she still couldn't bring herself to go through her mother's belongings.

"If you need any help, just ask. Helen and I can come by and give you a hand."

"Thanks, I'll keep that in mind." Although she was grateful for the offer, she wouldn't take him up on it. It had taken every ounce of strength to hold herself together at the funeral, and she wouldn't risk losing it in front of her boss and his wife. Tears only evoked sympathy, something Shoni despised. She tipped her head back. "God, I'm tired."

"You haven't taken any vacation since you started here, except for the occasional three-day weekend."

Something akin to disapproval twined through his voice, sparking her defensiveness. "I took time off for the funeral."

Bob's lips thinned to a grim line. "That was hardly a vacation. And you only took two days."

"Then I was put on desk duty."

"For attacking a fellow officer."

"Who didn't do his job." The anger and bitterness remained too close to the surface.

"He was suspended for a month without pay and given an official reprimand."

"And my mother's dead."

Bob shifted in his chair, suddenly uncomfortable.

"I'm serious, Alexander. You need a break—where you actually do something relaxing—or you're going to be the youngest officer to burn out."

Shoni rubbed at an imaginary spot on her thigh. She couldn't even remember how to relax, much less the last time she'd done so. "After this arson case is wrapped up, I'll consider it, sir."

Although her boss wasn't happy, she'd mollified him for now. "Meeting's in fifteen minutes, so I'd better pull my notes together."

Concern touched Bob's careworn eyes, but she couldn't afford to acknowledge it.

He made a shooing motion with his hand. "Go on. Get some work done so you can get your butt out of here at a decent time."

She gave him a halfhearted grin and left, closing the door behind her.

BOB picked up the top file from his in-box and opened it. He started to read through it, but couldn't focus on the words. Restless, he refilled his coffee cup, but even the rich, vibrant taste couldn't disperse the foreboding that clutched his gut. He cracked open the blinds at the window that faced the room filled with bustling detectives. Shoni was at her desk, the phone between her shoulder and ear while she typed at her computer.

Doubts assailed him. Had he made the right decision in allowing her to return to work? When she'd transferred over from the Special Crimes Unit to Violent Crimes and into his Homicide Section, he'd considered himself a lucky bastard. Despite her age, Shoni Alexander already had a reputation as a top-notch investigator. She had the second highest conviction rate in the division. He'd never questioned her drive, or asked her why she worked so relentlessly to put criminals behind bars. All he cared about was results.

However, in the time since Shoni's mother was struck and killed by a drunk driver, Bob had watched her attitude spiral downward. She was on the road to becoming the one thing he wouldn't tolerate in his section—a loose cannon.

When the dead body was found in the aftermath of a fire, the arson case was bumped up to Homicide. Bob had thought long and hard before assigning it to Shoni. Even though she didn't know it, this case was her chance to prove she could still handle the job.

Bile burned up his throat, and he grimaced. Bob reached into his desk drawer and shook two antacid tablets into his palm. His wife would tell him to cut back on his exotic coffees, but it wasn't the Tanzanian peaberry that gave him indigestion.

If only it were that simple . . .

* * *

A few nights later Shoni was no closer to finding the arsonist. There hadn't been a fourth fire yet, but her gut told her it was only a matter of time. Ever since Bob's ultimatum, she felt like she was watching an hourglass. With each falling grain of sand, she was another step closer to failing. If she couldn't find the arsonist, she'd be saddled with a feebie who'd probably take over. Couldn't have a local run the show even though this was *her* town and she'd taken an oath to protect its citizens.

She automatically reached for her cup and took a sip. Cold. Shuddering, she set the bitter coffee aside. The unit was nearly deserted, with only one other detective working. She glanced at the clock on the wall. Almost midnight.

The need to go watch *him* washed across her, sparking a surge of adrenaline. However, by the time she arrived, the house would probably be dark. She knew his routine, knew his wife went to bed at ten, but he stayed up drinking until after eleven. They got up early to drop off their kid at day care before going to work. The wife drove. His license was revoked. A minuscule punishment for taking a life.

She breathed deeply to dispel the rising rage. When her fingernails no longer dug into her palms, she closed the folders scattered across her desk and dropped them into her desk drawer. Pushing herself up, she managed to stifle a groan. She needed to get to the gym, and soon, before she lost all muscle tone except that in her ass.

She left the building, absently lifting a hand to the night desk cop. As she strode to her car, her breath misted in the cool air. The night seemed unusually still, and her footsteps thudded on the sidewalk. She could smell the fishy scent from the harbor and hear the low hum of traffic on the interstate. Laughter drifted down the block from a group of young men standing on a street corner.

Shoni was glad she didn't have to walk past them. Not

that she was frightened—she could take care of herself—but with her temper on a hair trigger, she'd shoot someone. Then she'd be stuck doing paperwork all night.

Her staid but dependable eight-year-old Toyota was parked between an older black Impala and one of the new hybrids. She slid behind the wheel, started the engine, and pulled onto the street. Closer to her mother's condo than her own apartment, she turned in that direction.

And suddenly remembered Iris Alexander was dead.

Her throat tightened, and welling anguish threatened to choke her. Unable to see through the moisture in her eyes, she swerved over to the curb and clutched the steering wheel. She'd already grieved for her mother, had accepted her death, so why the lapse? How had she forgotten?

She reached under the passenger seat, and her fingers brushed the locked metal box that hid it from prying eyes. Nobody knew she had it. Just another one of thousands of cheap handguns that flooded the streets.

Could she do it? Ever since she'd been a child, all she wanted was to be a cop like her father. Her hero.

What would he think of her now?

A shiver skidded down her spine. She glanced around, but nobody was there. Shoni straightened in her seat and buried the unease. Her father was gone, too. Justice was her responsibility.

She pulled back onto the road and wound her way through the maze of back streets. She braked at a red light and opened her window to breathe in the cold, saltwater-tinted air. It wasn't exactly fresh, but it cleared her head.

Then a childish, high-pitched scream shattered the night.

Chapter Two

SHONI made a sharp U-turn and braked at the mouth of a shadowed alley. As she jumped out of her car, a young girl raced out of the passageway, her dark eyes huge in the pale oval of her face.

Shoni caught her arms, and the girl squirmed and kicked. A toe caught Shoni's shin, and she gasped. "Take it easy. It's all right. I won't hurt you." She tried to restrain the kid without hurting her as she evaded thrashing legs and arms.

The girl, who was maybe seven years old, stopped struggling and clutched Shoni's sleeve. Despite the cold evening, she wore only a light jacket over a faded Shrek T-shirt and thin, oft-washed jeans. "They're hurting him!"

Shoni dropped to a crouch in front of the girl. "Who?"

"My friend. John."

"How many men are hurting him?"

"Three." The streetlight caught her face, revealing shiny tear tracks trailing down her caramel-colored cheeks.

"Get in my car and lock the doors. Don't open them for anyone but me."

Shoni pressed her toward the car as she drew out her cell phone and one-handedly dialed 911. The operator's professional, impersonal voice came on, and Shoni quickly gave her the information needed to gain assistance.

Once the girl was safely in the Toyota, Shoni turned and ran into the pitch-black passage. Her nape tingled, and she drew her standard-issue Glock 19 out of its holster at her back. A rustle made her freeze, and she leveled the pistol in the sound's direction. A cat's glowing eyes stared back at her.

"Damn it!" She raised the barrel of her weapon and nearly collapsed in relief. With adrenaline streaming through her veins, she ran deeper into the fetid alley.

Within moments, she picked up the unmistakable sounds of fist against flesh and the occasional moan and grunt. She was almost to the rear of the alley when she spotted shifting shadows. She crept closer, her heart hammering in her chest. Her eyes adjusted until she was able to make out three men surrounding another.

Rage surged through her at the uneven odds, and her finger curled around the trigger. A moment later, her brain caught up, and she realized the attackers seemed afraid to get too close to the single figure. She eased her finger's pressure and took the proper stance. "Freeze! Police!"

Three heads turned her way, but Shoni was peripherally aware of the victim, who kept his attention on his attackers. Seconds later, the bullies scurried away. One was holding his side and another was limping painfully as they made their escape. Shoni placed her weapon back in its holster.

"John!"

A blur rushed past her, and Shoni realized the little girl hadn't followed orders. She ran straight to the man and nearly knocked him down. Her arms wound around his waist and he hugged her, leaning over her.

"Shhh, I'm all right," he murmured soothingly.

The man's low, masculine voice sent a shiver of awareness through Shoni. Ignoring her unexpected reaction, she approached him tentatively and stopped a few feet away. With his head bowed over the girl, Shoni could see only thick, shaggy hair that covered the tops of his ears and brushed his collar. "Are you all right?"

The man straightened his spine, but kept a protective hold on the girl. He looked down a chiseled nose flawed only by a break that had healed with a slight crook. An untrimmed beard and moustache the same gold as his hair covered the lower half of his face, but it was his direct, silvery blue eyes that snared her.

He nodded in reply.

Caught by his direct gaze, it took her a moment to realize what his nod meant. She cleared her dry throat and fell back on police procedure. "I should still call an ambulance so you can be checked out at the hospital."

"No! No hospital." His voice was amazingly rich and deep.

Shoni's neck muscles tightened as she searched his expression. Despite her fairly impressive height of five foot ten, she had to tilt her head back to meet and hold his unwavering gaze. "I'm Detective Alexander with the Norfolk P.D."

The man's lips curled into a sneer. "And I'll bet you even have a shiny gold badge."

Taken aback by his vehemence, Shoni held up her hands. "I've got no beef with you. I was just passing by when I heard a scream." She glanced at the wide-eyed girl, her face blurred in the darkness, as she clung to him. "It was a good thing she yelled." She paused. "Did you recognize the men who attacked you?"

"No."

Shoni knew John hadn't spoken the truth, but she didn't dare call him a liar. His defensiveness was already notched up, but everything in her railed against letting the perpetrators get away. "If they're behind bars, they can't hurt anybody."

His expression turned ugly and he shook his head. "They'd be out on bail in less than twenty-four hours."

She didn't bother arguing and said quietly, "I'm trying to help you."

For a long moment, John studied her, then nodded as his granite expression eased. It wasn't much, but Shoni figured that from this man it was a huge concession. She reached into her pocket and the man tensed once more. "I'm just getting one of my cards," the detective said, keeping her voice calm.

Shoni withdrew one of her business cards and passed it to the man, who simply stared at it. She continued to hold it out, willing to give him time to judge her. Like an abused dog, this man didn't trust easily.

Finally, John reached out to accept the card from her grasp. His cool, callused fingertips brushed her hand, and a shock traveled up her arm. A core of restless heat settled in her belly. He stilled, as if he, too, felt it, and allowed the contact to remain for precious seconds longer.

When he drew his hand away, Shoni let out a gust of air and realized she hadn't breathed the entire time their fingers touched. What was wrong with her? Unshaven men who lived on the street weren't usually her type. So why the breathless-heroine act?

"If you need help, call me," she said.

"Why?"

She studied him and realized he wanted a real answer, not a canned reply. "I care."

He met her gaze and his distrust remained, but slowly, a sliver of acceptance stole into the icy blue depths of his eyes. He tucked the card into his jacket pocket.

Shoni noticed how he favored his right arm, but was

blocked from getting a closer look by what she suspected was a deliberate shift of his body. "Are you sure you're all right?"

"I'm fine." The distrust was back in full force.

The succinct reply reminded her too much of her own answer to Bob when he'd asked how she was doing. Shoni guessed John, too, was lying.

Restraining a sigh of frustration, she squatted down and spoke to the girl, who hadn't relinquished her hold on the man. "My name is Shoni. What's yours?" she asked, using the same soothing voice she used to defuse domestic disturbances and strung-out addicts.

"Lainey."

Bright, flashing lights invaded the alley and the blaring yowl of a siren filled the narrow passageway. Headlights illuminated the man and the girl, giving Shoni an unhindered view of them. But before she could catalog more than their basic physical characteristics, John scooped Lainey into his arms and loped away from the police cruiser. He moved with surprising grace, his stride long and confident. His second-hand jeans and jacket couldn't disguise his impressive body—well-proportioned but not muscle-bound shoulders that tapered to a narrow waist and nicely rounded backside. In fact, other than his unshorn hair and beard, and thrift store clothes, he didn't look like one of the desperate, hungry homeless who populated Norfolk's streets.

Two uniformed cops hurried over to Shoni's side.

"What happened?" one of them asked.

She stared into the blackness that had swallowed up the man and the girl. For a terrifying moment, she wondered if she'd allowed a sexual predator to escape with a child, but remembering the man's obvious protectiveness, she knew her instincts had been right.

"It was only a misunderstanding," she said. "Let's get out of here."

* * *

KEEPING up his guard, John guided Lainey through a maze of trash-littered alleys. He moved on the balls of his feet, his footfalls soundless, and the action was familiar in a way he couldn't pinpoint. But then, he didn't remember a whole lot these days. However, caution and wariness were second nature, traits he'd obviously retained even though he'd lost the rest of his identity.

"Are we going to Gram's?" Lainey asked.

John glanced down at the girl. "Yes."

"What about Mom?"

John managed to keep his antagonism hidden. "She shouldn't have taken you with her."

"She needed me."

The girl's defense of her mother made John's throat tighten even as fresh anger surged through him. The only thing Mishon needed was her fix. "Not tonight. She's working."

He wondered how much Lainey understood about what her mother did. Probably everything, which only made him more furious.

Lainey's great-grandmother, Estelle, lived in a rundown apartment building less than a block from the waterfront warehouses. It was the only inhabited building in a radius of three blocks. Everything around it had been bought by a developer who planned on creating another trendy, upscale area like the popular Waterside. The developer had tried to have Estelle and the few other stubborn tenants evicted but had lost the battle.

Despite the fact it was a weekday night, a handful of school-age boys and girls lounged on the apartment building's steps. The pungent and undeniable scent of marijuana tickled John's throat as he and Lainey climbed the warped wooden stairs. The kids watched them with suspicious inky-black eyes, the scant light caught by studs and hoops in pierced ears, brows, and lips. Although John wasn't a stranger to them, he wasn't the right color to trust either. However, Lainey was Estelle's great-granddaughter, and that was the only reason John wasn't hassled.

The combined odors of urine, stale alcohol, and vomit weren't pleasant, but they were familiar. There were holes in the wall of the stairwell, as well as descriptive—and pornographic—nouns and verbs scrawled across the faded pea green paint. John ignored them and kept his body between the wall and Lainey, even though he knew she'd seen the crude words numerous times, and probably understood them, too.

With a hand on Lainey's skinny shoulder, John steered her down the hallway, lit by only one dim incandescent bulb. He knocked on Estelle's door and listened to the older woman's shuffle as she approached. There was a pause, then the chain lock and two bolts were undone. The door was swung open by a leathery-faced woman with weary brown eyes and tight gray curls close to her scalp. She was a full foot shorter than John, but her weight probably equaled, or exceeded, his.

John gave Lainey a gentle shove into the apartment. Once they were inside, the woman wrestled the door locks back in place even though they wouldn't keep out a determined thief. But Estelle had a reputation as a tough bird; she'd lived in this building ever since it was built. Morey, her revolver, hidden close to the door, also served as a deterrent.

Wearing a shift that clung to her rolls of flesh, Estelle propped a fist on a generous hip. "You found her," she said in a sand-over-gravel voice.

John, conscious of the bleeding gash on his arm, held his cuff tight and bent his arm to keep blood from dripping onto the floor. Fortunately, his coat was black, so the blood didn't show, but he stood angled so Estelle wouldn't see the tear in the sleeve. "She was with Mishon."

Estelle's eyes narrowed, but all she said was "It's past your bedtime, Lainey."

The girl made a face. "I'm not tired."

"Don't care if you are or you ain't. Off to bed."

With a typical childish pout, Lainey trudged into the tiny bedroom she shared with her mother. She paused in the doorway. "'Night, Gram. 'Night, John." Then she closed the door behind her.

Estelle dropped into her chair that sagged from years of use. Her tiny apartment embodied the definition of clutter. A pile of old magazines and a basket of yarn with knitting needles in the middle of a project lay on either side of her favorite chair. Figurines of cats, dogs, children, pigs—whatever had caught Estelle's fancy over the past fifty-plus years—covered every available surface.

John picked up a ceramic black-and-white dog curled up on a pillow. An image flashed through his mind of a dog with the same colors, jumping to catch a Frisbee in its mouth. In his tattered memory, he heard laughter. He turned, but the image disappeared before he could see the girl's face.

"You're gonna bust it." Estelle's voice startled him back to the present.

"What?"

"The way your hand is curled around that dog. Looks like you're trying to crush it."

John immediately uncurled his fingers and set the figurine down.

"You remember somethin', Johnny?" Estelle asked, her gravelly voice almost gentle.

He shook his head. "Not really. Just pictures, pieces of a puzzle."

"It'll come. Don't force it."

The bird clock on the wall chirped twelve times, each chirp a little weaker than the previous one.

"So what happened tonight?" Estelle kept her gaze aimed at her knobby, arthritic hands.

John considered lying, but the old woman could smell a lie a mile off. "I spotted them on Mishon's usual corner. She'd just scored, and there was no way in hell I was going to leave Lainey there." He paused. "On our way here, Mishon's pimp, Jamar, and two of his goons jumped us in an alley."

Estelle's nostrils flared. "Bastards." She paused. "Guess I owe you one."

John smiled at her grudging tone. "Lainey's a good kid. Besides, *I* owe *you*."

Estelle harrumphed. "You don't owe me nothin'. I was just doin' what any decent human being would do."

John's gut told him there weren't very many of those left in the world. At least, not many who would care for a stranger with no name and no past.

"I care." Detective Alexander's soothing, solicitous voice echoed faintly in his mind. He didn't know if he could believe her, but a part of him wanted to . . . badly. However, he didn't dare take the risk.

After glancing into Lainey's darkened room, Estelle said in a low voice, "Jamar likes 'em young. Don't surprise me none that he wants Lainey."

The seven-year-old would bring a good price either in Jamar's stable or if he sold her to someone looking for a young virgin. Preteen girls were a valued commodity, but they were also high risk. If Jamar was caught pimping a girl like Lainey, he wouldn't last long in prison, provided he made it that far. John almost wished he'd told the detective the truth. But even if he had, she could only get Jamar for assault, which wouldn't give him what he deserved.

"If Mishon is desperate enough for a fix, she might make a deal with Jamar," John said, the words leaving a foul taste in his mouth.

Estelle glared at him. "No need to be tellin' me what I already know." Her wrinkles deepened. "As long as Lainey's here with me, Jamar knows better than to bother her. And if it comes down to it, I'll call the police."

He shifted his weight, and his injuries from the fight throbbed. "You and Lainey going to be all right?"

Estelle snorted. "As long as I got Morey, we'll be fine."

A corner of John's lips lifted in amusement, and he stepped toward the door.

"You goin' to that drafty warehouse where you been stayin'?" Estelle asked.

"Home sweet home."

She made a face that didn't leave any doubt what she thought of his comment. "I still think you ought to check with the cops, Johnny. Might be someone's lookin' for you."

A chill chased down his spine, although again he couldn't attribute it to anything specific. However, the scars on his body, the ease with which he defended himself, and the violent nightmares that haunted him warned him he was a dangerous man. Maybe someone the police were looking for, but not as a missing person.

"I'll think about it." It was the same answer he gave every time she brought up the subject.

Careful not to leave any blood behind, he undid the bolts and chain. "Lock up behind me."

Estelle grumbled and heaved her significant frame to her feet.

John closed the door behind him and waited until he heard the old woman rebolt the door.

"You can go now," she said, obviously knowing he remained on the other side.

John squelched a grin and walked away.

The front stoop was empty, and his shoulders sagged with relief. Although the kids weren't normally a threat, if they were hopped up on meth or heroin, that was another story.

And unpredictability yields the worst possible scenario.

The words drifted from that mysterious cache in his brain that remembered, but guarded its secrets zealously. Out of habit, he took a circuitous route to the warehouse he called home. In actuality it was located less than a block from Estelle's, but he walked four times that far to disguise his path. He didn't know why. . . .

With his injured arm, he awkwardly climbed the rusty ladder attached to the side of the warehouse and dropped noiselessly to the flat roof. A cold wind buffeted him and sliced through his clothing. Over two weeks after discovering the roof opening, John followed the familiar path and lifted a maintenance hatch door. Another ladder and he was inside the dim warehouse, his entrance sealed from the interior so no one else could access it.

There was an office on the second floor that he'd claimed. The space hadn't been abandoned long, since the couch and desk chair showed little sign of rodent activity and the water was still running in the bathroom. The only thing he didn't have was electricity, which would be a problem as winter drew nearer. And by the feel of the north wind tonight, winter was closer than he wanted to consider.

John tossed off his coat and ruined bloody shirt, shivering in the cold night air. In the bathroom he washed away the dried blood on his bicep, revealing a cut five inches long and half an inch deep. He suspected it could use stitches, but he had no insurance—let alone a last name—so it would have to heal on its own. That it would leave a scar was a given—one more for his collection.

But it's the first one I actually know how I received.

John dug around in his frayed backpack, which held all his earthly possessions. The first aid kit, left behind by the former office tenants, yielded a nearly flat tube of antibiotic cream. He slathered it on the cut, ignoring the discomfort. After placing a gauze pad on the wound, he used duct tape to hold it in place. If he was incredibly lucky, he was current on his tetanus vaccination.

He gazed in the smoky mirror, and a shaggy-haired stranger stared back at him.

"Who the hell are you?"

But the image didn't answer. Instead, his reflection blurred and he could almost feel a small hand on his cheek.

"Will I have to shave someday, Daddy?"

John whirled around, expecting to see a young girl standing beside him. But he was alone. Did he have a daughter out there . . . missing him?

The thought of a family made his gut twist in a knot. Maybe Estelle was right. Maybe he should visit the local police station and find out if someone was looking for him. It had been over three weeks now. Surely, if that family existed, they would've filed a missing persons report.

Torn by conflict, John rummaged in his backpack and pulled out his only other shirt, a black turtleneck. Grabbing the roll of duct tape again, he returned to the office. Laying out his jacket on the desk, he used the gray tape to mend the tear in his sleeve. When he was finished, the fix wasn't pretty, but it was efficient and that was all that mattered.

He slipped on his jacket and his hands slid into the pockets by habit. His fingers closed on the business card.

Detective Shoni Alexander. Homicide Section.

Despite the detective's tough attitude, he'd sensed a vulnerability in her that triggered some atavistic protectiveness. Ridiculous, considering she was a cop and he didn't even know who the hell he was.

"I care." The two words whispered across him once again. From anyone else he would've laughed, but his gut told him Detective Alexander was sincere.

A foreign scuffle from below caught his attention. Too loud for a mouse or rat. Not noisy enough for a dog. Either a clumsy cat or a human being. And, granted his memory was pretty much Swiss cheese, he couldn't remember ever meeting a clumsy cat.

Lowering into a stealthy crouch came as naturally as breathing. Although there were no lights in the warehouse, John had memorized the layout in between eating at St. Anne's soup kitchen and rummaging in Dumpsters.

He moved out of the office, onto the five-foot-wide walkway. He noiselessly crept to the railing to peer through the metal bars, down at the expansive space.

Another foreign sound—tinny, uneven. Then liquid being splashed against a surface.

Frowning, John crab-walked to the top of the stairs. A motion below caught his eye, and he used his peripheral vision to try to determine what it was.

But before he could, the unmistakable scent of gasoline drifted up to him.

What the hell . . .

A soft click and low laughter.

At a primal gut level John recognized the *whoosh* that followed.

Fire.

Chapter Three

WHEN Shoni finally arrived at her small, nondescript apartment, it was one A.M. Despite the acidic burn up her throat, she knew she had to eat something or she'd wake up with a headache. A *worse* headache.

She rummaged in a kitchen drawer and found the aspirin bottle. After dry-swallowing three tablets, she opened her fridge and found a carton of leftover Chinese take-out, three cans of soda, one bottle of beer, various condiments, and a quart of milk. She reached for the white carton and flipped it open to see if the food was still edible or if it had turned into a lab experiment. No fuzzies. She sniffed cautiously. No weird smell. Whatever . . .

She retrieved a diet soda and a fork, carried her meal the short distance into the living room, and dropped onto the couch. She switched on the television and found a *M*A*S*H* rerun she'd seen only half a dozen times.

After eating a few forkfuls of the leftover beef and broccoli, she set the take-out carton aside and tilted her head back, feeling boneless and empty. She hadn't cleaned her apartment in weeks and her laundry overflowed from the hamper in her bathroom. But she couldn't bring herself to care.

There were only two things that gave her a reason to get up in the mornings—tracking down the arsonist and ensuring that her mother's killer paid for his crime.

Maybe if her mom's death hadn't been so sudden and she hadn't been so young—only forty-nine—Shoni might have been able to deal with it better. Or had they been too close? Shoni's father had been killed in the line of duty when Shoni was thirteen years old. Between his insurance and the police department's financial compensation, Iris had bought a new condominium with cash and had enough left over to see to her and Shoni's needs indefinitely. However, the emotional burden was more difficult to bear, and Iris had turned to Shoni for support. The police department's counselor had suggested that Shoni had taken the role of mother in their relationship. Maybe that was true, but it didn't lessen Shoni's sorrow.

Grief was a raw, ragged wound in her chest, festering like an infection. Only the thought of punishing her mother's killer alleviated some of the pain. Perhaps she should've gone to his house tonight, watched him go about his life, oblivious to his executioner.

His murderer.

Shoni sucked in a sharp breath. Not a murderer. She would only be doing what the courts should've done.

That's not your job.

Her conscience spoke in her father's voice.

She shoved herself to her feet and stalked into the kitchen. She plucked the remaining beer from the refrigerator, twisted the cap off the bottle, and lifted it to her lips. In her mind's eye, she saw her mother's killer tipping up a bottle of beer and draining it.

Shoni threw the bottle into the sink. It clattered but

didn't shatter. White foam and pale yellow liquid flowed down the drain.

She clutched the edge of the sink and bent her head over it. Her control teetered on the edge, balanced like some high-wire artist at a circus. But there was nothing—no one—to catch her, no safety net.

Like John, she'd lost her trust in the system. Her mother's death left her dangling . . . lost . . . alone.

With a conscious effort, she unclenched her fingers and stepped back. John was a much safer subject to ponder than her own stuttering sanity.

She recalled his obvious concern for Lainey and his ability to defend himself against three attackers, like some hero in a comic book. Except John was no cartoon figure, but a flesh-and-blood man skilled in fighting. A soldier? Then why was he on the street?

Who the hell was John?

A phone shrilled loudly and Shoni jerked upright, confused. Where was she?

Not in bed. The couch.

Some infomercial about a fitness machine that also sliced and diced droned on the television. Her cell phone trilled again and she debated answering it. The calls that came in the middle of the night heralded nothing but trouble. Her sense of duty overcame her foreboding, and she nabbed it off the coffee table. "Alexander."

"We might have another one," Ian Convers, the arson investigator, said without preamble. "Looks like the fire started in a warehouse, then jumped across the street to an apartment building."

"Damn it." Shoni closed her eyes tightly and raked a hand through her mussed hair. Definitely bad news. "Victims?"

"None. A man warned the tenants and they all got out in time. He ended up with smoke inhalation and some minor burns."

Adrenaline dispersed the last remnants of sleep. "Maybe this guy is our fire starter."

"I don't think so," Ian said. "One of the older tenants knows the guy. He was living in the warehouse that was torched. He's refusing to allow the ambulance to take him to the hospital." He paused. "He's asking for you."

Shoni frowned, wondering how . . .

John.

Her heart somersaulted. "Where?" With only the illumination from the streetlights, she dodged into her bedroom. With her phone jammed between her ear and shoulder, she stripped off her jeans and tossed them onto her bed.

"Fourth and Lesley."

Less than six blocks from the alley where G.I. John had faced off against the three assailants. "I'll be there in fifteen, twenty tops."

Shoni punched the Off button. No time for a shower, but she pulled on clean clothes, stripped the elastic band from her hair, brushed the tangled curls, then tied it back again.

After grabbing her jacket and keys, she raced out of her apartment, locking the door behind her almost as an afterthought.

The waning crescent moon hung low in the sky, and Shoni sped down the nearly deserted streets with her lights flashing and her heater trying valiantly to churn out some warm air. Long before she arrived, she could see the fire's orangish glow. The acrid smell of smoke struck her six blocks before the burning buildings came into view.

She turned a corner and ran into a roadblock of emergency vehicles. The fire's glow and the headlights of the vehicles gave the whole area a nightmarish aura that sent a shudder skidding down her back.

She jumped out of her sedan and her gaze searched the flickering figures. Two local television stations had reporters and camera crews, and she recognized another reporter from the local paper. Four police officers were keeping the media and curious onlookers back.

Shoni's gaze came to rest on Ian, who stood by an ambulance behind the police line. She showed her badge to one of the cops and ignored the questions from the press. Weaving between vehicles and jumping over hoses, she finally reached Ian's side.

She returned his nod, and her gaze latched onto the man perched on the end of the ambulance. He held an oxygen mask to his mouth and nose, and what she could see of his face bore soot smudges and grime. The duct tape on his right jacket sleeve hadn't been there earlier that evening.

"You should really be examined by a doctor," one of the EMTs said to him, as if lecturing a child.

John pulled away the clear mask and shoved it at the EMT. "No. No hospital. I'm fine." His voice was both raspy and surly.

He stood and grabbed the ratty backpack at his feet, grimaced, then shifted the straps from his right hand to his left. It was obvious he'd been injured when the men attacked him earlier. His intention to escape now was equally obvious.

"Seems to me I've heard that before," Shoni spoke up.

He turned sharply and pierced her with his gaze. They were the same icy blue eyes she'd met earlier that night.

She stepped closer. "How are you really doing?"

"Cold, tired, and homeless, but since I was homeless and cold before, just make that tired," John answered, his tone rife with sarcasm.

"He won't let us examine him," the EMT grumbled.

John glowered at him.

"Where do you have to go?" Shoni asked before John could speak.

His gaze flicked to her, his eyes so intense she nearly gasped. "I want to check on the people from the apartment building."

Shoni turned to the patrol cop who stood behind Ian. She recognized him, but couldn't recall his name. "Has the Red Cross been called?"

"Already here, Detective." Obviously he recognized her, too. "They set up a block east of here."

"Good." She shivered, realizing the air held a taste of winter. "How many displaced?"

"Twenty-one."

"Everyone accounted for?"

"Yes," Ian replied. "The Red Cross is setting them up in temporary shelters."

Shoni turned back to John. "See? They're being taken care of."

He narrowed his eyes. "I want to see them."

Shoni stifled her exasperation. "If you see them, will you let the EMTs check you out?"

His mouth was barely visible as a thin line between his beard and mustache. "No promises."

In other words, "No way in hell." However, his concern for those who'd lost their homes was genuine. And admirable.

"Fair enough," Shoni said. "I'll walk over there with you."

He scowled, but didn't argue.

They walked in silence, in contrast to the chaos surrounding them, traveling through pockets of warmth created by the blaze. The firefighters concentrated their efforts on containing the fire since the apartment building was already a lost cause, as was the warehouse. Shoni trembled, but this time it wasn't from the cold. If John hadn't warned the residents, many, if not all, would've perished.

"Why did you ask for me?" she asked.

"They weren't going to let me go."

"And you figured I would?"

He stopped and speared her with a look. "You said to call if I needed anything. I needed to get the hell out of here."

"You should spend the rest of the night in a hospital, let them take care of you."

He grinned, a frigid, hurtful grimace. "And how do I pay for it? 'Sorry, nurse, my Blue Cross seems to have expired.' "

"They wouldn't turn you away."

His only reply was to continue walking.

Shoni stifled her frustration and followed. "So you lived in the warehouse where the fire started."

He continued to stare straight ahead, but a muscle flexed in his cheek, telling her he'd heard her.

"Well?" she pressed.

He glanced at her, his lips turned downward and his gaze arcing fire. "I didn't hear a question."

She wondered if he had to practice being so damned exasperating. "Did you live in the warehouse that was torched?"

"Yes."

Okay, questioning him was going to be like rolling a boulder uphill. "Did you see who started the fire?"

He sidestepped a puddle of water.

Shoni narrowed her eyes as she studied his profile. She was usually pretty good at reading people, but he defied her. She stumbled, jarring herself out of her thoughts, and John caught her arm. "Thanks," she muttered, embarrassed.

He released her immediately. "Watch your feet."

His curt command irritated her.

"About the fire," she said, annoyance sharpening her tone.

"It started in the warehouse. Wind must have carried it across the street."

John's stride lengthened, forcing Shoni to run to keep up with him. He didn't pause by the Red Cross van, but continued to where the displaced apartment dwellers stood in clumps. He finally halted beside an elderly black woman and the same girl he'd protected earlier that night. Both had blankets wrapped around them, hands clenching the corners.

Shoni remained about six feet behind John, close enough to hear their conversation but far enough away to give the illusion of privacy.

"Why ain't you on the way to the hospital, Johnny?" the older woman asked, her irritation clear.

Shoni immediately liked her.

"Nothing they can do for me that I can't do myself. How're you and Lainey?"

"Everything's gone. Fifty years." The woman's dark expression crumbled, but her tone was more angry than upset.

"I'm sorry, Estelle. I wish I could've stopped him," John said.

Shoni tensed. "You saw the arsonist?"

John ignored her. "Did Mishon ever show up?"

The woman he called Estelle shook her head. "No." Bitterness twisted her mouth. "Won't she be surprised when she comes home in the mornin'?"

"I'm cold," the girl said.

John lifted her as if she weighed nothing. She pressed her face into the curve where his shoulder met his neck and wrapped her thin arms around his neck. "That better?"

The girl nodded.

John's concern for Lainey was obvious in his solicitous tone. If only he'd open up with her, she might actually get a straight answer out of him.

Shoni drew nearer and tucked the girl's blanket around her narrow shoulders. The youngster tipped her head slightly and stared at Shoni with accusing brown eyes. "You're that cop."

"That's right. Don't you like the police?"

"They're assholes."

"Lainey Montrose," Estelle scolded, "you been raised better'n that."

Lainey's cheeks turned dusky.

The short, stout woman faced Shoni and lifted her chin. "I'm sorry for what she said."

Shoni bit the inside of her cheek to keep from smiling. She shrugged. "I know a few cops that I'd call the same. I like to think that most of us are better than that, though."

Estelle tipped her head to the side to study Shoni, her ebony eyes probing. Shoni looked away, uncomfortable under her scrutiny.

Shoni dug her notebook and pen out of her pocket. "Did you see anything suspicious tonight?"

Estelle snorted. "'Round here, if I *didn't* see anything suspicious, I'd be suspicious."

Shoni smiled. "Yes, ma'am. Did you see anybody who didn't belong? Someone you've never seen before in the area?"

"Can't this wait?" John broke in, furious blue eyes pinning Shoni. "They just lost everything."

As much as Shoni sympathized with them, she had a job to do. "I realize that, but I want the arsonist caught before he can do more damage." She paused. "Maybe kill someone."

Estelle rested a blue-veined hand on John's arm. "Let the woman do her job, Johnny."

His thunderous expression told Shoni what he thought of her job. She deliberately turned away from him and gave Estelle her full attention, although she was aware of John staring daggers at her back.

Shoni wrote down Estelle and Lainey's full names and former address. "When were you first aware there was a fire?"

"When Johnny come pounding on my door," Estelle replied. "Next thing I know, he's herding me and Lainey out, along with everyone else in the buildin'."

"Did you see anyone other than your fellow tenants or John?"

Estelle shook her head. "No." Her expression hardened. "But if I had, I woulda used Morey."

"Morey?"

Estelle reached into her bathrobe pocket, and John caught the old woman's wrist.

"They didn't see anything," John stated.

Shoni glanced at the lump in Estelle's pocket and suspected she knew who—or what—Morey was. Her eyes collided with John's and she read the message in them as clearly as if he'd spoken aloud. Her duties as a cop vied with her empathy for a woman trying to protect her own. Three months ago she would've gone by the book, but that was before . . .

A shuttle bus arrived and those who'd lost their homes climbed aboard.

"Do you know where you'll be staying?" Shoni asked.

Estelle held out a piece of paper with an address written in ink. "Said there's room for me and Lainey there."

Shoni recognized the motel's name and wrote it down. "It's a nice place. I think you'll like it. Were you insured?"

Estelle pursed her lips and rolled her eyes. "With all my expensive antiques and diamond jewelry?" She snorted. "Most of what we had was what you'd call junk."

"But it was yours," Shoni said softly.

Estelle blinked and looked away, but not before Shoni caught the sheen of moisture in her eyes. "We're alive and healthy. That's all that matters."

It wasn't, but Shoni respected the old woman's grit. "Thank you for your help. If you think of anything, please call me." She handed Estelle her business card.

The woman tucked the card into her pocket beside Morey.

"If you tell me where I can find Lainey's mother, I'll get her, tell her what happened, and bring her to your temporary residence." Shoni didn't miss the look Estelle exchanged with John, and suspected Lainey's mother wouldn't be found waiting tables or serving drinks. "I won't hassle her," she reassured.

John set Lainey down. "You and Gram get on the bus. I'll find your mom and bring her to your new place."

"Promise?" Lainey asked.

As John drew an X on his chest, Shoni caught his slight grimace. Obviously, the duct tape on his jacket sleeve was covering more than a simple tear.

"I promise. Go on." John gave Lainey a gentle shove.

"You already done enough tonight, Johnny," Estelle said in a low voice.

"I promised Lainey," he said.

"And you never break your promises," Lainey said solemnly.

John smiled, and Shoni's breath caught at the transformation from chiseled ice to tender warmth.

He ruffled Lainey's thick, curly hair. "That's right, Short Stuff."

Estelle laid a leathery hand on John's arm. "Thank you."

"Go on, before you get left behind," he said gruffly, urging them aboard the bus.

Once they were inside the vehicle, John began to stride away. Surprised, Shoni hustled to catch up to him. She laid a hand on his right shoulder and he spun away, falling into a defensive crouch, the type she saw only among trained professionals.

He straightened shakily and glared at her. "What the hell do you want from me?"

"Who are you?" she asked, puzzled by the mysterious man.

He peered past her. "John McClane."

The name sounded familiar, but she couldn't place it. "How do I know you didn't start the fire?"

"I didn't." No hesitation.

"But you saw who did."

"What if I did?"

Shoni's heart skipped a beat. "Then you need to come down to the station and give your statement, as well as a description of the suspect."

"No."

Frustration tore through Shoni. John could be the key to cracking open the case. "If this person is the same one who torched three other warehouses, you'd be helping us put away a murderer."

John's eyes widened then narrowed.

"We found a body at the second scene," Shoni explained.

John stared at the blaze that was slowly being overcome. Shadows flickered across his face, etching and erasing angles and curves. As still as he stood, he could've been an ice sculpture.

Finally, he brought his attention back to her. "I'll tell you what I know after I find Mishon."

"Lainey's mother?"

He nodded.

Shoni considered his proposal. He'd told Lainey that he kept his promises.

"Deal."

John tilted his head, surprised she'd capitulated. "I'll meet you at the station after I take care of Mishon."

Shoni crossed her arms and shook her head. "No. We'll both get her and deliver her to Lainey."

John opened his mouth, but Shoni cut him off.

"Either we do it my way, or I take you to the station now and book you for loitering."

"Then I don't give you shit."

"It's not shit I want. It's a murderer. Do you know what it's like to be burned alive?"

John stiffened and his gaze became unfocused. The

hand that wasn't holding his backpack curled into a tight fist. And his pale face went milk white.

Alarmed, Shoni stepped closer and touched the back of his left hand. "Hey, John, you with me? McClane!"

He blinked, and awareness flowed back into his features along with some color. "Yeah, I know."

Shoni replayed their conversation in her mind and froze when she realized what he meant. "How?"

"I don't know." Before she could demand more of an explanation, he went on. "You have a car?" She nodded. "Where?"

"This way."

They retraced their route. She spotted Ian standing by the engine farthest from the fire. "I'm going to tell them I'm leaving," she said to John.

Perspiration sheened his brow, and she could sense his struggle to hide his exhaustion. Making a snap decision, she dug her car keys out of her pocket and handed them to John. "It's just around the corner. An eight-year-old blue Toyota four-door."

His eyebrows hiked upward. "I could steal your car."

She shook her head, hoping her gut wasn't playing her wrong. "You won't. I'll be there in a few minutes."

He stared at her, as if trying to determine if it was a trap. He tossed the keys in the air, caught them, and walked away.

After a moment, Shoni joined Ian, who was out of the main cacophony. "The homeless guy who warned the residents saw the arsonist."

Ian's expression lit up, but caution quickly overtook it. "Is he a reliable witness?"

"He's our *only* witness."

"You've got a point. Are you taking him down to the station?"

"After we run an errand." Ian frowned. "He promised a

little girl he'd find her mother," Shoni answered the unspoken question. "I made a deal with him—I help find the mother, then he comes in to give his statement and puts together a picture of the suspect."

Ian didn't look happy. "What if he's playing you?"

"I don't think so."

"Where is he?"

"He's waiting in my car."

"You didn't give him the keys, did you?"

Shoni glanced away. "Yes."

"When did you get to be such a pushover?"

She scowled. "Think what you want. He's the break we needed."

"Do you even know his name?"

"John McClane."

Ian chuckled without humor. "A Bruce Willis fan."

"What?"

"John McClane. The character Willis played in the *Die Hard* movies."

Shoni sucked in a sharp breath. "Damn—"

A rifle shot cracked, splintering the night.

Chapter Four

JOHN found what he figured was the cop's Toyota and shook his head. A sleek Corvette or a classic Mustang seemed more her style—all smooth lines and kick-ass acceleration. Like the woman herself.

A wave of exhaustion rolled over him and he paused by a patrol car, the Toyota's keys slipping from his icy fingers to clatter to the broken concrete. His head throbbed from both the knife wound and the smoke inhalation, and he considered following the keys to the ground. To simply close his eyes and give in to his fatigue sounded like nirvana. However, sitting on a cushioned car seat sounded like a better plan, so he clenched his jaw and leaned over to pick up the keys.

Glass exploded above him. Instinct sent John diving to the pavement. By the time his brain registered what his body had recognized, he was on the far side of the patrol car.

There was another sharp report and a bullet skimmed the hood, less than a foot from John's head. He rolled and pressed his back against the driver's door, fighting a conflicting barrage of reactions, with pissed off being at the top of the list. His fingers closed around an imaginary weapon and he could almost feel cool steel cradled in his hands, and smell the trace of gun oil and the tang of blood.

Despite the survival instinct that told him to stay hidden, another instinct, more powerful, urged him to his knees to peer around the car. To find the son of a bitch with the rifle. Another shot struck the front bumper. John dropped back behind the car's protection and swore. A nearby streetlight acted as a spotlight for the sniper, but left John basically blind. And vulnerable.

His fingers went to his neck, searching, but his night goggles weren't there. *Damn it! Where did I leave—*

Running footsteps snapped him back to the present. The detective and two uniformed cops raced toward him, their guns drawn. For a chilling moment, he stiffened, expecting one of their bullets to find him.

The detective dropped to a crouch beside him, and the two cops took cover behind another police cruiser. Alexander's shoulder pressed against his, her warmth seeping into him, heating parts of his body like single malt whiskey. He shifted enough that they no longer touched and he could think with his brain instead of the part of his anatomy that had picked a hell of a time to take renewed interest in a woman.

She cast her gaze around them. "Where'd the shot come from?"

Thankful for the distraction, he pointed in the general direction. "Don't know exactly where. Didn't catch a muzzle flash."

She shot him a glance. "You okay?"

"Yeah."

"Stay here," she ordered.

Every muscle in John's body rebelled, but he held himself in check and nodded. She kept low as she scurried to the back end of the car, then rose and dashed to the cover of her own car.

John closed his eyes and concentrated on his breathing, on the smooth flow of air in and out of his lungs. The repetition was familiar and the adrenaline seeped away, leaving him shaky but no longer wired.

There was no more gunfire, and some minutes later, Detective Alexander returned. Corkscrew tendrils curled around her face, and her lips were pressed together in a thin line.

"He's gone." She glared at him. "Who wants you dead, McClane?"

He frowned at her scornful tone and added a heavy dose of sarcasm to his reply. "Everybody loves me."

"Bullshit. Somebody was gunning for you."

Her eyes sparked an intriguing blend of green, blue, and gold. He tugged his gaze away before he got lost in the fireworks. He started to shrug, but the motion was aborted when his injured arm protested. "You said yourself that the arsonist is a murderer. Probably wants to get rid of the only witness."

She leveled her catlike eyes on him. "Arsonist and sniper usually don't go together."

He glared at her. "I wouldn't know."

A flash blinded John and he ducked, bringing up an arm to cover his eyes.

"Jenkins, get Jimmy Olsen out of here," Detective Alexander shouted, derision coloring her tone.

A patrol cop grabbed the camera wielder's arms.

"Ah, come on, Shoni, for old times' sake, give me something here," the reporter said.

John rubbed his watering eyes and slowly brought the blurred man into focus. He was a head shorter than John and built along more slender lines, like a swimmer or runner. Unlike John's clothing, it was doubtful that his sharply pleated khakis and polo shirt came off a secondhand store rack.

"If I do anything for old times' sake, it'll be tossing you in jail for obstruction," Alexander said, anger and something else twined in her tone.

"That wasn't my fault."

"Nothing is ever your fault." She sighed, the something else congealing into weariness. "Get him out of here."

"This is the fourth one. When are you going to tell the public there's a serial arsonist out there?" the blond man shouted as he was escorted away.

Detective Alexander muttered some creative phrases under her breath. John didn't think half of them were anatomically possible.

"Old boyfriend?" John asked dryly.

She jerked her head up, confirmation in her surprised features, but it was quickly masked. She took stock of the damaged car. John followed her gaze to the windowless door. Glass shards littered the backseat. It was pure luck that his brains weren't spattered there, too.

Her gaze turned to him and something akin to concern flitted across her face. "You cut? There's glass in your hair."

"Nah, don't think so." He leaned over and shook his head. Small, sparkly chips drifted to the street.

"Get in my car. I'll be right back."

Before he could argue with her curt command, she spun around and joined the circle of cops. Sighing, John picked up his backpack, then searched for the keys and found them on the ground in front of the patrol car's rear tire. He unlocked the Toyota's passenger door, tossed his pack onto the backseat, and slid inside. Tipping his head back against the headrest, he closed his eyes and surrendered to a heavy sigh.

He rubbed his whiskered jaw and grimaced. Damn, he wanted to shave, but that same instinct that had sent him diving for cover also told him to leave the beard. It hid his features, made him more difficult to identify, which shouldn't have made any sense. Didn't he want to know who he was?

Not if I don't want to know that person.

Frustrated with chasing his thoughts in an endless circle, he tilted his head to look out the side window. He had a clear view of the back of Detective Alexander as she spoke with the cops. His gaze roamed over her curly hair, tied back in a loose ponytail falling to the middle of her shoulder blades. The short brown jacket snugged around her slender waist, and gave him an unhindered view of her denim-encased backside. He imagined sliding his hands into those jeans pockets curved so enticingly around her ass. . . .

Realizing he had a hard-on for the first time in his limited memory, John didn't know whether to celebrate or damn his libido for its lousy timing.

Detective Alexander strode toward the car and John tugged down his jacket to cover the telltale bulge behind his zipper.

She folded herself behind the wheel and held out her hand. "Keys."

John dropped them in her palm. "What did you do?"

She shoved the key into the ignition and the engine turned over without a cough.

"Called in more personnel to search for the sniper's position," she replied.

"Even if they find his nest, I doubt they'll find any evidence."

Her fingers curved around the steering wheel. "Probably not, but we might get lucky." She studied him through narrowed eyes. "I didn't expect you to be so calm and cool after having a bull's-eye on your back."

John found he couldn't hold her gaze, and stared out the windshield at the dying fire's glow. He had the fleeting sensation of a rifle settled comfortably in his hands, and he pressed his fists into his lap. For all he knew about his own past, *he* had been a sniper. She had the resources to find out who he was. But if he was so accustomed to weapons, what did that say about him?

"Maybe I just hide it well." He lifted a shoulder. "If the arsonist is the sniper, he had lousy aim. Or maybe you're dealing with two psychos."

The fierce scowl on her face looked incongruous with

her delicate features. "One's more than enough. So where's the girl's mother?"

It took John a moment to switch gears. "Probably the corner of Palmer and Thirty-eighth."

Alexander pointedly stared at him.

"What?" he demanded.

"Buckle up."

Rolling his eyes, he pulled the seat belt across his chest and muttered, "You must have kids."

"Nope." She wheeled her car around and wound her way between emergency vehicles. "I've seen more than my share of car accident victims. Most of the dead ones wouldn't have been dead if they'd buckled up."

Once away from the scene, she stepped on the accelerator and they flew down the nearly deserted streets. "What about you? Any kids?"

John stared straight ahead. "None that I know of."

Alexander's lips curved downward in disapproval. He could live with her thinking he was an irresponsible jerk if it kept her from suspecting he was a criminal.

The heater's warmth and the rhythmic slap of tires against the pavement threatened to put John to sleep. It had been a long night, starting with the disagreement with Mishon's pimp and his hired muscle, and ending with getting shot at. And don't forget about meeting Detective Shoni Alexander, who might or might not be one of the good guys.

"People are calling you a hero," Detective Alexander said, breaking the silence.

John snorted. "That and a quarter won't even get a decent cup of coffee."

She glanced at him. "Don't be too sure of that. I'll introduce you to my boss."

One corner of her lips quirked upward, like it was a private joke. John didn't plan on sticking around for the punch line.

They arrived at Mishon's usual corner, but it was empty.

"Now where?" Alexander asked.

"There's an old hotel around the corner."

"The Ecstasy. Hourly rates."

It didn't surprise him that she knew of it. He figured it was on the cops' top ten list of places where people got laid in Norfolk. The detective drove around the block and parked in front of the rundown hotel.

"Something tells me she's not working the front desk," she said dryly.

"I hope not," John muttered as he shoved open his door. "A bed's more comfortable."

Shoni barely muffled her snort of laughter. After his stoic act, she didn't think he possessed a sense of humor.

The Ecstasy was well known as a "meeting place" for prostitutes and their customers. Shoni had done a tour of duty in this area as a beat cop and had gotten to know the characters inhabiting it. As long as they didn't draw undue attention to themselves, they were more or less left alone.

She felt a hand on her arm and halted. "What?" she asked, annoyed with herself for noticing the warmth and width of his palm.

"I'll do the talking," he said.

"Why?"

"You scream *cop*."

"So? It won't be the first time they've been rousted."

"I don't want Mishon to get in trouble."

Shoni's irritation grew. "She's a hooker."

John's blue eyes turned stormy gray. "She's Lainey's mother."

Shoni peered at him, trying to figure out if there was more going on between him and the girl's mother, but he was impossible to read. "All right, but if he doesn't tell you anything, I do it my way."

Although John didn't look happy—tough luck—he

nodded. He led the way into the lobby, going through the door first but holding it open for her.

The place hadn't changed much in five years. The muddy brown shag carpet held stains of every imaginable—and unimaginable—origin known to man and woman. It stank of stale cigarettes, staler liquor, and urine. Not exactly the Ritz.

The man behind the desk matched the décor. Four lank strands of greasy brown hair crisscrossed his head, and Shoni doubted he'd ever made the acquaintance of a toothbrush. A faded pink shirt dotted with grease and what she hoped was ketchup covered his concave torso.

"Twenty bucks an hour or a hundred 'til checkout time," the clerk said in a bored, nasal voice.

Shoni shuddered at the thought of checking into a room. Who knew what kind of bodily emissions were left by past visitors?

"You seen Mishon tonight?" John asked.

The clerk squinted at John. "You've been here before."

"I'm a friend of Mishon's."

The lecherous dick gave John a wink and a nudge with his bony elbow. "She's got a lot of friends."

John snatched the guy's shirtfront and hauled him halfway across the desktop. "I'm a *special* friend. What room is she in?"

"Twenty-five. Upstairs and to the right." The clerk couldn't answer fast enough.

John released him with a shove, and the man pinwheeled his arms as he struggled to keep his balance. He lost the battle and tumbled to the floor behind the counter, ass first.

"Remind me not to piss you off," Shoni said as they climbed the narrow stairs with only a low-wattage bulb lighting their path.

"You already have."

"I hope the fact that I'm a woman didn't inhibit your response," she said dryly.

John stopped in the hallway and canted a crooked grin. "Nah. I was in a good mood"—he surveyed her from head to toe, pausing on the swell of her breasts—"and I like feisty women."

Shoni wished she had something to fan her suddenly burning cheeks. The man was frustrating as hell. One moment cold and aloof, the next making her blush like some junior high schoolgirl.

John continued down the hall, leaving Shoni staring at his back. Although it was a very nice back—taking into account all the parts—she hurried to catch up. Her hand automatically checked the Glock at the small of her back.

The two of the number twenty-five hung upside down. Instead of the more modern key card, there was a doorknob with a keyhole. There was also a dull, rhythmic pounding against the wall. Shoni didn't need a cue card to tell her what was going on inside the room.

"Shouldn't put the beds so close to the wall in these places," she grumbled.

"Saves on the Do Not Disturb signs," John said.

"Good point. You want to break up the budding romance or should I?"

Instead of answering, John stepped back then launched forward, kicking the door directly above the knob. The wood shattered under his heel and the door swung inward. John pressed his left arm against the door, holding it open, and Shoni peered under his bicep to see the room's occupants.

The client scrambled out of bed and she caught the flash of a flat, pasty white ass. Her gaze flicked down to John's jeans-covered buns. No contest there.

"What you d-doin' here?" the woman asked.

"Looking for you," John replied with no sign of embarrassment.

The client tugged on enough clothes that he wouldn't violate indecency laws and made like a tornado escaping the room. Once he was gone, McClane stepped inside and Shoni followed, closing the door behind them.

Which was a mistake, because the tiny room reeked of sex. Holding her breath, Shoni opened a grimy window, and the screech told her no fresh air had entered this room in a very long time.

"The apartment where Gram lived burned down," John said to the hooker.

Mishon seemed to have trouble focusing on both John and his words. "What?"

"The apartment building." Impatience crept into his voice. "It's gone, burned to the ground."

Mishon sat up and the sheet slipped down, exposing her breasts and more than one scar from an overly enthusiastic customer. She didn't seem to notice her nudity. "L-Lainey?"

"You remember her?" John's tone could've cut diamonds. He took a deep breath and bent over to tug the sheet up to cover her exposed chest.

That small but thoughtful gesture spoke volumes about the man, and Shoni's respect for him climbed a notch.

When John spoke again, his voice gentled. "Lainey and your grandmother are fine. But they're staying in a different place. Lainey wanted me to find you and take you there."

"I'm workin'." Irritation crept back into the hooker's voice.

The lack of focus, the seesawing of moods, and the dilated pupils didn't come as any surprise to Shoni. She'd seen enough prostitutes to know that most of them were also addicts. It was a fairly cheap and easy way for a pimp to control his stable.

Gritting her teeth, Shoni gathered the young woman's scant clothing and dropped it on the bed. "You're done for the night. It's time to go see your daughter."

Mishon tried to stare her down, but failed. The hooker threw aside the blankets, exposing her undernourished body, and grabbed her panties. John turned away, giving Mishon the dignity of dressing without an audience, but Shoni didn't feel so generous. She crossed her arms and made sure Mishon didn't try to escape.

It didn't take Mishon long to throw a thigh-length knit dress a size too small over her bikini underwear. Shoes with three-inch heels completed her working attire.

"I gotta give Jamar the money," she said, picking up her purse.

"Later." John took hold of her thin arm. "Right now I'm taking you to Lainey."

Mishon made a feeble attempt to escape then allowed John to lead her out of the room and down the stairs. Shoni followed, marveling at this marshmallow-soft side of McClane. He obviously cared for Lainey and her small family. How had he met them? Why was he so devoted to them?

As they walked through the lobby, the clerk, his four strands of hair askew, swore at them. Shoni considered busting him for disturbing *her* peace, but didn't want to deal with the mandatory paperwork.

Following John through the exit, Shoni nearly bowled into his back when he came to an abrupt stop.

"What—" she began. Then she saw the reason for his sudden halt.

Son of a . . .

Chapter Five

. . . BITCH.

John yanked Mishon back and shoved her behind him. Jamar had cleaned up since their less-than-friendly exchange in the alley. Wearing a purple silk shirt open to his navel and tight black leather pants, the pimp exuded crude sensuality. No surprise, considering his line of work.

"She's done for the night," John growled.

"Not until I say she is." Jamar fingered the puckered scar that zigzagged his left cheek.

"My little girl needs me," Mishon said, picking a rotten time to stand up to her handler.

John swore inwardly as the pimp's eyes lit with perverted lust.

"Little Lainey." Coming from Jamar's lips, her name was an obscenity.

"I'm taking Mishon home," John said. "Now."

The two thugs who'd been with Jamar earlier emerged from the murky darkness.

"We'll escort you." A cold smile twisted Jamar's features. "It's not safe on the streets this time of night."

The detective stepped forward. "I think we can handle it."

Jamar's eyes narrowed. "This isn't any of your business. Cop."

Alexander smiled with no hint of amusement or surprise that he recognized her. "Sure it is. I'm protecting the good citizens from garbage like you."

The pimp's nostrils flared as his two henchmen took a step toward her. Jamar lifted a hand, halting them in their tracks. "If you want to waste your time protecting these 'good citizens' "—Jamar made a production of stepping aside—"go right ahead."

Gnashing his teeth, John tugged Mishon along behind him. He had no doubt Detective Alexander was watching his six.

The Toyota was still in one piece and John assisted Mishon into the front seat. He crowded in beside her as Alexander slid behind the wheel. Tires squealed, leaving rubber on the pavement.

Mishon's head lolled and her eyelids were at half mast. She was so high John suspected she didn't even know she was in a moving car.

"She needs help," the detective said.

"She's quit a couple of times, but can't stay away from it. I suppose you've seen a lot like her."

"Too many."

Although her tone was matter-of-fact, John spotted the compassion softening her expression.

"It's a good thing her mother is willing to look after Lainey," Alexander said.

"Grandmother. Estelle is Lainey's great-grandmother. Mishon's mother died of an overdose about nine years ago, when Mishon was eleven."

John could almost hear Alexander's mental calculations.

"Mishon was what, thirteen, fourteen when she had Lainey?"

"Thirteen. And no, she doesn't know who Lainey's father is," John answered before she could ask.

As John had recovered from his head wound, Estelle had sat beside him, telling him about her own family. It had given John something to dwell on besides the empty darkness in his mind.

The inky night cocooned them in the vehicle and Mishon's soft snores were the only sound except for the tires rolling over broken pavement.

"So, what's your story, John McClane? How do you know Lainey and her family?"

Detective Alexander's voice was lower, more husky, and it arrowed straight south of John's gut. He peered out the side window, at the empty sidewalks and little shops interspersed with homes no middle-class family would ever consider living in. "They helped me when I needed help."

"Simple as that?"

"Yep." He found he didn't want to lie any more than was necessary.

Five minutes later the detective pulled into a motel's parking lot, the address the Red Cross had given Estelle as their temporary shelter. It wasn't the Marriott, but it was definitely more reputable than the Ecstasy.

"Wait here. I'll ask the desk clerk what room Estelle and Lainey are in," the detective said.

Twenty minutes later, John and Alexander were back in the car, sans Mishon. Both Estelle and Lainey had been awake, waiting for them. John had half-carried the barely coherent Mishon inside then deposited her in one of the two bedrooms. He and Alexander had made short good nights and returned to the car.

As they sat in the car, John was aware of the cop's scrutiny but chose to ignore it. She'd kept her end of the bargain to retrieve Mishon. Now it was John's turn to make good on his part. "Let's get this over with."

"It's after four. You should get some rest before we go in to the station," she said.

Bitterness brought a scowl to his face. "Sure. Drop me off at the nearest park. I'm sure there's an open bench."

Her lips curved downward. "Make it easy for the shooter to succeed this time? I thought you were smarter than that, McClane."

"I didn't know you cared, Detective."

She glanced away. "Didn't believe me, huh?"

I care.

It seemed like ages ago that she'd spoken those two powerful words.

"Look, you're our only witness, McClane, and someone is after you. That means you need police protection until this guy is caught," the detective said.

Panic flooded through John. "Forget it. Just take me back to the neighborhood. I'll find my own hiding place." He reached for the door handle.

Alexander reached across him and grabbed his hand. Her shoulder pressed against his chest and a small but soft breast flattened on his abdomen. He willed his libido to behave. The way she was laid out across him, she'd have no trouble feeling him.

"I'm not going to risk losing you," she said, her face turned upward to meet his gaze. "You're too important to the case."

The case. That was all that mattered. It shouldn't have bothered him, but it did. "Let's go to the station now. I'll give you a description of the guy, and then you won't have to worry about me any longer."

"We'll need you to identify him from a lineup when we pick up a suspect."

Frustrated with her, his body's treasonous reactions, and

the loss of his home, John gripped her wrist, his fingers automatically finding the pressure points.

She yelped and released him. Pressing back against the door, she rubbed her hand. "What the hell was that?"

"Just letting you know I can take care of myself."

"All right. I get it. You can take care of yourself. But right now, you're exhausted. You need someplace safe to sleep." He opened his mouth to argue, but she held up a hand. "No safe house. No police protection, other than me. Acceptable?"

The blinking amber Vacancy sign from the motel haloed her dark head, and the color of her eyes kept shifting, from gold to green and back. Mesmerizing, like a cat's eyes. He shook himself before falling prey to the predator.

No doubt about it, he was tired and aching, and his lungs felt like they were filled with smoky phlegm. Damn Alexander for being right. But could he trust her?

Could he trust himself?

She remained still, giving him time to think, to decide. He ran a hand over his injured arm and stifled a flinch.

"Where would you take me?" he asked.

"I know a place. No one will find you there."

He didn't have much of a choice.

Detective Alexander drove away from the motel and he closed his eyes.

"Wake up, McClane. We're here," Alexander said.

He opened gummy eyes, surprised to realize he'd fallen asleep, and that they'd stopped in a well-lit, fenced parking lot.

"Think you can navigate on your own?" she asked.

"No problem." Some inner sense told him he'd maneuvered under far more extreme conditions.

Despite his assurance, she came around to his side and opened his door. However, she didn't attempt to help him. Smart woman.

He dragged himself out of the car and remembered to

snag his backpack from the backseat. The detective bent over and pulled a metal box from under the passenger seat. She tucked it under her arm and crossed the street to a fancy multistoried building. She paused in front of the spotless glass entrance door and a buzzer sounded. Pulling the door open, she entered and John followed.

A twentysomething man wearing a sharply pressed security uniform smiled. "You're up early, Shoni."

"Make that up late, Pete. It's been a busy night."

"Anything to do with that fire?"

She smiled crookedly. "Listening to the police band again?"

Pete grinned with boyish chagrin. "Who's your friend?"

"Pete, this is John. John, Pete."

John nodded at him, wary of anybody in a uniform, even a rent-a-cop. Pete's lips turned downward but he didn't voice his disapproval.

"John will be staying in the condo for a little while," the detective said.

The security guard turned his attention back to her. "I check it every evening when I come on duty. It might need an airing out, but otherwise everything's fine."

"Thanks. I appreciate it."

"No problem, Shoni."

The way Pete looked at the detective reminded John of a puppy. The kid had it bad.

"Elevator," the detective said to John, leading the way.

The doors swished open immediately. Shoni punched number twelve and the car rose with soundless efficiency.

"You live here?" John asked.

She pressed her lips together and shook her head.

Puzzled, John tried to read her expression, but she veiled her thoughts well.

The elevator glided to a gentle stop and the doors swished open. Again, John followed the silent detective down a hallway that smelled fresh and flowery. Thick carpeting muffled their footsteps and subdued lighting gave the impression of understated elegance. Compared to Estelle's apartment building, this place was obscenely opulent.

Detective Alexander halted and fumbled with her keys before finding the right one to unlock the door. She swung it open and motioned for him to precede her.

He stepped across the threshold and froze.

The foyer's ceiling was more than ten feet high and pale gold wallpaper covered the walls. On the floor was a rich tapestry rug that seemed too extravagant to walk on. A bronze and glass lantern-style wall lamp lit the entrance with a soft glow.

He was vaguely aware of the detective slipping in behind him and closing the door.

"You can hang your coat in there," she said, pointing to a closet on the left.

Moving gingerly, he removed his duct-taped jacket. The turtleneck's long sleeves hid his bandage, but he suspected the detective already knew he was injured.

As he hung up his jacket, she went around him and flicked on the lights in the first room, which turned out to be a spacious kitchen. It was neat and tidy, with an array of high-end appliances scattered across the granite-topped counters. A computer with a flat-screen monitor sat on the built-in corner desk.

"Let me give you the ten cent tour," the detective said.

He nodded, and wondered if he should pinch himself to ensure he wasn't dreaming. She led him into the dining area, which had a glass-topped table with an empty vase in the center of it. One wall was covered by mirrored panels that reflected the city lights streaming through sliding glass doors that led out to a balcony. The mirror taunted him with his shaggy appearance—long hair, untrimmed beard, and filthy jeans. He had a difficult time reconciling that person with the image he carried of himself in his fractured memory. He deliberately turned away.

The dining room's hardwood floor and the living room's beige carpet were the only separation between the two rooms. A fireplace sat in the far corner with two comfortable chairs and a small table artfully arranged in front of it. A flat screen television hung on the largest living room wall, and a sofa and love seat were placed in an L-shape around it.

The faint scent of some herb tickled his nose and he sneezed.

"Bless you," the detective said.

"What is that smell?"

She glanced away self-consciously. "Sage. Mom was into aromatherapy and cleansing auras and stuff like that."

Pragmatic Detective Alexander's mother was a New Age disciple? It boggled John's mind.

She opened a set of French doors off the dining room. "You can sleep in here."

John peeked inside the room, not surprised to see it was furnished as tastefully as the rest of the condo. However, it was obviously a woman's bedroom. "Whose room is this?"

She pressed her lips together and looked past him. Her detective mask dropped, revealing haunted grief. "My mother's. This was her place. She died a couple of months ago."

"I'm sorry," John said awkwardly. "I don't have to stay here."

Her cop persona snapped back in place. "It's just sitting here empty. No reason for you not to take advantage of it."

John could've argued with her, but the lure of sleeping in a real bed was too powerful.

"There's a master bathroom you can use," she added. A warm smile made her look younger, more approachable . . . sexier. "Use all the hot water you want."

Now he definitely couldn't resist.

"Thanks." It was hard for him to say the word, but he managed.

Before he woke and found himself back in his cold warehouse office, John strode into the bathroom and closed the door behind him. For a moment, he thought he'd stepped into the wrong room. The bathroom was nearly the size of the kitchen, with two sinks, a soaking tub, and a separate shower. Marble tile and gold fixtures gave the illusion he was in some sort of storybook castle. And he was the bewitched prince. Or the beast . . .

His mind suddenly foggy from exhaustion, John dropped his backpack on the floor and started the water. By the time he'd undressed, steam rolled through the bathroom. He stepped into the shower and pulsing streams of hot water massaged him.

Paradise.

AS Shoni stripped the bed, she heard a long, drawn-out moan from the bathroom. John must be in the shower. That brought an image to mind that was anything but professional, and she reluctantly banished it.

Shoni concentrated on removing the sheets that had been on the bed for over two months. The faint scent of her mother's favorite lotion wafted around her and she turned, half expecting to see Iris Alexander standing in the room. But the bedroom remained empty except for Shoni's memories. She sank onto the edge of the mattress, the sheet clutched between her hands.

Futility raged through her. Her mother's murderer still walked around free, never to be punished by a system that racked and stacked in favor of the criminals. She used to believe in innocent until proven guilty. Her father had instilled in her that sense of justice, and she'd lived by that creed for as long as she could remember.

Until her mother's death.

Shoni took a deep, shuddering breath, willing herself to ignore the memories evoked by the familiar scent. Feeling the lure of soul-deep exhaustion, she pushed herself upright and finished making the bed with clean linens.

As she smoothed the last wrinkle from the comforter, the bathroom door opened. John exited amid a cloud of steam. He wore the same filthy clothes, but his clean feet were bare. With wet hair plastered to his scalp and whiskers covering the lower half of his face, Shoni shouldn't have had any hormonal flare-ups. So how did she explain the heat crawling through her belly?

"Do you have something to get out a splinter?" he asked, holding his right hand in his left.

She looked closer and saw blood pearling on his forefinger. "Mom has, uh, had some tweezers." She searched a dresser drawer until she found them.

He thrust his hand toward her. "Piece of glass. Must've been in my hair."

Her heart thumped against her ribs as she cradled his hand in hers and bent her head over it. She tried to find the splinter through the scarlet drop but failed. "Blot the blood away."

John plucked a tissue from the box on the dresser and dabbed the liquid. His warm, minty-fresh breath wafted across the side of her neck, and she shivered.

"Can you see it?" he asked, yanking her attention back to her task.

Squinting, Shoni spotted the silvery splinter. She gripped his hand a little tighter. "Here goes." She grasped the end with the pincers and withdrew the tiny glass sliver.

John pressed the tissue against his finger and nodded his gratitude.

She rinsed the tweezers under the faucet in the bathroom while John put a bandage on the cut. After pouring some alcohol over the tweezers, she set them aside and returned to the bedroom.

John stood in the middle of her mother's room, looking out of place amid the feminine decor. "She had good taste," he said.

Shoni examined the room as if seeing it through John's eyes. "I was always too much of a tomboy to get into the frilly stuff." She shrugged. "Guess I still am."

She crossed her arms and his gaze fastened on her chest. Realizing he could see her nipples outlined by her knit shirt, she dropped her arms to her sides. "Are you feeling better?"

"Much. I don't remember the last time I got to indulge in a long, hot shower."

She smiled at the genuine pleasure in his tone. "I put clean sheets on the bed."

"You didn't have to do that. I'm used to making do." He glanced around the room. "Not that staying here is any hardship."

"Are you hungry?"

"Yes, but I don't think I'd stay awake long enough to eat."

She studied him more closely, noting the pallor of his face and the slight tremor in his hands. "I'll make something for you when you wake up, then."

"You don't have to."

"It's no problem. I'll be staying."

"Nobody's going to get to me here."

"That's right. Nobody is." Steel threaded through her voice. She turned to the door but paused before leaving. "If you need anything, I'll be in the bedroom on the other side of the living room."

She closed the door behind her and wandered into the kitchen. Placing her hands on the counter, she leaned into them and hung her head. Why had she brought him here? She should've checked him into the same motel that his friends were in.

The last time she'd been in the condo was a month ago, when she'd tried to start the cleaning-out process. She had lasted all of five minutes surrounded by her mother's things. She glanced at her mother's prized Tellurium clock sitting on the mantel—going on forty-five minutes in the condo. A new record.

A jaw-cracking yawn caught her off guard. It had been a long night, compounded by her suddenly overactive libido. She worked with and met men every day, some worth more than a sneak peek, so why was she attracted to John McClane?

John McClane. Even his name should've put her off.

Her intuitive female brain trusted McClane. A man could fake a name, but he couldn't fake his basic character for long. He'd saved the lives of everyone in the apartment building and brought a young girl's mother home safely.

However, her logical cop brain told her she had no reason to trust him. If McClane was hiding his real name, what else was he hiding? The fighting skills he'd shown in the alley when she'd first met him weren't moves the average person would know. His catlike stealth and coolness under fire were also not commonly found among the homeless.

Didn't catch a muzzle flash.

Recalling his comment after the sniper attack, Shoni furrowed her brow. What kind of person would talk about muzzle flashes with such easy familiarity? Those associated with law enforcement and the military.

And possibly criminals.

Sleep. That's what she needed. Twenty-four hours of uninterrupted bliss.

Not going to happen.

Maybe two or three hours, if she was lucky. She stumbled across the floor to her bedroom and flipped on the light. Keeping her mind blank, she unclipped her holster and gun and set them on the nightstand. Although it was unlikely they'd have any visitors, she wasn't going to take any chances. She undressed mechanically and pulled on an oversized T-shirt from the dresser drawer.

Her gaze strayed to the top of the dresser, where a neatly folded pile of clothing sat. Since the condo was closer to the station than her own apartment, Shoni had sometimes crashed here instead of making the longer drive.

Consequently, she always kept spare clothes here. Her mother had never once complained about doing her adult daughter's laundry.

Shoni ran her fingertips along a shirt on top of the pile. This was probably the last load of laundry her mother had done before going out to be struck down, the victim of a drunk driver.

The memory of her mother's broken and bloody body on the pavement sucker punched her.

Chapter Six

JOHN lay staring at the unfamiliar ceiling. After knowing only a rigid couch these past few screwed-up weeks, it was damned near impossible to get comfortable on the soft mattress. Maybe if he slept on the floor. . . .

A muffled sob from the living room startled him, driving away his restlessness. The idea that the tough-as-nails detective was crying was as unlikely as Mishon swearing off drugs. But who else would it be?

He rose, wearing only his tattered boxers, and glided across the plush carpet, his bare feet luxuriating in the hedonistic pleasure. He cracked open the French doors. The sunrise lent a coral glow to the spacious outer rooms, and the dusky light was more than enough for him to see Detective Alexander's hunched-up figure on the love seat. Why wasn't she asleep?

Because she's surrounded by memories of her dead mother.

He couldn't remember his past and she couldn't forget hers. It would've been funny if it weren't so true.

Even as stealthily as he moved, something alerted her to his presence and her head came up sharply, her gaze pinning him from across the expansive room.

"Why aren't you sleeping?" Her expression didn't reflect the tears that thickened her voice.

He opened the French doors wider, unconcerned about his state of undress. As a cop, she'd more than likely seen worse. "That's what I was going to ask you," he said.

She grabbed a decorative pillow and clutched it to her chest. Classic self-protective gesture.

And how the hell do I know that?

"I'm not tired." The dark crescents beneath her eyes gave lie to her words. Her gaze moved over him and she grimaced. "Is all that from the fight in the alley?"

He glanced down at his torso, surprised by the colorful bruises. "I guess."

"You could use a fresh bandage on the arm."

"It's fine."

She sighed and her mask slid away, revealing a weary, heart-stricken woman. "Go back to bed, John."

Even though he couldn't remember the specific circumstances, he knew what it was like to be alone with grief. However, he also recognized the emptiness of well-meaning words. Yet everything in him resisted leaving her alone with her pain.

Before he talked himself out of it, he approached her. As he drew closer, he noticed slender bare legs folded beneath her. He sucked in a breath, realizing that only an oversized T-shirt covered her body. However, the telltale glimmer of a single tear trail scattered his X-rated imaginings.

He sat on the love seat beside her, forcing himself to lean back in a casual pose. "Want to talk about it?"

Misery lanced her expression before she could hide it, and she turned her face toward the window, giving him her profile. "What's to talk about?"

"Whatever's bothering you."

She glared at him. "So you're a shrink?"

The idea that he might be a psychologist or counselor made him smile wryly. "How did she die?"

Her gaze skittered away again. The clock on the mantel ticked loudly in the heavy silence.

"She was hit by a drunk driver," she finally replied in a husky voice.

He recognized the detective's unnatural stiffness. Recognized the battle to lock in the sorrow, to move past it without surrendering.

He lifted a shaking hand and placed it on her shoulder. Her muscles shifted beneath his palm, growing impossibly tighter.

She blinked, and a tear rolled down her cheek. She scrubbed it away with her hand. "I hate crying." The anger in her voice contrasted with the desolation in her eyes.

"So do I."

Her shoulders jerked once, then again. John slipped his arm around her and drew her close to his side. She pressed her face into the curve of his neck and laid her arm on his waist. Her skin was hot against his, but not as scalding as the tears that dampened his shoulder.

He expected wracking sobs, but her silent cries were even more excruciating to bear. Tightening his embrace, he wished he had the ability to absorb some of her pain. He rocked her in his arms and crooned reassuring words. Even if she didn't hear what he said, he hoped the soothing tone might calm her.

As the sun cleared the horizon, Shoni grew still and silent. However, she didn't attempt to move out of the circle of his arms.

Now that the emotional storm had passed, John became aware of a small but soft breast pressed against his side. Her bare thigh touched his, and it took every ounce of control not to run his palm over her silky leg. He hadn't comforted her in an effort to get in her panties, but that didn't mean he wasn't tempted to take advantage of the situation. Hell, he was only human.

Disgusted with himself and the inappropriate but undeniable flare of arousal, he eased her up and away from him.

"Do you think you can sleep now?" he asked her.

Her damp eyelashes were matted together and her eyes were red and puffy, but John's awakened libido didn't care. He still wanted her and wished like hell he'd thrown on his jeans. A pair of boxers hid only so much. . . .

"I think so," she said, her voice raspy.

He stood, anxious to put some distance between them, and kept his gaze firmly fixed on her face. "All right. We should both go to bed. Our own beds . . . separate." His cheeks flared with heat. Damn, he sounded like a kid with equal amounts of raging hormones and embarrassment.

A tiny, amused smile tugged at her lips. "Good night, John."

"Good night, Detective."

He fled toward his room.

"Thank you," she said.

He paused and looked over his shoulder at her. "You're welcome." He closed the French doors with a definitive *snick* and climbed back into the soft, warm bed.

However, the sensation of Shoni's soft, warm body lingered and sleep was long in coming.

IT was the tantalizing smell of freshly made coffee that brought John out of a deep, dreamless slumber. Disconcerted, he lay motionless as he tried to determine where the hell he was. It wasn't the couch in the warehouse, and it wasn't his own be—

A soft knock sounded on the door. "McClane?"

Detective Shoni Alexander. The events of the previous night—and early morning—returned in startling clarity.

"Uh, yeah. Just give me a minute."

"Take your time. I'll make breakfast."

John's stomach growled loud enough that he wouldn't be surprised if she'd heard it. However, the noises coming from the kitchen told him she'd already moved away from the door.

Breakfast and coffee without having to raid any Dumpsters was a luxury in itself. And the only reason good enough to leave the cozy warmth of the bed.

He sat up and stifled a groan. His injured arm was stiff and painful. He threw off the covers and headed for the bathroom, moving with all the grace of an elephant on rollerblades. After taking care of the first order of business, he squeezed some toothpaste on a finger and brushed his teeth. Studying his image in the full-length mirror—which was a hell of a thing to put in a bathroom—John eyed the dark blue and purple bruises across his chest and abdomen.

Superficial.

No internal damage.

Ignoring the clinical voice in his head, he unwrapped the bandage from his wounded arm, hissing as the material stuck to the cut. The area around the laceration was reddish and swollen. Just his luck to end up dying from an infection.

He replaced the old bandage, relegating the concern of infection to the back of his mind, then finger-combed his shaggy hair and smoothed his beard. The shower beckoned, but the lure of hot coffee and food easily won the toss-up.

Returning to the bedroom, he noticed a large plastic shopping bag sitting inside the French doors. It hadn't been there earlier that morning. John picked up the bag and deposited it on the bed. Inside were clothes from a chain discount store.

He drew out a pair of blue jeans and read the tag. His size. There was also a pair of black jeans, a dark blue V-neck sweater, two turtlenecks, and a brown fleece shirt. Even bags of socks, underwear, and T-shirts. Buried at the bottom were a comb, toothbrush, deodorant, and razor.

What the hell?

"Five minutes," she called from the other side of the door.

Uncertain if he should be grateful or pissed off by her generosity, John glanced at the only set of clothes he owned, which were grimy and reeked of smoke. His pride rolled with the punches and the scales tipped in favor of gratitude.

After removing the tags from the new clothes, he dressed as quickly as he could with his clamoring aches and pains. At least his lungs didn't feel like someone had poured hot, lumpy oatmeal into them. Grimacing, he slipped his white-stockinged feet into his filthy, tattered tennis shoes.

He swung open the French doors. The condo looked even more impressive in the full light of day, with bright sunshine filling every corner up to the ceiling. Warbling chimes caught his attention and he spotted a glass-encased gold clock on the mantel.

Twelve noon.

"Good afternoon."

John turned around to face the detective, who looked more like a woman than a cop today. A navy blue knit top hugged her slender upper body and was tucked into low-rise khaki jeans. A wide belt accented the curve of her hips. Instead of tying her hair back, Shoni had left it free to curl around her face and soften her features.

She cast her gaze across him. "Glad to see the clothes fit."

His cheeks heated at her perusal. "Uh, yeah, they do. You didn't have to . . ."

"No big deal, McClane," she said gruffly. "They're nothing fancy. No designer labels."

Her embarrassment made his lips twitch with amusement. Detective Alexander was back. "Well, gee, back on the street I always wore Brioni and Zanella."

Shoni snorted, hearing the sarcasm in his bland tone. However, her spidey-cop senses went on full alert. After dating fashion-conscious Mack St. Clare, she'd come to know the high-end labels, but how did John know of them? Maybe he was one of those homeless who'd been well-off at one time, but through fate or design had lost everything. It might explain why he used a fake name, too.

"Ready to eat?" she asked.

She motioned to the breakfast bar. Steaming plates filled with scrambled eggs, sausage, and toast were set at each place, along with a cup of coffee and a glass of water. When she'd gone out earlier to buy the clothes, she'd swung by a grocery store to get enough food to last a few days.

John perched on a stool, his movements stiff. She'd worked around men for the last eight years and recognized the signs. He'd sooner admit to being a cross-dresser than being in pain.

Stupid macho men.

"Cream or sugar?" she asked.

His rusty laugh startled her. "Hey, I'm just happy when I can get hot coffee."

Way to go, Alexander. Guy's been living on the street, probably grateful to get one hot meal a day. "Helluva way to live."

"Not much choice."

She wanted to ask him why, but as skittish as the man was, he'd probably fly out the door, never to be seen again. Besides, he was staring at the food like it was a woman and he'd been trapped in a monastery for months. She owed him, too, for holding her while she'd cried, even though she shied away from the subject, and planned to keep it that way. "Dig in."

John didn't waste any time. He kept his head down, interspersing sips of coffee with forkfuls of eggs and sausage. He spread peanut butter across a piece of toast, his expression one of rapture. Yet despite his obvious hunger, he ate like a man accustomed to formal dining.

Zanella, Brioni, impeccable table manners . . .

Who are you, John McClane?

He finished his food and Shoni glanced down at hers. She'd eaten little, yet couldn't eat another mouthful. She pushed her plate toward him. "Here."

"You should finish it."

"I'm not hungry," Shoni said, and upped the ante. "Either you eat it or it goes down the garbage disposal."

John hesitated a few moments more, then stacked her plate on his empty one. "Shouldn't be wasting food," he muttered, then attacked the remaining food.

She rotated her stool until she faced the balcony windows, sparing John an audience while he scarfed down the food. However, awareness of his solid body next to hers was harder to ignore. A shower and new clothes had done wonders for a body already gifted with broad shoulders and narrow waist and hips—attributes she'd witnessed up close and personal early that morning. The powder blue turtleneck complemented his eyes just as she imagined it would. His longish light brown hair had dried in thick waves with a few graduating to curls. All he needed was a trip to the barber to get rid of the beard and mustache.

Blinking aside her personal fantasy, she swiveled back to face him. "I wish I could've let you sleep a little longer, but my boss wants me in at one."

John dabbed at his lips with his napkin. "I had enough sleep."

She carried their empty plates into the kitchen and stacked them in the dishwasher, too aware of John's gaze on her. Was he feeling sorry for her? It had been years since she'd cried in the presence of another person. But her embarrassment was tied up with anger. While she'd been acting like some weak female and crying on John's shoulder, she'd left him and herself vulnerable. What if the man who'd shot at John had learned where he was? It would've been her own stupidity that would've gotten them killed.

She retrieved the coffeepot, refilled their cups, and remained standing on the other side of the breakfast bar to drink hers. Spying the slight bulge beneath John's upper sleeve, she remembered the less-than-sanitary bandage around his arm.

"Did you change the bandage on your arm this morning?" she asked.

He blinked, as if startled. "No."

"I'll do it now."

His eyes darted about. "It's almost one o'clock. You'll be late."

She rolled her eyes. "You're the key to the case. My first priority is to keep you alive and well."

He glanced away. "It's just a scratch."

"Why don't I believe you?" She went around the bar and into the bathroom by her bedroom, returning with a first aid kit. "Take off your shirt."

"Are you coming on to me, Detective?" John asked, his voice low and sexy. The kind of voice a man used to get a woman into his bed.

Shoni's belly fluttered and waves rippled through her. What was it about this man that pushed all her buttons? And why was she letting him sidetrack her? "Lose the shirt, McClane."

He scowled, and stood to tug the sweater over his head. The turtleneck came with it, leaving him bare from the waist up. Although she'd seen his torso that morning, she'd been too surprised by the bruises to notice his cut abs and defined pecs. How did a homeless man end up with a six pack that would be the envy of gym junkies?

"You gonna change the bandage or stare at me all day?" McClane asked in irritation.

If she had a choice . . . She cleared her throat. "Sit down."

He did so, and she reached for the duct tape that covered the injury. The adhesive was loose and she eased the gray tape away from his skin; the bloodstained gauze bandage came with it. The gash was larger than she'd expected. "Why didn't you get this stitched up?"

He glared at her. "Either put a new bandage on it or slap the old one back on."

Shoni pressed her lips together and managed to rein in her temper. Where was the man who'd comforted her that morning? She carried the ball of tape and gauze to the wastebasket, then ran hot water into a bowl, grabbed a clean cloth, and returned to his side.

"This'll hurt," she said.

"Needs to be done."

Grasping his elbow with one hand, Shoni wiped dried blood from around the wound. She smoothed the damp cloth up and down his bicep, and muscle flexed beneath golden skin. She concentrated on her task, refusing to give in to the impulse to press her lips to his warm skin.

"When was your last tetanus shot?" she asked.

"Can't remember."

"We'll stop on the way to the station and get you one."

"I don't have any insurance."

Shoni bit her tongue. She'd make sure he got a tetanus shot and anything else he needed, whether he wanted it or not. "So, this come from the fight in the alley?"

"Yeah," he replied reluctantly. "I zigged when I should've zagged."

"When I saw you, you seemed to be doing a pretty good job of both zigging and zagging. Where did you learn to fight like that?"

He stiffened. "Here and there," he replied vaguely.

"Mystery man to the end, huh?" She smiled, hoping the gesture would unravel his knotted muscles.

Although the crooked smile appeared forced, some of his tension melted away. "I hear women prefer the strong, silent types."

Shoni chuckled. "You've read too many books." She held a towel against his arm, beneath the bottom of the gash. "Time for the hydrogen peroxide."

He clenched his teeth and nodded shortly.

Shoni grimaced in empathy as she poured the peroxide into the reddened wound. The only visible sign of John's discomfort was a tic in his jaw.

When she was satisfied it had been irrigated enough, she set the brown bottle on the bar and dabbed around the cut.

She bent down to look into his pale face. "How're you doing?"

"Fine," he replied through gritted teeth.

Like hell he was. Shoni applied a new bandage and wrapped his arm. "I'll be right back."

She closed her bedroom door behind her and placed the first aid kit back in her bathroom. Digging the cell phone out of her pocket, she punched in a familiar number.

McClane is going to be majorly pissed.

Chapter Seven

THE moment Shoni was out of sight, John pressed a hand to his stinging arm. The peroxide burned more than the infection.

"Suck it up, soldier," John muttered to himself as he donned his turtleneck and pullover.

As much as he hadn't wanted the detective to see his wound, he was glad for her assistance. Maybe the cleansing would kick the infection in the ass.

He glanced in the direction Shoni had gone and frowned. How long did it take to put a first aid kit away? He walked across the living room to her bedroom's closed door and heard her muffled voice. Frowning, he drew closer and tried to make out her words.

"He won't be happy, but I'll have him there in twenty minutes. See you then."

John darted back to the breakfast bar before she caught him eavesdropping. Had she been talking to her boss?

"Ready to go?" she asked, returning to the kitchen.

"The police station?"

She headed to the foyer, avoiding eye contact. "That's right."

Although the detective hadn't given John any reason not to trust her, his internal alarm buzzed. The phone call was probably to let her boss know they'd be late. So why had she made the call behind a closed door? And why was she avoiding his gaze? He ducked into his room to get his backpack that now bulged with the new clothes.

"You can leave that," she said. "I'll bring you back here after you've given your statement."

"I'm taking it." If he had to make a fast escape, he wanted his pack.

She shrugged. "Suit yourself."

After donning their jackets, Shoni locked the condo behind them and they rode down in the elevator in silence.

An older security guard at the front desk glanced up as they approached. "I didn't know you'd stayed at your mother's place, Shoni." He eyed John with an arched brow. "With a guest."

Her cheeks burned, but she didn't correct his assumption. "It was late when we got in. We'll be back later today, after a trip to the department."

The gray-haired guard picked up a pen. "Guest's name?"

"John McClane," John said before Shoni could answer.

The guard jotted it down. "As long as you vouch for him, he can come and go."

She smiled, although to John's eyes, the gesture appeared tenuous. "I will."

"As long as you know what you're doing. . . ." The security man's voice trailed off, his meaning clear.

Shoni bristled. "I'm a big girl now, Robert."

Before he could sputter a response, Shoni strode away.

John lengthened his stride to catch up to her. "What's with him?"

Shoni sighed. "He's worked here since I was in high school. He still thinks of me as a kid."

"So you grew up here?"

"More or less."

Although curious about her ambivalent reply, John didn't pursue any more answers.

As they neared her car, he recalled the metal box Shoni had retrieved from under the passenger seat and taken into the condo. "You're leaving your backup here?"

Blankness met his question.

"I figured that box under the seat held your backup piece," he elaborated.

An expression close to guilt passed across her features. Averting her gaze, she opened her car door. "I'm just going to be in the office today. I figured I didn't need it."

As gung-ho as she was about protecting him, John was surprised at her lack of concern for a second weapon. He'd always carried more than one. . . . The memory ghosted away.

"You gonna stand there all day, McClane?"

Her impatient question galvanized him into action and he slid into the car. She paused at the exit and stuck a card in the slot. The arm lifted, and she drove out into the lunch hour traffic.

"Can you remember what the arsonist looked like?" she asked.

That was one of the few things he *could* remember. "You'll get your description. How many fires has this guy started?"

She tipped her head to the side, sending a springy tendril of hair across her forehead. Using a delicate hand, she brushed it back. His groin tightened unexpectedly.

"Last night's was the fourth. The second killed a man, which is why the case landed on my desk."

"How do you know the fires are connected?"

"Need to know, McClane."

Need to know. The words stumbled around in his mind's

maze, and a man with piercing brown eyes and short gray hair flashed through his memory. Again John attempted to cut through the static, but like all the times before, the near-memory slid away.

"John, you with me?"

Shoni's concerned voice scattered the tatters away.

"Yeah." The word came out as a growl. He hated the elusive memories, hated that his own mind conspired against him.

"How'd a guy like you end up on the street?" she asked.

I wish I knew.

"Things happen."

She turned in to the parking lot of a medical clinic. He glanced around, his suspicions returning. "Why are we stopping here?"

The detective parked the car and took the key out of the ignition. "You have a doctor's appointment."

"I don't have any insurance or money."

"I do." She opened her door and stepped out.

John remained in his seat. Shoni jerked his door open and leaned in. "You aren't scared of a little needle, are you, McClane?"

"Your insurance doesn't cover me."

"It does here. Come on." She took hold of his wrist and tugged.

Ever since Detective Alexander had entered the picture, his life—such as it was—had been thrown into chaos. Almost burned alive. Getting shot at. Was Alexander involved? But if she wanted him dead, she could've done away with him any time she chose.

So having a blank slate makes me a little paranoid. I'm allowed.

Surrendering, he allowed her to pull him out of the car. Instead of the front door, she took him around to a nondescript side entrance, increasing his wariness. She knocked, and it was only a few moments before a man in his mid-fifties wearing a white smock swung open the door. He immediately pulled the detective into a hug.

"It's good to see you, Shoni," he said.

"Nice to see you, too, Lance."

John frowned, observing the man's sincerity and Shoni's awkwardness.

The doctor released her and motioned them inside. His name tag read *Dr. Norman.* "Is this my patient?"

"John McClane, Dr. Lance Norman," Shoni said by way of introduction.

"I'm afraid I have only ten minutes so let's get you in a room," Dr. Norman said.

Confused, John followed mutely with Shoni tagging along behind him.

Once in the exam room, the doctor donned his professional persona. "Let me take a look."

Shoni leaned a shoulder against the door, her arms crossed. Her expression was blank, but her seemingly nonchalant stance radiated awkwardness.

John removed his jacket and sweaters, then sat on the edge of the exam table. Dr. Norman perched a pair of glasses on his nose and undid the bandage. He didn't comment, although it was obvious he was curious. After disinfecting the area, he held up a needle and thread. "Do you want a local?" he asked.

John shook his head. He'd been stitched up before, under more adverse conditions, but why and when, he had no idea.

"You were supposed to call me," Dr. Norman said as he closed the wound.

Startled, John glanced at him but realized the comment was directed to Shoni.

"I did," she replied.

"For my help." The doc continued his task. "Not that I mind."

John frowned. Wasn't he a little old for her?

"Things got busy," she said, and even John knew it was a lame excuse.

Dr. Norman tied off the catgut and snipped the end. He held a roll of bandage out to Shoni. "Wrap it while I get a couple syringes."

Shoni took the roll from him and the doc left the room.

"An *old* boyfriend?" John asked, even as he knew he had no right prying into her private life.

"My mother's."

The flat reply punched the air from his gut. "Oh."

"He said if I needed anything, to call him." She shrugged. "So I called him."

"That probably wasn't what he meant."

"He made the offer."

Shoni tied off the bandage, tucking the end between two layers of cloth.

Dr. Norman returned. "Arm first."

John hardly noticed the needle's sting.

"Now the pants," the doc said.

John glared at Shoni's twinkling eyes. "Turn around," he muttered.

She did so, but not without a smirk.

The second shot wasn't as pain-free.

"The first was a tetanus, the second an antibiotic." Dr. Norman held out a bottle of pills. "Take one twice a day until they're all gone. The stitches will dissolve."

John took the prescription bottle reluctantly. Just another debt he owed. As he donned his sweaters for the third time that day, he listened to Shoni and the doctor's exchange.

"I assume you're back at work already," Dr. Norman said.

"It's been two months. Why wouldn't I be?"

"You haven't processed her death yet."

Shoni's fingers curled into her palms. "I've done all the processing I needed. Work is the best thing for me now."

"Your mother said you used your work to hide from unpleasant things you didn't want to face."

Shoni's hands curled into fists at her sides, but her tone was steady. "This isn't the time or the place for this conversation. I'll call you and we'll go out to dinner."

"If you don't, I'll call you."

She took a deep breath and exhaled. "I'm all right, Lance. It's just that I've got this case and it's taking all of my time."

John caught the doctor's deliberate look in his direction.

"Is he involved in your case?"

"Right now, he's the most important part of it."

Dr. Norman sighed. "All right. But I'll be waiting for your call."

Shoni nodded. "Send me the bill."

"I'll take care of it."

Shoni opened the exam room door and Dr. Norman led them back to where they'd entered the clinic.

"Thanks," Shoni said. "I owe you."

"Yes, you do." A kind smile tempered his words.

"Thank you, Doctor," John said.

"You're welcome. You might want to try some aromatherapy and meditation, too. It's amazing what holistic medicines can do."

"'Bye, Lance," Shoni interjected.

They made a hasty exit.

"Seems like a nice guy. A little fruity, maybe, but nice," John remarked once they were back in her car.

Shoni laughed. "Yeah. He's into prescribing aromatherapy and meditation." Her amusement died. "My mom believed in that stuff. She taught me how to meditate when I was five years old."

He tried to imagine her as a curly-headed imp sitting still and quiet. He couldn't do it. "What about your dad? He meditate, too?"

Shoni pulled out of the parking lot into traffic. "My

dad's idea of meditation was sitting in his favorite chair while he zoned out during a football game."

"That kind of meditation I could get into." John didn't miss the past tense. "What happened to him?"

"He died. Line of duty."

John's eyebrows shot upward. "He was a cop?"

"He's the reason I became one," she admitted.

"A cop with a New Age wife. Strange combination."

She shrugged. "A case of opposites attract, I guess."

Some minutes later the police building loomed into view. Nervous energy rippled under John's skin. His hand settled on the door handle, his fight-or-flight response screaming. But he'd promised to give his statement, and his word was the only thing he now possessed.

Shoni parked on the street, less than half a block from the building. John commanded his body to unfold from the car and he fell into step beside her.

She nodded at the cops they passed, but didn't seem inclined to talk. She opened the door and John hesitated before following her inside. What if someone recognized him?

"We don't have all day, John," she said.

With a start, John crossed the threshold. His heart thumped in his chest and his palms grew damp. However, although he received some curious looks, nobody seemed to be scrutinizing him.

She stopped at the front desk, where a tall, reed-thin cop stood. "I need a guest pass."

He held out his hand. "ID?"

"He doesn't have any. Lost it in a fire last night," she lied.

The policeman frowned, but this obviously wasn't the first person to come through the front doors without identification. "Name?"

"John McClane," she replied.

"Reason for visit?"

"Give a statement."

The cop scrawled the information across a form on a clipboard. "Address?"

John tensed.

"Twenty-five hundred Hampden Lane," she replied without missing a beat.

Her mother's condo.

A few minutes later John had a visitor badge clipped to his sweater. She led him to the elevator. The doors slid open and a woman about Shoni's size but with brown eyes and a mocha complexion stepped out.

"Shoni, girl, how have you been?" the woman asked.

"Busy. You know how it goes," she replied. "What's going on at my alma mater?"

"The usual. Had a bad one yesterday. Man killed his girlfriend and her kid, then shot himself."

Standing so close to Shoni, John felt her shudder.

"I hate it when a child is involved. That's why I had to get out of SCU," Shoni said.

The awkward silence was broken by the woman. "This your new partner?"

"Witness," Shoni replied. "Lesley, this is John McClane. John, this is my former partner, Lesley Hayes."

He sent her a guarded nod.

Lesley laughed. "Doesn't look like Bruce Willis."

"Don't let his looks fool you. I'd rather have this McClane on my side any day," Shoni said. "Catch you later, Les."

Startled by Shoni's defense, John was almost left behind as Shoni abruptly boarded the elevator. He hurried in after her.

John kept his injured arm close to his side as the elevator glided upward. "What's SCU?" he asked.

"Special Crimes Unit. Domestic and family crime."

John stared at their distorted reflections on the metal doors. "That'd be tough."

"It was."

"Lesley still there?"

"Yep. She knows how to turn it off."

"You don't?"

Shoni turned to him and met his gaze. "Didn't want to learn. Things like kids and women getting punched around isn't something I wanted to get desensitized to."

Before John could process her surprising confession, the doors whisked open.

A man wearing a dark blue pinstripe suit with an immaculate white-collared shirt and coordinating tie stood waiting for the elevator. He grinned. "Slept in, Alexander?"

"Up yours, Raff," she shot back without heat.

The man named Raff chuckled as he entered the elevator. "Delon made the coffee," he said as the doors shut behind him.

Shoni groaned.

Frowning at the cryptic words and her response, John followed Shoni through a set of doors with a sign that read VIOLENT CRIMES UNIT. Going from relative quiet to the bustling of the sprawling room, John felt a wave of vertigo wash through him. Voices buzzed, phones rang, and computers beeped. The scent of burnt coffee, sweat, and competing aftershaves threatened to give him a worse headache.

Seeing the coffeepot, John veered toward it, but Shoni caught his sleeve.

"You don't want any of that crap. My boss has some that I can guarantee you'll like better," she said.

As they wove between the desks, a man in a fluorescent green shirt with tiny blue, red, and yellow guitars bumped John's injured arm. John bit the inside of his cheek.

"Heya, Shoni. How's it hangin'?" the fashion-challenged man asked.

Shoni squinted and made a show of donning her sunglasses. "Are you trying to blind Norfolk's finest, Delon?"

The detective grinned, his teeth brilliant white against his ebony skin. "Someone has to show Raff how to dress." He glanced at John. "This your witness from last night?"

"Word gets around," Shoni said, and John could tell she wasn't pleased.

Delon shrugged his wide shoulders. "Ian Convers stopped by earlier to talk to the lieutenant."

Shoni grimaced. "Crap."

"Yep. Your ass is grass, and the lieutenant is a big bad lawn mower."

"Thanks for the reassurance."

"Me and Raff started the background work on last night's fire. Raff went to interview the warehouse owner. We got the reports of the apartment tenants from the scene cops, but nothing jumped out. You want us to re-interview them?"

Shoni shook her head. "Just run the usual background checks on them. Thanks, Delon."

"No prob." He wandered back to his desk.

As Shoni led him to her boss's office, John kept his head lowered, torn between wanting to be recognized and wanting to remain anonymous.

They stopped by a door with a nameplate that read LT. BOB TYLER, HOMICIDE SECTION, and Shoni knocked.

"Enter," a gruff voice replied.

Shoni opened the door and motioned for John to step inside first. His gaze fastened on the bald man behind the desk. The image was overlaid by that of another bald man, but this one wore a uniform.

Dizziness washed through him.

Chapter Eight

When John braced a hand against the doorway, Shoni scowled and moved around him into Bob's office. However, one glance at her witness's chalky complexion told her it wasn't rudeness that had him blocking the entrance. Maybe it was an adverse reaction to one of the shots Lance had given him.

"John? Are you all right?" Shoni asked, concerned by his glassy gaze.

"Get him in a chair," Bob ordered. He stood and poured a glass of cold water from a sweating pitcher on the windowsill behind him.

Shoni managed to ease John into a chair and closed the door to curious onlookers. She accepted the ice-cold water from her boss with a grateful nod.

"Drink this." She helped John lift the glass to his mouth, and he swallowed some water before pushing it away. Color sccpcd back into his sallow chccks.

"You all right, son?" Bob asked him.

"Yeah," John rasped.

"What happened?"

John blinked and focused on the lieutenant. He rose, stiffened his spine and drew back his shoulders. "Sorry, sir. It won't happen again."

Bob looked at Shoni for answers, but she had little to give him. In fact, she had no idea what to think of John's strange behavior. "Lieutenant Tyler, this is John McClane, the man who saw the arsonist last night," she said.

Bob picked up a folded newspaper and slapped it down in front of Shoni. "He looks just like his picture."

Shoni picked up the paper and studied the black-and-white photo of John and her. Fortunately, John's face was turned to the side and his hair obscured the features his beard didn't. Still, she hated that Mack had even gotten the picture. "That son of a bitch. I should've smashed his damn camera."

"I shouldn't have had to learn about your witness in the newspaper, Alexander. You have a cell phone. You damn well better learn how to use it." Bob's razor-sharp reprimand cut deep.

Shoni flinched inwardly. "I screwed up, sir."

John placed his crossed wrists at the small of his back. "If anyone's to blame, it's me. I blackmailed Detective Alexander into helping me with a personal problem first, which prevented her from calling you."

Bob's eyebrows shot upward. "You blackmailed her?"

"No, not blackmail," Shoni said quickly. She flashed John an irritated look. "It was a negotiated deal. I help him, he helps me."

Bob rolled his eyes heavenward. He pointed to the chairs in front of his desk. "Sit down, both of you."

Shoni perched on her chair and John followed suit. Meanwhile, Bob filled three cups of coffee from his personal stash. Shoni figured a cup of one of Bob's exotic coffees was almost worth the dressing down.

"Thanks," she said, taking a cup from her boss.

John merely sent him a nod, but his nostrils flared as he caught the rich scent.

Bob sat down in his chair, his own mug held between big-knuckled hands. "Talk to me," he said to Shoni.

She described last night's events, keeping it succinct, knowing she'd go into more detail in her written report. Bob listened without comment until she finished.

"How do you know McClane didn't start the fire?" Bob asked her point-blank.

"I didn't," John said without hesitation.

Bob's laser gaze latched onto him. "Is John McClane your real name?"

Shoni's stomach clenched.

John merely stared at the lieutenant, his chin lifted at a defiant angle.

Bob narrowed his eyes and his voice was edged with steel. "If you're lying about your name, how do I know you're not lying about the fire? That you didn't start it and that you're making up a suspect for us to chase around like a puppy chasing its tail?"

"I didn't start the fire. I did see who did. If that isn't good enough for you, fine. I'll leave." John slammed his cup on the desk, sloshing coffee over the rim, and rose.

"Sit down." Bob's quiet command was more effective than a shouted one.

John stared at him, a battle of wills. Finally, he lowered himself back to his chair, but his backbone remained ramrod stiff.

Shoni had been a cop long enough to question John's innocence, but she also trusted her instincts. "If he's the arsonist, how do you explain him being shot at?" she asked her boss.

The lieutenant stared at Shoni, then switched his attention to John, who matched his steady gaze. "Say I believe you about the fire. What were you doing in a deserted warehouse so late at night?"

John's jaw muscle clenched. "I lived there."

Bob leaned back in his chair and his granite expression eased. "Why? You look capable of holding down a job."

"Look, I'm here to give my statement and a description of the suspect, not to answer personal questions."

Impatience flared in the lieutenant's plain features, but there was also a hint of respect. "Drink your coffee, McClane. Nothing I hate worse than wasting a decent cup of coffee. Especially when it's Jamaican Blue Mountain."

At John's startled expression, Shoni hid a smile behind her own cup. Bob was an expert at keeping a person off balance.

Tyler turned his gaze on Shoni. "This is the first time something other than an old warehouse burned."

"Arsonist probably didn't realize the wind would carry the fire," she said. "It's a good thing John was in the warehouse. If he hadn't been, everyone in that apartment building might've been killed."

Bob grunted, which told Shoni he wasn't convinced John was innocent. She glanced at her witness, who'd finished his coffee. "Let's go out to my desk, and I'll take your statement," she said.

John nodded and stood, anxious to leave the lieutenant's office. As he went through the doorway, Bob said, "Alexander, a minute."

She cursed under her breath, but her sense of duty reigned.

"My desk is over there." She pointed it out to John. "It's the one with the mountain of folders on it."

When she was assured he was headed to the right one, she returned to Bob's office. Crossing her arms, she stood in front of his desk.

"What do you know about him?" Bob asked.

She knew her boss wouldn't let it rest. "Only that he's homeless and lived in the warehouse. And he knows an older woman who lived in the apartment building with her granddaughter and great-granddaughter. He saved them and everyone else."

"So basically you know nothing about him, yet he's your star witness?"

Dread settled like lead in her belly. "I trust him."

"I'll bet he has some military in his background."

Shoni blinked at the non sequitur. "Why's that?"

"The way he snapped to attention." Bob shrugged. "Besides, I was one myself. I recognize the type."

Norfolk was full of ex-military, and many cops, including Bob, Raff, and the desk sergeant, were veterans. That John might be one was a possibility Shoni had considered. It also explained how John had held off the three men in the alley. "I'll see what I can learn from him. Is there anything else?"

"I'm putting in that request for a profiler," he said bluntly.

She planted her fists on his desk and leaned forward. "Why? I have a witness."

"Even if he is reliable—which I'm not as willing as you to believe—all you'll have is a general physical description. You need more than that to get this guy, Alexander."

She shoved away from the desk and spun about in frustration. "Damn it, Lieutenant, I've been busting my ass to get this guy. You bring this fed in, and he's going to take over."

Bob's level stare unnerved her. "Maybe that's not a bad thing."

Shoni froze. "You're saying I can't do my job?"

"No, I'm not saying that. What I *am* saying is that your judgment has become impaired. You should've called me last night."

She flung her arms out. "So I made a mistake. Sue me."

Tyler's face reddened and he thrust a finger toward her. "You make a mistake in our business and it could cost a life. Maybe more than one. We have to stop this arsonist before he kills again. And if that means calling in a federal official, I'm damn well going to do it." He paused, and his voice quieted. "Because I'd rather bruise your ego than see another person die."

Unable to deal with the shame and anger twining through her, Shoni gathered her ragged composure. "Yes, sir."

Bob opened his mouth as if to add something more, but abruptly shut it. Instead, he motioned for her to leave. Shoni didn't hesitate to escape.

She wended her way to her desk, her heart pumping like a freight train. As if sensing her mood, everybody scrambled out of her path.

John sat beside her desk, a cup filled with Delon's nightmare version of coffee. She plopped in her chair and glared at the leaning tower of files.

"He ought to get his room soundproofed," John commented.

Hot embarrassment flooded her face. "Wonderful. Now everyone knows the lieutenant doesn't trust me."

There was a trace of sympathy in John's cool eyes. "I doubt anyone could make out the words."

"That's a relief. Not." She shoved aside the paperwork and punched on her computer. The thought of a profiler coming in to steal her case burned in her gut. Yet she recognized the validity of Bob's argument. If bringing an agent in saved just one life, it would be worth it. It didn't mean she had to like it. Because she didn't. Not one damn bit.

JOHN steeled his taste buds and took another sip of the horrendous coffee. It was even worse than anything he'd had on the street. No wonder so many cops had an attitude.

Shoni laid the paper down on the desk in front of him. "Read through your statement, make sure everything is correct. Then sign it."

Ever since her blowup with her boss, she'd been as prickly as a cactus. She hadn't veered from her task in the nearly two hours of digging as much information out of him as she could. She'd also gone through every detail of his statement at least five times.

Sighing, John read through the report and, despite himself, was impressed by her writing skills. She'd managed to condense his rambling replay into a concise account. He signed the form with the only name he knew and passed it back to her.

She stood. "Now let's get the sketch done."

With his sharp recall, John didn't have any trouble coming up with a likeness of the man who'd started the fire. John studied the hard copy of the suspect's image—short hair, wide nose, heavy dark eyebrows, and clean-shaven face.

"You recognize him?" Shoni asked, perching on a corner of her desk beside him.

Her scent—soap and pure woman without a trace of perfume—sidetracked him. "I don't think so." Was that husky voice his?

"Maybe you saw him around the neighborhood?"

John cleared his throat and shook his head. "That doesn't feel right."

She gazed down at him, her green eyes curious, probing. "What about your life before the street?"

The solid wall rose up in his mind. Why could he remember every detail of the arsonist, but not a damn thing about his past? "No," he replied. "Am I done here?"

She rubbed her brow. "Yes, but you're going to remain under poli—*my* protection."

Although that thought held a world of pleasurable possibilities, John chafed at anyone getting too close. Besides, staying at the condo made him feel . . . normal. Like a man. A man who couldn't remember the last time he'd gotten laid, yet had no problem imagining hot, horny, no-holds-barred sex.

With Shoni.

Mind out of the bedroom, Mon—

The name skittered away from him.

"Damn it," he muttered.

Shoni stiffened beside him. "I didn't think staying at the condo was that much of a hardship."

He blinked, realizing he'd lost the train of the conversation. "Uh, no, I was thinking of something else. Are we done here?"

"I'm not, but you are. I'll give you a ride back to the condo if I have your word you won't leave it."

"I thought you weren't going to let me out of your sight."

She shrugged. "You want to sit around here all day, be my guest. But I figure it's safe enough during the day, with the condo's security, to leave you there alone."

As much as John hated to be penned, a gilded cage was better than being caught in the open. "Fine. I'll go."

SHONI finished the last of her phone calls. Earlier, she'd sat down with Raff and Delon and gone over their progress. The bottom line was that no connection had been discovered between the two buildings that had burned last night and the previous three.

What if she was operating under a mistaken assumption? What if the fires were set by different people? Gasoline was the most common accelerant.

No. Ian said each was identical in regard to the pour pattern, too. He'd sounded as tired as Shoni felt when she'd talked to him earlier in the evening. She'd told him about bringing a fed in from the Behavioral Analysis Unit, and Ian had thought it a good idea. His acceptance felt like a betrayal, but objectively, she understood. Any help they could get to catch the criminal should be welcomed. If only she could get her head wrapped around it without her pride butting in.

Sketches of the arsonist had been sent out to the field operations divisions and units, to be distributed to the patrolmen who worked the streets. It would take another shift for the picture to be disseminated to everyone, but by tomorrow morning the entire Norfolk police department would be on the lookout for the suspect.

Her cell phone buzzed, and she drew it out of her pocket. Glancing at the number, she thrust the phone back. The fifth call in two hours. Mack never did know how to take no for an answer, but that was what made him one of the best reporters in the city. He was desperate for the arson story, and with his ex-girlfriend in the thick of it, he was going to try to sweet-talk an exclusive.

Fat chance, bub.

Shoni looked at her wristwatch—seven forty-five. It wasn't as late as she usually worked, but then she usually didn't have someone waiting for her. Not that John would care one way or another when she returned, but she felt antsy leaving him alone for too long. The condo's security was high-tech. She had no reason to worry, yet . . .

She rose and donned her jacket, unable to deny a burst of anticipation at seeing John again.

SHONI juggled the Chinese take-out bags as she dug in her pocket for the keys to the condo. Across the hallway, Mr. Levinson's television blared through the walls. The elderly man had probably forgotten to put his hearing aids in again.

Shoni unlocked the door and stepped inside, closing it behind her. She basked in the relative silence, until she realized John wasn't in sight. Her heart thudding, she deposited the food on the breakfast bar and checked in the living room and dining room. Nothing.

Dread spiraled in her gut. What if she'd been wrong about him? What if he was the arsonist, just as the lieutenant suspected?

The French doors to the bedroom were open and she paused in the doorway. Running water in the bathroom caught her attention and she strode toward it, then froze as relief swept through here.

John stood in front of the vanity, a razor in his hand. He spotted her via the mirror and the part of his cheeks that weren't covered with soapy lather reddened. "When did you get back?"

Was there a huskiness to his voice?

Regaining her composure, Shoni waved a hand. "Just now. I didn't see you." She hadn't meant it to come out as an accusation.

John's expression returned to its normal inscrutability. "Did you think I ran out on you?"

Shoni crossed her arms, feeling way too exposed. "I didn't know." Suddenly impatient at her childish reaction, she drew her shoulders back. "What are you doing?"

"What does it look like I'm doing?"

She noted two small cuts on his neck. "Trying to slit your throat?"

He held up the disposable razor. "If I wanted to do that, I'd find something more efficient. Like a butter knife."

Shoni squelched a grin and leaned her shoulder against the doorway. "What made you decide to shave?"

He faced the mirror again, his gaze locked on his reflection. "That newspaper picture. If someone's out to get me, getting rid of the beard might make me less recognizable."

Guilt banished her amusement. "I'm sorry, John. I should've stopped Mack."

His gaze found hers in the mirror. "The reporter's name is Mack?"

Glancing away, she nodded.

John resumed shaving. "So this Mack the reporter is an old boyfriend."

"How'd you know?"

His hand holding the razor stilled. "I didn't, until just now. Isn't that like sleeping with the enemy?"

She raked her fingers through her curls. "You sound like my boss. He didn't care much for Mack either." She sighed. "Of course, the lieutenant was right. It wasn't my looks that attracted Mack."

"You were his inside scoop."

"That's a polite way of putting it." She couldn't hide her bitterness.

"I'm sorry."

The sincerity in his voice caused her to glance up. He'd turned toward her again, and through the lather and uneven whiskers, his expression was sympathetic.

Uncomfortable, she motioned toward his injury. "How's the arm?"

He flexed it and smiled. "Better, thanks to you and your granola-head doctor friend."

She laughed. "Sounds like something Dad would've said. He was always teasing Mom about her New Age friends." Her amusement faded and her gaze turned inward. "When I see how many cops have bad marriages, I realize that what my parents had was pretty special."

"So why aren't you married?"

"Because I want what Mom and Dad had, and after dating a few losers like Mack, I've pretty much given up."

He studied her silently with cool, fathomless eyes.

"So, you need any help?" she asked, embarrassed by her confession to a virtual stranger.

"I'm good."

"So what's with the slasher impersonation?" Shoni plucked the razor from his hand. "If you're determined to get rid of the beard, I'll do it."

John made a grab for the razor, caught Shoni's wrists, and swept her arms behind her back, which brought them chest to chest. He suddenly recalled with startling clarity how a woman's breasts felt in his hands, soft and full and feminine, and how drawing her nipples into his mouth made her moan with desire.

Stunned by the vividness of the picture, he released her and clenched his hands close to his sides. "I can shave myself."

"Without a bum arm I'm sure you can." She paused, and for a moment he thought she'd capitulate. "Let me do it."

John was prepared to argue with her, to spare them both the embarrassment of his uncontrolled reaction to her proximity. However, her softly worded plea proved more potent than his libido. "I suppose I don't have to worry about your hand slipping, since I'm your prize witness," he said wryly, hoping to hide his unease.

Shoni wanted to tell him he was more than that, but the words died in her throat. She knew little to nothing about the man, yet she respected and trusted him. For a cop who never took anyone or anything at face value, Shoni found the position an odd one.

Of course, he was also incredibly hot. While she'd been up close and personal with his abs of steel, her hormones, which had been AWOL for months, returned with a vengeance. Not that she was going to let some body chemistry turn her into a sex fiend, but John McClane was definitely damned tempting. And totally off limits.

Shoni reached for the shaving cream, and John remained motionless as she scrubbed the lather into his beard. The whiskers caressed her palms, arrowing tingles up her arm. She ignored the shivers gathering in her belly and focused on her task, reminding herself he was simply a witness. She stifled a snort at her attempt at self-delusion. John had ceased simply being a witness the moment she had brought him to her mother's condo.

She rinsed her hands under the faucet, then picked up the razor. Noting the height difference, she pressed John back a step and hopped onto the vanity. Sitting on the counter, Shoni was at eye level with him.

"Come here," she said.

John eyed her warily, like an animal unsure whether it was being lured into a trap. He took one step toward her, still leaving far too much distance between them.

"I won't bite. Promise," Shoni said, hoping she could keep her word.

With a resigned sigh, John stepped into the space between her thighs.

Ignoring the heat that pooled below her belly—and more or less succeeding—she placed the razor against his cheek. She drew it downward slowly, leaving behind a narrow path of smooth, pale skin. After swishing the razor in the sink, she repeated the motion. More skin was revealed with each track of the razor.

The left side of his beard disappeared first, and Shoni couldn't resist running her fingertips along the newly exposed skin. John cleared his throat a moment after Shoni felt a slight pressure against her inner thigh.

Her face hot with embarrassment, she concentrated on the remaining whiskers. Each stroke revealed another strip of the real John McClane. Finally, Shoni finished removing the last of his beard. Her hands shook as she dampened a washcloth and wiped away the remaining lather. Arousal, which had been on low simmer, skyrocketed to boiling.

She'd suspected John McClane was a good-looking man beneath the scraggly beard, but even she hadn't been prepared for the real thing. A sinfully sexy mouth that begged to be kissed; a strong jawline angling down to a squarish chin with a slight cleft; and damn, if that wasn't enough to make her squirm, the man had dimples.

Praying that McClane wouldn't notice her uneven breathing and trembling fingers, she tossed the washcloth into the sink. Forcing herself to remain objective despite the lust rippling through her, she examined his face for any whiskers she missed and spotted a bit of shaving cream above John's upper lip. She drew her thumb across his lip to wipe it away, but when her eyes caught John's, her hand stilled in midmotion.

John's breath stuttered against her hand and his pupils nearly eclipsed the blue irises. This time she couldn't ignore the hard flesh pressing against her thigh. Her fingers uncurled and curved around his fresh-shaven cheek. She inhaled the fresh scent of soap and John's unique maleness. Electricity arced through her veins as his warm breath washed across her lips.

Shoni's heart raced, and she fought the urge to press her mouth to those lips that should be outlawed in most states. Then the tip of his tongue touched his lower lip. It was erotic as hell, and the need to kiss him became a burning imperative. She angled her head and shifted enough to bring her lips to his.

For a moment, John's mouth remained stiff. A brush of her tongue against his lips and John latched onto Shoni's arms, jerking her against him. He moved his mouth over hers, the firm press of flesh against flesh. Shoni framed his smooth-shaven face in her palms, her thumbs stroking those incredible dimples. It wasn't enough. She wrapped her legs around him, crossing her ankles at the small of his back and tugging him close. His erection throbbed against her dampening center, threatening to throw her over the edge despite the layers of clothing between them.

Shoni's cell phone jangled.

Chapter Nine

SHONI dropped her legs, freeing John. Frustration made her hands clumsy as she retrieved the phone from her pocket. She glanced at the caller ID and swore.

"Your boyfriend?" John asked, his tone icy.

She glared at him, refusing to acknowledge his flushed face and slightly swollen lips she'd just tried to devour. "*Ex*-boyfriend."

"You gonna answer it?"

"No."

What Shoni wanted to do was continue where she and John had left off, but by his implacable expression, the mood was definitely shattered. Besides, it had been a mistake. She'd already screwed up once; she didn't want to make it twice.

Except I just did.

Keeping her gaze averted, she hopped down from the vanity. "I brought dinner. We should eat it before it gets any colder," she said in a passably normal voice.

She escaped the suddenly too-small room and strode

into the kitchen. She was still so damned turned on that her hands shook as she opened the refrigerator. John appeared in the kitchen and Shoni forced herself not to stare at his impossibly handsome face and lean body.

She held up a bottle of water, and he nodded. She brought out two and passed him one, careful to avoid touching his fingers. After unscrewing the top, she tipped the bottle up and drank, hoping the cold water would douse her frustrated libido.

"What's in the bag?" John asked.

"Dinner. Hope you like Chinese." She hoped her voice didn't sound as strained as she felt.

"I think so."

"You *think* so?"

John shrugged. "I haven't had it in a while."

He retrieved two plates while Shoni watched him. Even if a person hadn't eaten something in a while, wouldn't he remember if he liked it or not? Frowning, she set the take-out boxes on the breakfast bar and motioned for him to dig in, even as her own stomach rebelled.

John filled his plate and carried it to the dining room table, where he sat with his back to the mirrored wall. Shoni was certain it was deliberate. She sat across from him and stirred her food around with her fork. What had looked and smelled so appetizing earlier only made her stomach churn now.

She tried not to stare at John while he ate, but the physical transformation was almost shocking. However, his aloof manner remained. The only time that had disappeared was while they'd kissed. Why was John so standoffish? Why was he living on the street? What had happened to him?

He lifted his gaze and caught her studying him. She should've looked away, shouldn't have been caught in the first place, but, God help her, she wanted him. The scent of soap and lather wafted over the aroma of the food. The air hummed with the attraction, grew dense with need. It would be so easy to reach across the table and touch his jaw, trace those lips. . . .

Shoni abruptly shoved back her chair and stood. She had to get out of here, away from John. Away from this overpowering—and totally inappropriate—temptation.

"I—I forgot something at my desk." She grabbed her jacket and made her escape.

SHOCKED by Shoni's abrupt departure, John didn't have time to do or say anything. She left a void in the condo, a vacuum that made it feel emptier than before she'd arrived. He wasn't gullible enough to believe she'd left something at work. She'd wanted to get away from him. John didn't know whether to be relieved or insulted.

He carried his plate to the kitchen and put the leftover Chinese food in the refrigerator. Funny how he knew he'd eaten sesame chicken and beef and broccoli before, but couldn't remember when or where.

Listening to the muted silence, he wandered into the dining room and stared at his reflection in the mirrored wall. The hair was still too long, but this was the man John knew. Recognition goaded him, but every time he tried to grasp his identity, it slipped away. Flashes of scenes and people, snapshots like a PowerPoint presentation on fast forward, rushed through him. His head ached with trying to slow the images.

John forced himself to ponder a memory he did possess—Shoni shaving him, her touch driving him crazy with lust but not wanting it to stop. Yet even that was tainted with déjà vu. He could recall a child, a girl, sitting on the counter watching him as he shaved. Questions, always questions. Yet he couldn't remember her voice or what questions she'd asked. Or who she was.

And when Shoni had kissed him, there'd been the shadow of someone else with them. Shoni's kiss would've totally undone his hard-fought control, if not for that vague sense of another woman. What if he had a girlfriend or even a wife? But if there was a significant other in his life, why wasn't she looking for him?

Maybe she is, and you're too chickenshit to find out.

John longed to leave the condo, take a walk, and clear his head. It was the only way he knew to dull the edginess. However, he figured Detective Alexander would have something to say about him skipping out.

A blonde woman flashed in his mind and pain stabbed deep. He clutched his head between his hands and bent over at the waist.

Tiffany.

Who the hell was Tiffany?

SHONI'S nerves fired beneath her skin, a running commentary on her frustration, both physical and emotional. She managed not to sprint to her car, but it was a near thing. Once outside the lot, she gunned the engine, taking the twists and turns like a NASCAR pro. Car lights and streetlights flashed by her and she automatically stopped at the red lights and continued on the green. She allowed the familiarity of the steering wheel in her hands, the ebb and flow of the accelerator beneath her foot, to subsume the feelings John had dredged up.

Some time later, she was shocked to find her aimless driving had brought her to her mother's killer. She pulled up to a curb across the street and stared at the innocuous-looking house. The drapes were pulled over the front window, leaving only a sliver of light exposed. She opened her window a crack and listened to the familiar neighborhood sounds—a dog barking down the block; a door slamming; tires rolling over pavement. Just normal people living their normal, everyday lives. Did they know a murderer lived in their midst?

She reached under the front seat and her fingers curled around the metal box. She drew it out and set it on her lap. After she'd returned John to the condo that afternoon, she'd managed to retrieve the box without him seeing her. She unlatched it, lifted the cover, and picked up the cheap handgun. Although the metal was cool, it seemed to burn her palm.

She would do it tonight.

A child cried within the house she observed. Tony Durkett's young son was upset about something. Probably didn't want to go to bed. Typical kid.

He'll grow up without his father.

Was that such a bad thing? His father was a killer.

Who made you judge and jury?

Her father's voice made her cringe.

"I did," she whispered hoarsely. "He killed Mom."

Your job isn't to execute, but prosecute.

"My job sucks."

It's who *you are. If you do this, you'll have nothing left.*

Shoni stared at the nondescript gun in her hand, then lifted her head and tilted it back. She barely noticed the dampness trailing down one cheek. *You left us years ago, Dad. You have no right telling me what to do now. So just leave me the fuck alone.* But there was no force behind the thought, only anguish and bitterness.

Silence filled the car. Had her father abandoned her again? Or was she simply going insane, bit by bit?

It was only nine thirty and lights shone in most of the houses. However, there was a good chance no one would see her, or if they did, it would be too dark to discern any details. Eyewitness accounts were generally unreliable, with two people seeing two totally different things. She'd taken enough reports to know.

Still, it might be better to wait a couple more hours, until Durkett's wife and son would be asleep. Durkett would be alone in the living room, drinking. She settled back in her seat, the gun cradled in her hands.

Having pulled a few stakeouts, Shoni knew how to blank her mind to everything but what she watched. But tonight, her thoughts were too chaotic. The memory of kissing John, touching John, was too potent to ignore.

John McClane. A homeless stranger. A man who'd risked his life for a child not his own. The first man who made her forget everything, even her responsibilities, in the blinding need to touch him.

A man who was also her sole witness in an arson investigation.

Insanity. It was the only thing that explained hearing her father's voice and falling for a witness she hardly knew.

Headlights turned onto the street and Shoni spotted the light bar on the car roof. She slid down in her seat. The patrol car moved past hers slowly and she kept low. She held her breath until the cops were gone.

She worried her lower lip. If she took care of Durkett tonight, there was a chance the patrolmen would remember her car. After her infamous meltdown after Durkett's release from jail, the trail might lead to her.

Cursing under her breath, Shoni placed the gun back in its box and under the seat.

She started her car but took a moment to give the house one final look. "Soon," she promised.

Without haste, she drove out of the neighborhood. Faced with the prospect of seeing John at the condo, Shoni realized she couldn't do it. Not yet. He'd be safe there. Even if the shooter knew John was there, which was highly doubtful, the secure building would scare him off.

No, it would be better for both her and John if she spent the night at her own apartment. She'd call him once she got to her place and let him know she'd be by in the morning for breakfast.

Shivering, Shoni headed to her apartment. Her reserved parking space was vacant, and she pulled into it with a tired sigh.

After locking the metal box in her trunk, she trudged into the building that was from the same cookie cutter mold as over half of the apartment buildings in the city. Her place was on the second floor of the three-story building and she climbed the stairs, exhaustion making her tread heavy. The recessed lights illuminated the hallway but weren't harsh enough to cast light under doors.

She stopped in front of 215 and fished the keys out of her jacket pocket. Just as she was shoving the key in the lock, she noticed a note tacked to her door. Recognizing the scrawl as her elderly neighbor's, she read it.

A nice young man stopped by and fixed your cable television today. He wasn't wearing a wedding band. Mrs. Brogan.

It wasn't Mrs. Brogan's attempt at matchmaking that brought a silent curse to Shoni's lips. She left her key in the lock and went to the far end of the hall. Leaning against the wall, she took a deep breath. She hadn't called the cable company, but maybe it had been scheduled maintenance. Yet she didn't remember receiving any notification.

Maybe I've been a cop too long and it's only an overdose of paranoia.

Gut instinct said otherwise. Knowing she might end up getting razzed for overreacting, she punched her third speed dial number and waited for the officer at the front desk to pick up. Once he did, she asked for backup and a bomb technician. Her next call should have been to her lieutenant.

The phone at her mother's condo rang and rang. After counting twenty rings, Shoni hung up, swearing.

Frantic with worry, she made another call and got the number for the security desk at the condominium.

"Pete, it's Shoni Alexander. Did you see John McClane leave there in the last hour or two?" she demanded.

"About ten minutes after you left, he walked out the door."

Shoni's heart sank. "Did he say where he was going?"

"No. What's going on?"

She forced a lightness to her voice. "Probably nothing. Could you have him call my cell phone when he comes back?" She gave him her number, then hung up.

A siren wailing in the distance was growing louder, coming closer. Knowing she didn't have much time before backup arrived, she quickly called the lieutenant's cell phone.

"Tyler," came the groggy reply.

In as few words as possible, she told him about the cable technician.

"You sure you didn't call them?" the lieutenant asked, his voice more alert.

Shoni rolled her eyes. "I can't remember the last time I even turned on my television." She dragged her hand over her curly hair, tugging a few strands in her frustration. "After that shooter last night, I'm thinking someone is serious about killing John. And if that person saw John with me . . ."

"So you think someone booby-trapped your apartment to get McClane?"

"Maybe. I don't know." Shoni paced in tiny circles. "I might be totally wrong here, but I've got the bomb squad coming."

"Good. Where's McClane?"

"Safe," she replied, unwilling to confess he'd been staying at the condo. Or that he'd disappeared from it.

"Give me a call when you know anything more."

"Will do, sir."

Just as she slid her phone back in her jacket pocket, two firefighters tromped up the stairs. She explained the situation to them and they began the task of vacating the building.

As frightened, pissed-off, and hastily dressed men and women exited the building, personnel from the police department arrived. The two patrolmen immediately pitched in to help the firemen with the evacuation. Sergeant Montoya and three Bomb Squad members showed up moments later. They were already garbed in Kevlar vests and padding, as well as helmets.

"What do you have, Alexander?" Montoya didn't waste time on niceties.

Shoni sent a curt nod to the twenty-three-year veteran of the force, grateful for his no-nonsense attitude. She gave him a quick rundown.

"Did you open your door?" the sergeant asked.

"No. I had my key in the lock when I saw the note on my door."

"As soon as everyone's out, we'll check it out."

She called her mother's condo again, in case Pete hadn't given John her message, but there was no answer. Her nerves stretched taut and her muscles tensed. She could drive over there and see if anything was amiss, but Pete had said John had left the building. By himself.

Besides, this possible crime scene was hers. Her home. Her apartment. Her life. She couldn't up and leave.

"I don't need this crap," she muttered, helplessness giving way to anger.

A Community Services van arrived with blankets and hot drinks. Needing something to do, she joined the workers in distributing the items and offering reassurances. But even as she helped, concern for John lurked.

Where are you, McClane?

WITH his hands buried in his jacket pockets, John strolled down the relatively quiet sidewalk. Traffic wasn't heavy, but it was steady. Probably shoppers leaving the mall at closing time.

When he'd first left the condo, he didn't have any destination in mind. All he wanted to do was walk away the frustration that burned in his belly. The flashes from his past; the inability to push aside the curtain; the sniper; the arsonist; Shoni, wrapped around him, kissing him. Everywhere he turned, there were questions. Always questions. But no answers.

Realizing he was headed in the direction of Estelle's temporary home, John figured it was early enough that he could drop by and see how she and Lainey were doing. It would be good to talk to someone who knew him, accepted him as he was.

When he arrived at the motel, he knocked on their door. He could picture Estelle shuffling to the door, peering through the peephole, and undoing the locks.

The door swung open and Estelle, wearing a dress John hadn't seen before, stood in the entrance. Her eyes saucered.

"Johnny! Look at you. All cleaned up." Estelle's surprised smile gave way to irritated concern. "What in the world are you doing out in the cold? Get your skinny ass in here before it falls off." She grabbed his arm and tugged him inside.

The heat of the room and Lainey's small figure hit him at the same time, and John smiled in genuine pleasure. "Hey, kiddo. How's it hanging?" he asked the girl.

Lainey looked up at him and her mouth dropped open. "You look bitchin'."

"Is that a good thing?"

She nodded, her dark eyes twinkling. Then she stepped back and held out her arms. "My hero Captain Jack Sparrow."

Her new pajamas had a picture of the pirate from the popular movie. John feigned disappointment. "And here I thought John McClane was your hero."

"Jack Sparrow is only pretend. You're my real hero."

Her ingenuous reply tightened John's throat, but he managed a grin and a wink. "Good answer, Short Stuff."

Estelle smiled gently, as if understanding how her great-granddaughter's simple words affected him. "Lainey, girl, would you get me and John a cup of tea?"

The seven-year-old dashed into the kitchenette.

John took a moment to survey their temporary home. He'd been here the previous night when he and Shoni had brought Mishon in, but he hadn't seen much beyond the tiny bedroom where they'd deposited the drugged-out woman. It was larger than his first impression, with two small bedrooms and a bathroom off a kitchen area, which held a refrigerator and microwave, as well as a range and a sink. There was a table where four could sit comfortably in the middle of the kitchenette. A room half the size of the condo's master bathroom held a couch and a fairly nice recliner, both facing a television that sat on a wood cabinet.

The woman motioned to the sofa while she plunked herself in the chair. John sat on the couch, finding it disconcerting that Estelle wasn't surrounded by her animal figurines, knitting needles, yarn, and magazines.

"I been wondering about you. Hoping you was okay," the woman said.

"I'm fine."

"Where you stayin'?"

He smiled self-consciously. "I'm under police protection. I can identify the arsonist."

"They think this fellah's gonna try to get you?"

John glanced into the kitchenette, making sure Lainey wasn't listening. "He already tried. At least, we think it was the same person." He kept his voice low.

"So what're you doin' out here all by yourself? Shouldn't you have one of them police escorts?"

Anger flared in Estelle's careworn face, but John knew it was concern that prompted it. "It's a long story."

Lainey arrived with his steaming tea and he accepted it with a thanks. Once Estelle had her cup, Lainey joined John on the sofa.

"How're you doing?" John asked before Estelle could interrogate him in front of Lainey.

"A lady from Social Services stopped by this afternoon. Helped us fill out some forms and whatnot. There's some new housing goin' up on the other side of town. Said we qualify, so she's puttin' us on the list."

Puzzled by Estelle's reluctance, John asked, "That's a good thing, right?"

"I guess. It's just that I spent all my seventy-nine years in the neighborhood. Don't know if I want to be movin' into a whole new part of the city at my age."

"But isn't the old neighborhood pretty much gone already?"

Estelle sighed. "You're right, Johnny. That apartment building was the only thing stoppin' them rich developers from putting up their fancy stores and restaurants."

John nodded and spoke to Lainey. "What do you think of moving to a new neighborhood?"

Lainey grinned, all white teeth and shining dark eyes. "Gram says I'll get my own room and I won't have to share with Mom. You'll have to come over after we're all moved into our new home. There's even a place to play, with new swings and a jungle gym."

"Higher, Daddy! Push me higher!"

Giggles and shrieks of laughter.

"John, what's wrong?"

A small hand on his arm and Estelle's concerned voice dispelled the picture of the girl on the swing and her high-pitched laughter.

He rubbed his brow, not surprised to find it damp with sweat. Glancing down at the girl's worried face, he gave her a reassuring smile. "I'm all right, Chelle."

The girl's worry turned to a scowl. "I'm Lainey, not Chelle."

John registered curly dark hair and brown eyes, instead of golden hair and blue eyes. He blinked and opened his mouth, but didn't speak. Didn't know what to say.

"It's time you get ready for bed, Lainey," Estelle said, breaking the awkward silence.

"But Gram," Lainey began.

"No arguments. Go on, now."

With a stubborn pout, Lainey slid off the couch and stomped to her room.

"What was it, John?" Estelle asked, her sand-over-gravel voice gentle.

"A girl. On a swing. I was pushing her." John's tongue stuck to the roof of his mouth. "She called me Daddy."

"So you have a little girl." Estelle's voice was gentle, pleased. "Named Chelle."

John's heart hammered in his chest, threatening to bust out. But it didn't feel like happiness. It felt more like dread. Like there was a door he had to open, but knew something terrible was on the other side. "I d-don't know."

"Shhh, it's all right, Johnny. Don't push it. It'll come in its own time," Estelle said.

But John wasn't certain he wanted to know. The pain of ignorance hurt, but he suspected the knowledge might be even more painful. But why would having a wife and child be so distressing?

Estelle leaned toward him and patted his knee. "Ask the cops, Johnny. Ask them to help you find out who you are."

Before John could reply, the door opened and Mishon entered. Beneath her thin jacket, she wore a short skirt that barely covered her backside and a blouse two sizes too small. Her working clothes. Yet it was awfully early for her to be home if she'd been tricking.

The vacuous look in her eyes told him she'd scored that evening. Nothing new there.

"Didn't figure you'd be back for another few hours," Gram said, her disappointment and disapproval obvious.

"Business's slow. Only got one customer in two hours." Mishon wandered into the kitchenette.

"I should be going," John said. "If the detective hasn't come looking for me yet, she will soon."

Estelle narrowed her eyes. "That pretty little cop you were with last night?"

"Detective Alexander probably wouldn't appreciate being called pretty or little." He shook his head. "Brass balls on that one."

Estelle chuckled. "Good. She can keep you in line."

"She's trying."

"You in some safe house?"

John shook his head. "Her mother's condo. She died a couple of months ago. Shon—Detective Alexander has the key to it."

Estelle's lips twitched, as if fighting a smile. "You tell Detective Alexander hello from us."

"I will."

Estelle heaved her bulk up and walked John to the door. "Don't you worry 'bout us. We're doing fine," she said.

John kissed her leathery cheek. "If I didn't say it before, thanks."

"And like I said before, no thanks is needed."

John turned to leave, but Estelle touched his arm and he paused.

"Tell that detective gal about your amnesia. She'll help you."

John took a deep breath and let it out in a shaky exhalation. "I'll think about it."

Then he turned and strode away from the motel. The roads were quieter, pedestrians almost nonexistent as he hiked back to the condo. His breath misted in the cold air. He jammed his fists deeper into his jacket pockets and hunched his shoulders.

The giggling blond girl haunted him. Chelle. Just as he knew he liked Chinese food and long hot showers, he knew the girl was his daughter. He should be ecstatic to know he had a family. But her memory was tinged with bleakness. Maybe he was divorced and didn't get to visit her very often. No, that didn't feel right. It was something else. . . .

Lost in his thoughts, he didn't see the car swerve toward him.

Chapter Ten

After a bomb was discovered and disarmed, Shoni called her boss. He pushed for a safe house for her and John. She pushed back, confessing John was at her mother's condo, which was just as secure, if not more so, than a safe house. Lieutenant Tyler reluctantly capitulated after the standard warning to remain professional. Then he threw in police security. Shoni talked him down to extra patrols around the condominium.

However, the lieutenant's last order was one she had every intention of obeying.

"Don't let McClane out of your sight."

Only she'd already lost him, which meant she had to find him first.

Leaving the firemen and patrol cops to get everyone back into their homes, and the bomb technicians to handle the evidence, Shoni raced back to her mother's condo. John still hadn't returned.

Where would he go?

She was aware of only one of John's acquaintances, the

old woman from the building that burned. Had he gone to see Estelle? If so, how had he gotten there? The motel was at least three miles away.

Gripping the steering wheel like it was a lifeline, she drove the pedestrian-friendly route instead of the interstate shortcut. There were few people out, so if John was walking, she should see him. When she spotted his tall, lean figure with shoulders hunched against the cold ten minutes later, her entire body sagged. But anger came quickly on the heels of relief.

She stepped on the accelerator and lurched to a halt as she swung her Camry against the curb. John lifted his head and fell into a defensive crouch, the movement almost instinctive. The skilled and graceful motion, his composure after the shooting, his amazing physique . . . It all pointed to a professional, a man trained to fight and defend himself.

Determined to get to the bottom of the mystery, Shoni opened the car door and stepped out. She eyed him over the Camry's roof. "You gonna stand there all day or get in the car?"

It was as if she'd flipped a switch and John straightened out of his warrior's persona. Without a word, he slid into the front passenger seat.

Shoni got behind the wheel, but instead of driving back to the condo, she turned in her seat to face him. "That was a stupid thing to do."

At least John wasn't foolish enough to pretend he didn't understand. "I had to take a walk, clear my head."

"You went to visit Estelle."

"She's a friend." He turned toward her and an approaching car's headlights lit his blue eyes, making them appear almost translucent. "She doesn't demand more of me than I can give."

"What does that mean?" Shoni didn't like being cast as the bad guy. Especially when she was missing part of the script.

Frustration gave his voice an edge. "You needed a description and statement, and I gave them to you. You wanted me to stay at your mother's condo so you could guard me, and I did it. You kissed me and I kissed you back. Then you ran."

Shoni's face burned under his accusation. "I've never run away from anything."

A cold smile tugged at his lips. "So what was it that you forgot at the station?"

She was determined to learn the true identity of John McClane, but honesty was a two-way street.

"Nothing," she replied softly. "You're right. I ran."

John appeared startled by her sudden confession. "Why?"

"You're a witness, John. I'm a cop. I broke regulations." Impatience crept into her tone.

"I'll bet me staying at your mother's condo isn't exactly regulation either."

"No, but my boss approved it, so only the lieutenant, you, and I know where you're staying."

John glanced away and ran a hand along his freshly shaven face. "I told Estelle. Not the address, just that it was your mother's place."

"Will she tell anyone?

"No. I told her the arsonist might be trying to kill me."

His words reminded her that she had to tell him about the bomb, but not here. Back at the condo, where a beer would make the news go down easier and where they'd be safe from arsonists, snipers, and bombers.

Shoni snapped her seat belt in place and waited until John did the same, ignoring his exasperated eye roll. After putting the car into gear, she made a U-turn and drove back the way she'd come. Her passenger remained mute, but the silence that filled the car wasn't awkward or oppressive.

She parked in the same space she'd had earlier, then she

and John walked side by side to the entrance. Still quiet. Still comfortable.

"I see you found him," Pete said as soon as they entered.

John arched an eyebrow. "Didn't know I was lost."

"The detective called a couple of hours ago looking for you. She didn't sound happy."

Shoni sent the security guard a glare and the tips of his ears reddened. He got the hint.

Shoni and John stepped into a waiting elevator.

"So why didn't you come looking for me two hours ago?" John asked.

Shoni watched her distorted reflection in the shiny elevator walls. "I was busy."

"Doing what?"

She didn't answer, counting silently with the lighted numbers above the door as the elevator rose. Finally, they stepped into the hallway, and moments later were in the condo.

The beer her mother kept on hand for guests was still in the refrigerator and Shoni pulled out two bottles. Without asking John, she handed him one, then walked into the living room.

Folding herself into a corner of the love seat, she twisted the cap off the longneck and took a healthy swig. John joined her, sitting on the comfortable recliner at a right angle to the love seat. He tilted his head back and lifted the beer to his lips.

Shoni's gaze followed the glide of his Adam's apple up and down his whisker-free neck. She clutched the bottle between her hands, willing them to remain there.

"So what happened?" he asked.

Shoni lined up her thoughts, sending those involving John, bare skin, and wet heat to the back of her mind. "I went to my apartment. It was booby-trapped with a bomb."

John's eyes widened and his gaze swept across her, obviously searching for injuries. "You didn't get hurt."

She couldn't tell if it was a question or a statement, and

settled for shaking her head. "A neighbor had tacked a note to my door. Said a cable tech had been there." She peeled a shiny silver strip from the beer label and dropped it on her thigh, then continued to remove the label, piece by piece. "I hadn't called for service. Bomb techs came and took care of it."

"How sophisticated was it?"

Startled by the unexpected question, Shoni glanced up to see John leaning toward her, his elbows on his knees. The intensity of his gaze sent warning signals up and down her spine. "What do you mean?"

"Was it the kind somebody could make off the Internet? Or something more complicated?"

"Why?"

John's intensity eased and his brow furrowed, as if he was trying to figure out a puzzle with half the pieces missing. "Just curious."

The weak answer did nothing to assuage Shoni's wariness. She was also getting tired of dancing to John's off-key tune. "Someone is out to get you, John. Not me. *You*."

Not a flicker of surprise. For that matter, his expression revealed nothing. "We already knew that."

Shoni's temper climbed. "Arsonist. Sniper. Now a bomber. Three totally different types of criminals. And you're mixed up smack-dab in the middle of them. What the hell is going on?"

John jumped to his feet and Shoni jerked back, sending the silver paper strips fluttering to the floor.

"I don't know!" he shouted. "I wish to hell I did, but I don't." He turned his back to her, every line of his body vibrating.

John's outburst shocked Shoni. He'd always been nothing less than in total control—while fighting off three men in an alley or losing the place he called home. The only time he'd dropped the mask was during their kiss. She'd tasted his hot passion, known his coolness was only a cover for what burned beneath the surface. But that hadn't been anything like this blaze of temper.

Shoni forced herself to remain on the sofa, to give him the illusion of control. "Who are you, John?" she asked softly.

The answer was equally quiet. "I don't know."

The way he said it, she knew it wasn't some lame-ass comment on existentialism. Faint tendrils of realization curled through her, bringing a hint of the truth. She rose and set her beer bottle on the coffee table. Coming up behind John, she forced herself to ignore his long, lean figure.

"Tell me the truth," she said.

When he turned around, she almost gasped at the anguished eyes, the lost expression.

"I don't know who I am," he confessed in a husky whisper. "Over three weeks ago I woke up near the waterfront, soaking wet, beat up, and with no memory. Lainey found me and took me to Estelle's. They took care of me."

A thousand questions filled Shoni's mind and she filtered through them, prioritizing them. "Why didn't you go to the hospital? Or the police?"

His gaze slid away. "I was scared."

Shoni placed a hand on his forearm, the heat of his skin tangible through his sleeve. "Of what?"

Impatience flicked across his features. "You saw how I held off Jamar and his two thugs in the alley."

"So? What does that have to do with anything?"

He grabbed her upper arms and pressed his face closer to hers. "I have flashes of memories. Guns, knives, blood, men dying and dead. What the hell kind of person am I to have those pictures in my head?"

Shoni grasped at straws. "Maybe they're not real memories. Maybe scenes from movies or pictures from newspapers and magazines."

John laughed, the sound broken and chilling. His fingers pressed into her arms. "I can smell it, too. The blood. The sweat. The piss and shit. It's all in my head."

Shoni fought down a wave of fear. Not for herself, but for John's sanity. "Look, John, we can find out who you are. We'll go to the station and look through the missing persons reports. If that doesn't work, we'll check your fingerprints."

"And when you find out I'm a wanted criminal, what then?"

The man was like a bird dog locked on its quarry. "Damn it, John, you don't know that." She recalled Tyler's comment about the military. "Maybe you're a soldier."

"So you're saying this is some kind of post-traumatic stress?"

She wanted to shout, but kept her tone steady. "I don't know what this is. We won't know until we learn who you are."

John stared at her and the feral fear eased into resignation. As if suddenly realizing how firmly he held her, he dropped his hands to his sides. "Sorry."

Shoni rubbed her arms, where John's grip would probably leave marks, and didn't know if his apology was for that or for his outburst. "It's all right."

He didn't appear convinced, but lapsed into stony silence.

"Maybe you should get some sleep. We'll go in tomorrow morning and figure out who you are."

"I'm not tired."

Shoni stifled a sigh of exasperation. Her stomach took the moment to growl loud enough that it made John look up. His lips quirked upward.

"There's leftover take-out in the fridge," he said.

With all the excitement of the night, it felt like forever since she'd eaten. "You interested?" she asked, heading for the kitchen.

He shrugged. "Sure. Wouldn't want you to have to eat alone."

She sent him a grin over her shoulder, relieved that he'd put the possibility of being some kind of killer out of his head. At least for now. She busied herself with dividing the remaining sesame chicken and beef and broccoli between two plates. John sat on one of the stools, his clasped hands resting on the counter.

"You didn't answer my question about the bomb," he said.

She glanced up from her task and met his curious eyes. "Sophisticated. The type a pro would use."

Shoni stuck the first plate in the microwave and hit Two. Bending at the waist, she rested her forearms on the counter across from John. "Tell me what you're thinking."

His crooked smile traveled straight to her heart, and for an insane moment, all she wanted to do was hug him. "I'm thinking that I wish I could remember who I am and why I figured the bomb would be a pro job."

"Might just be the fact that the sniper was also a pro, and since we're assuming the two attempts are related . . ." She let it drop with a lift of a shoulder.

The microwave dinged and she retrieved the steaming plate and set it in front of John. After placing the second plate in the microwave to heat up, she grabbed another bottle of beer for John and a soda for herself.

"How do you know the shooter was a pro?" John asked.

"Nothing was found on the roof of the building where the shots came from. No shell casings, no footprints, no fingerprints. Nada. Zilch." Shoni took her food out of the microwave and sat on the stool next to John. "I don't know many amateurs who'd be that thorough."

"Tell me about the arsonist," John said.

Shoni stuck a forkful of broccoli in her mouth as she debated whether or not to answer his request. Technically, he was a suspect yet she had never seriously thought he was involved in the arsons.

"There's not much to tell. He's burned four deserted—supposedly deserted—warehouses in two weeks. A man died in one of them. And last night, those people in the apartment building would've died if you hadn't gotten them out."

A flush stained his cheeks. "Anybody else would've done the same."

She aimed her fork at him. "No, they wouldn't have. Most people don't want to get involved. You risked your life for Lainey. You got everybody out of Estelle's building while you were suffering from smoke inhalation. You're working with us to get the arsonist despite the fact some shooter with a fancy rifle is trying to kill you, as well as a bomber who doesn't need the Internet to build a bomb." She tipped her head to the side. "You're not a killer, John. I'd stake my badge on it."

He lifted his face, met her gaze with skeptical blue eyes. "And if you're wrong?"

"I'm not."

Even as she savored the sesame chicken, she wondered at her own certainty. Was she allowing her attraction to him color her judgment? *Duh.* How could she not? Yet the first time she'd seen him, she'd been impressed by his compassion and concern for Lainey. Then seeing him with Estelle and Mishon solidified that impression.

A man might lose his memory, but he didn't lose his basic nature. John McClane was a protector. The people he cared for automatically had his protection. And he would never ask for anything in return. It was who he was.

"Do all your memory flashes involve violence?" she asked.

John tipped his head to the side and his vision turned inward. "A little girl. She used to watch me shave."

"So, you have a daughter." She managed to keep her voice steady.

"Maybe. I don't know." He squeezed his eyes shut and rubbed his head.

Concerned, Shoni laid her hand between his shoulder blades. "What's wrong?"

"Headache. Getting worse."

"C'mon. I'm taking you to the hospital." She tried to help him up but he resisted, remaining seated.

"I'm not going to a hospital."

"Amnesia is usually caused by a blow to the head. What if the blow was hard enough to do more than give you amnesia?"

He grabbed her hand and squeezed it gently. "It's caused by the memories. The more flashes I get, the worse the headaches, and over the last day or two, they've gotten a lot worse."

Although Shoni considered herself composed and in control—being a cop had its perks—she found herself on the verge of panicking. "You don't know it's as simple as that. It could be something life-threatening."

He smiled wryly even though the pain lines at the corners of his eyes remained. "Worried about your only witness?"

She wanted to punch him. "To hell with the case. I'm worried about *you*."

"Be careful, Detective Alexander. You might actually convince me that you care."

If she hadn't been watching him so closely, she would've only heard his words and not seen the teasing warmth behind them. Her frustration melted away and she sank back onto her stool.

His thumb brushed across the back of her hand and quicksilver slid through her veins. Even the possibility that he had a daughter couldn't stop the wave of want that washed through her. A lot of single men had children.

"Estelle told me I should trust you," he confessed.

"She's a smart woman." Shoni paused deliberately. "Even if she does keep a concealed weapon without a permit."

John stiffened, but must have seen the tolerant amusement in her expression because he relaxed again. "Morey keeps her safe, or as safe as she can be, living in that part of the city."

"She named her gun?"

A lift of his sensuous lips nearly made Shoni groan.

"Don't tell me you don't have a nickname for your Glock."

Shoni wasn't surprised he knew the kind of gun she carried. She also wasn't going to share that personal tidbit. "How's the headache?"

"A little better."

"You should get some rest. Tomorrow's going to be a long day."

"For you, too," John said.

Keeping her gaze averted, she shrugged. "Most of my days have been long since Mom died."

"You were close." It wasn't a question.

"After Dad died, it was only the two of us. We relied on each other."

Mom relied *on me.*

The clock chimed on the mantel. Midnight. The witching hour. Aptly named with John holding Shoni's hand, rubbing his thumb across her knuckles. She didn't know if he realized what he was doing, but it felt too good to interrupt.

"We should go to bed," John said. Was his voice rougher than usual?

Shoni nodded but didn't make any effort to stand. John's knees were tangled with hers, his hand held hers, his face was close enough that she felt his breath across her cheek. She didn't want to lose the feeling of rightness, of familiarity with this man who didn't even know himself. Yet she knew the important things. The things that made him who he was, with or without a name.

She lifted her free hand and brushed back a tendril of hair from his brow. Thick and wavy, soft beneath her fingers.

John didn't appear surprised by her dare of intimacy, yet uncertainty remained. "You don't know me," he said, the same husky quality in his voice.

"I know enough."

He shook his head and captured her hand that glided down to his cheek. "I don't want to hurt you."

"I'm a big girl. I know what I'm doing."

John blinked and his breath hitched. "Maybe I don't."

Shoni's heart continued its erratic rhythm, but she made an attempt at levity. "It's like riding a bicycle."

"I'm not talking about sex." His jaw clenched. "I remember a woman, too. Her name is Tiffany. I think she's my wife."

Chapter Eleven

SHONI stood and gathered their plates, keeping her eyes on anything but him. "It's time we both got some sleep."

"I'm not *sure* the woman is my wife," John said, then wished he hadn't spoken at all since the words came out needy and desperate.

Shoni scraped the remains from their plates into the garbage disposal and deposited them in the dishwasher. She leaned her hips against the counter, crossed her ankles and arms. Every line in her body radiated defensiveness. "You're right, we shouldn't do this. And not just because you might be married, but because I'm a cop and you're involved in an active investigation. I keep telling myself that you're innocent and that I'm not jeopardizing my case."

She licked her lips and John clenched the edge of the counter to keep from vaulting over it, to follow the trail of her tongue with his own.

"But the fact is, we're both having trouble remembering

who we are." Shoni shoved away from the dishwasher. "I'm going to bed. I'll see you in the morning."

And with that, she strode past him.

John placed his elbows on the breakfast bar and dropped his head in his hands. Maybe he shouldn't have told her about the woman, but how could he live with himself if he slept with Shoni when he was already married?

And despite what he'd said to Shoni, he was convinced he was, or had been, married to this Tiffany. She was blonde and beautiful, a woman any man would be proud of loving, yet it was odd to think of a stranger as his wife.

Unlike Shoni, whom he knew and wanted to know better. She was smart and savvy, and had more integrity and compassion than he expected from a cop. He respected her, cared for her more than he should. And if his libido was any indicator, he wanted to strip her and make love to every inch of her hot, smooth skin. Kiss the moist haven between her thighs until she writhed beneath him, begged him . . . He shifted, carefully adjusting the hard flesh that pressed painfully against his jeans.

He had it bad. Or maybe it was simply a case of being celibate for too damned long.

John stifled a groan, then stood. He checked the condo's locks, as well as the patio windows, even though he knew Shoni had already done so. Although everything that made him who he was had been ripped from him, he couldn't stop feeling responsible for Shoni, Estelle, and Lainey. Even Mishon.

By the time he stripped to his underwear and crawled into bed, his erection had faded. However, he knew it wouldn't stay that way if he allowed his thoughts to stray to the woman in the other bedroom.

John lay on his back, his arms folded beneath his head. Tomorrow he'd learn who he was. Tomorrow he'd discover who the woman and child were that haunted him. Tomorrow he'd either be reunited with his family or be arrested. He didn't share Shoni's faith that he was squeaky clean. A man didn't know over a hundred ways to kill with his bare hands unless there was some blood on those hands.

But for the first time, that conclusion didn't frighten John. Facing the truth of who he was had to be better than this purgatory he was trapped in.

Only one fear remained. How much would the truth hurt Shoni?

DESPITE John's cool attitude the following morning, Shoni knew he was fearful of learning his identity. It was in the way his eyes would slide away when hers met them, and how he couldn't sit in one place for more than a minute or two.

She didn't push him, knowing how much courage it had taken to ask for her help. If there turned out to be a warrant issued on him, he was setting himself up for prison. In spite of what he'd told her about his fractured memories, she couldn't believe he was a criminal. She'd known enough to recognize the type, and John was definitely not one of them.

It was the possibility that he had a wife and family that kept Shoni awake long into the night. She'd been tempted to crawl into his bed and have one night with him. If John wanted her as much as she wanted him, it wouldn't have taken much to sway his honorable intentions. But she hadn't been able to do it. Maybe she was old-fashioned, but marriage vows still meant something to her.

"Are you taking your antibiotics?" she asked as they finished their coffee.

He nodded and flexed the injured arm. "It's not as sore as yesterday."

He finished his coffee and stood, stretching his arms above his head and exposing a thin strip of flesh between his shirt and jeans.

Shoni quickly glanced away, but not fast enough. Her hands trembled as she rinsed their cups in the sink.

As they donned their coats in the foyer, she noticed the creases in John's brow and at the corners of his mouth. "More memories?" she asked.

He managed a wan smile. "I think so. Headache's a bitch."

She reached into her jacket pocket and tossed him a small bottle of aspirin.

He caught it one-handed. "Thanks." He dry swallowed four tablets and returned the bottle.

Five minutes later they were on their way to the precinct. The sun shone brightly but there was a crispness in the air heralding the coming of winter, and Shoni had the car's heater cranked up.

She parked in the official lot, and as she reached for the door handle, John's voice halted her.

"I want to thank you for all your help," he said quietly.

Shoni's heart tripped and she forced a smile. "Hey, you aren't going to get rid of me that easily. You're still the star witness in my case."

"I know, but things will be"—he searched for the right word—"different."

"You'll still need police protection. And if you have a family, they'll be protected, too." It hurt to say it aloud, but Shoni was first and foremost a cop. Her personal feelings didn't matter.

John reached across the seat and clasped Shoni's hand. "I'm grateful for everything you've done. I just wanted you to know."

Moisture stung Shoni's eyes but she shook her head, smiling wryly. "It's not like you're dying or anything, so spare me the chick flick moment."

John chuckled and it actually sounded sincere. "I thought you chicks liked sensitive guys."

"Yeah, well, maybe this chick is a masochist who likes guys who growl at her."

John shook his head, smiling. He squeezed her hand one last time before releasing it.

The attempts on John's life were foremost in her mind as she unfolded herself from the front seat and searched the surroundings for any sign of danger. They met at the back of the car, and John's hawklike gaze and loose-limbed stealth told her he didn't take safety for granted either.

Their approach to the building was uneventful and Shoni breathed a sigh of relief. The same sergeant was on duty at the desk, and it didn't take long for John to get his visitors pass. They entered the relatively quiet bullpen a few minutes after seven o'clock. The smell of fresh coffee filled the room and Shoni glanced around but didn't see Delon. That meant the coffee might actually be tolerable.

"Go ahead and sit down," she said to John. She picked up her mug from the desktop. "Do you want coffee?"

She read a half shrug, half nod as an affirmative and brought him some. Sitting behind her desk, Shoni found herself reluctant to begin the missing persons search. After a sip of not too horrible coffee, she booted up her computer and typed in her password. Intensely aware of John's gaze on her, she focused on her task. Within moments, she had the files at her fingertips. Using the search option, she typed in the date and place John was found and his physical characteristics.

Blue eyes. Light brown hair. Approximately six foot two. One ninety.

Sexy dimples. Abs of titanium. World-class ass.

She cleared her throat. "Do you have any distinguishing marks?" she asked without looking at him.

"Scars. Right side, left thigh, and left shoulder."

Shoni's fingers curled into her palms. Those scars were more evidence of a violent past. She took a deep breath and input the scar information. "Any tattoos? Birthmarks?"

"None that I could see."

She resisted the urge to offer to check him out and punched the Search button.

John leaned forward in his chair, his attention trained on the computer screen. His expression gave nothing away, but Shoni had taken a few lessons in McClane-speak. The stiff spine, braced shoulders, and clench of fingers around his coffee cup broadcast his tension.

The search brought back five names.

Her palms sweaty, Shoni double-clicked on the first one. The picture that came up wasn't even close. She went to the next. Again, no match. Shoni let out a gust of air when the fifth one yielded the same result.

She slumped in her chair and met John's bleak gaze. Her heart thudded dully. "I'll expand the search to all of Virginia."

As the computer raced through the numerous missing persons reports, the lieutenant's door flew open and he bellowed from the doorway. "Alexander. My office. Now."

Her computer beeped, letting her know the search was complete. Twenty-six possibles.

"His timing sucks," Shoni said, glaring at Bob's open office door. She debated shutting down her computer, but didn't want to start the search from scratch. "Don't touch anything. I'll be back in a few minutes."

John looked like he wanted to argue, and Shoni didn't blame him. "I shouldn't be long," she assured him.

She grabbed the arson file, allowed her hand to rest on John's shoulder a moment. She meant the gesture as reassurance for him, but she found herself bolstered by the brief contact. She wove a line between the desks to Bob's office. Once inside, her boss didn't waste any time.

"Your witness actually looks reputable now," Bob commented, lifting his chin in the general direction of her desk.

"Amazing what a simple shave will do."

"Get anything more out of him?"

She glanced down, knowing she'd have to fish or cut bait at some point. She had hoped she'd have more time, maybe learn John's real identity before having to tell Bob.

Dropping into a chair, she licked her suddenly dry lips. "He's on the street because he lost his memory."

"What?"

Bob's roar could probably be heard in the Special Crimes Unit, two floors away.

Keeping her voice calm and detached, she told him what John had confessed last night. "We're going through the missing persons reports now to see if we can figure out who he is."

"You realize his entire statement and suspect description are now contestable?"

Shoni jumped to her feet and paced to the window that looked down on the busy street. Although she'd thought it a possibility, she'd hoped it wouldn't become an issue. She spun around and placed her hands on Bob's desk. "Why? He remembers everything from the point he woke up with amnesia, and that includes the arsonist's face."

Bob lifted his outstretched arms. "I'm not saying I think it's right, but that's the way it is."

"What if we determine who John is? What then?"

Bob tapped his lower lip with his forefinger. "Twenty-four hours. If you haven't figured out who he is by then, I'll have to call the DA's office and find out where we stand."

Relieved by the reprieve, Shoni straightened. "Yes, sir."

"Now sit down and tell me what you have. I'm going to take it to the captain and see how much should be released to the press," Bob said.

Shoni opened the arson file and wondered if she dared ask for a cup of his special brew. One look at his dark scowl gave her the answer.

ALTHOUGH Shoni had told John to wait until she returned, the names on the screen beckoned him. Was he Randolph Lewis? Or Jeff Sanders? Maybe William Nordby?

He glanced around, and the few detectives in the large

but cramped area paid no attention to him. Moving like he had every right to be there, John shifted over to Shoni's chair in front of the keyboard. He clicked on the first name.

Twenty minutes later, he'd gone through all twenty-six names and not a single picture was even close. So either he wasn't from Virginia or nobody missed him. He hoped it wasn't the latter.

He tried to pull back the curtain in his mind, but he was smart enough not to search for any specifics about his life. Instead, he focused on generalities. How familiar was Virginia? Did it have the ring of "home" to it?

Pain arrowed through his brain and he clamped his hands against the sides of his head. Every time he pushed for his memories, something in him fought back. And it was getting worse. And the random images were growing more frequent.

A touch on his shoulder startled him and he jerked, which did nothing for the sharp ache in his head.

"Damn it, you went through the—you look like a ghost," Shoni said, annoyance flipping to concern. She squatted down beside him, her slender but strong hands on his arms, and asked quietly, "Headache worse?"

"I'm all right," he muttered.

"Sure you are, tough guy," Shoni said, not without a trace of fond exasperation. "You want me to take you to the clinic or back to the condo?"

He glared at her, or at least tried to. "I want to find out who I am."

Shoni dropped back on her heels. "I assume that means none of those twenty-six men were you?"

He didn't bother to reply. "Run my fingerprints."

"Are you sure?"

"Yes." He could barely speak through his clenched teeth.

Half an hour later John's fingerprints were scanned and stored in the lab's computer.

"How long?" Shoni asked Tasha, the lab geek on duty.

The platinum blonde pressed her black-rimmed glasses up on her nose. "Depends. Where's the paperwork?"

"There isn't any." Shoni winked. "A favor?"

Tasha's kohl-lined eyes twinkled. "Oooh, a detective owing me a favor." She nodded and her glasses slipped down her nose again. "Twenty-four hours. Maybe less. That's provided his fingerprints are in the system."

"Thanks, Tash." Shoni handed her a business card. "Oh, make sure to run them through military records, too."

As Shoni and John left the lab, she glanced back at Tasha, only to find her gaze locked on John's ass. Possessiveness surged through Shoni and she barely stifled the impulse to get between him and Tasha's predatory gaze. If she reacted this strongly to another woman simply eyeing John, how would she react to a wife who had every right not only to ogle her husband, but to make love to him as well?

Her stomach churning, Shoni led the way back to the VCU. John held the door for her and she sent him a quick nod.

"I'll take you back to the condo," she said once they were at her desk.

"What about you?"

"I have work to do."

"I can walk back," John said.

"The hell you can. If you haven't noticed, someone is trying to kill you."

"What crawled up your ass and died?"

Shoni clamped her mouth shut. She *was* angry, and she didn't even know why. She took a deep breath to calm her buzzing nerves. "All I'm saying is that I can't let you wander off alone. Whoever wants you dead is serious enough to have a professional gunning for you. We don't know when he'll try again."

"Maybe he gave up."

"Are you willing to take that chance? Because I'm not." Shoni glared at him.

"Maybe you two should take the lovers' quarrel someplace more private," Rafferty said, sotto voce, from his desk across the aisle. "You're putting on quite the show."

She glared at Raff, who had removed his Armani suit coat. However, one glance around the room proved his words. More than a few detectives were watching them with the same eager expectancy as a Dr. Phil audience.

"Fine," she said in a low, tight voice. "And even though it isn't any of your business, it isn't a lover's quarrel."

Raff lifted his hands in surrender. "Whatever."

"Come on," Shoni said to John. "I'll take you back to the condo."

The stubborn thrust of John's jaw didn't bode well for a hassle-free exit, but he nodded and followed her out the door. Despite her simmering and unexplainable irritation, Shoni kept her vigilance as they made their way to her car.

"I'm not helpless," John said, breaking the silence as Shoni drove.

"I never said you were."

"You didn't have to."

She glanced at him, noting the muscle flex in his cheek and the implacable flat line of his mouth. *A man and his pride.*

"Look, I know you can take care of yourself. But fighting three men in an alley is a whole lot different from fighting an unseen enemy. Next time it might be a hit-and-run, or an anonymous mugger with a knife. We don't know what he'll try next."

"Why?"

The single word question startled her. "Why what?"

"Why am I on someone's hit list?"

"Because you can ID an arsonist." But even as Shoni said it, she realized she didn't believe the simple explanation.

"I came up with a picture of the suspect, but we both know the chances of finding this guy in a city the size of Norfolk is a long shot. Why would he take the chance of getting caught trying to take me out? Why doesn't he just leave Norfolk and play with matches in some other city?"

Shoni considered half a dozen replies, but all had serious logic flaws. "I don't know."

"There's more going on here than just some guy starting fires."

"Like what?"

He shot her an annoyed look. "If I knew that, I'd know what it was."

"Point taken. Any theories?"

He shook his head and his bangs flopped over his forehead. He shoved them back with an impatient hand. "I need a haircut."

Shoni chuckled. "As theories go, that one pretty much sucks."

John's smile didn't touch his eyes. "Were the warehouses owned by the same company?"

Shoni's amusement disappeared. "That was the first angle we checked. All different owners."

"Arson for hire?"

"Doubtful. All were insured, but only one had a payoff that would make it worthwhile. The others were covered for liability only."

"That doesn't make any sense." John paused. "You said someone was killed in the second fire."

Shoni nodded. "That's right. Still a John Doe. The body was burned beyond recognition. Couldn't get any fingerprints and it takes time to run dental records."

John shifted in his seat and stared out the windshield. "That could've been me," he murmured so softly Shoni almost missed it.

She shot him a worried glance, then pulled up in front of the condo's entrance. "But it wasn't. And you'll know who you are soon." Her heart climbed into her throat. "I promise."

A tic in John's jaw was his only acknowledgment.

Shoni held back a sigh. "I'll be back around six this evening, provided nothing comes up." She paused. "I know I can't force you to stay here—"

"I won't leave." John turned his head toward her. "You have my word. You'll call me if my fingerprints bring back a name?"

"You have my word," Shoni said, intentionally repeating John's promise. "Get some rest. You look like hell."

"You say the sweetest things, Detective."

Relieved he'd climbed out of his funk, Shoni gave his shoulder a playful shove. "Go on. And remember to lock the door and don't let anyone in."

After a visual reconnoiter, John stepped out of the car but leaned in with a smirk. "I won't take any candy from strangers, either."

Shaking her head in amusement, Shoni watched the unfamiliar guard buzz the door open for John, then wave him past the security desk.

She headed back to the station, her mind on the number of things she had to do when she returned. She'd have to make a list.

List. The security guard at the condo hadn't checked his list before letting John in.

Chapter Twelve

SHONI made a tire-squealing U-turn, barely avoiding a head-on collision with an SUV. She muttered an apology to the gape-mouthed driver and raced back to the condo, using her siren to cut through the sluggish traffic. Braking sharply in front of the building entrance, she rocketed out of the sedan and palmed her Glock.

The guard was no longer at the front desk. Keeping her weapon aimed downward with one hand, she punched in the door's security code with the other. She shouldered the glass door open and slipped inside, bringing up her gun with a two-handed grip, her arms straight.

Nobody in sight.

Shoni's gaze roamed the lobby. Had he followed John to the twelfth floor?

Remaining vigilant, she drew her phone out of her pocket and hit the speed dial. It seemed to take forever for the call to go through, then another eternity as she waited for John to pick up. Only he didn't.

Her mother's serene voice clicked on. "I'm sorry you

missed me. Please leave your name and number, and if our karmas are destined to connect, I'll return your call."

Shoni's eyes stung. But even as renewed grief rolled through her, concern for John bulldozed it aside. "John, if you're there, pick up."

She counted eighteen rapid pulse beats before John's voice came on.

"I'm here," he said.

Shoni nearly collapsed in relief.

"Did you get the results from my fingerprints already?" John asked, trepidation in his voice.

"No, I—"

A door down a short hallway to her left opened, and Shoni dropped her phone to swing her weapon toward the hall. A uniformed man zipping his fly walked toward the desk. He raised his head and froze, his round eyes reminding Shoni of Wile E. Coyote suddenly realizing he'd run off a cliff.

"What's going on? Where are you, Shoni?" John's tinny voice came through the cell phone.

She snatched it up and put it to her ear. "Everything's fine. I just wanted to make sure you made it safely up to Mom's place."

"I did." He sounded puzzled, but Shoni could give him the details of her paranoia later. "I'll call you if I hear anything. 'Bye." She clapped the phone shut and dropped it into a pocket.

"Wh-Who are you?" the pimply-faced security guard asked.

Shoni holstered her Glock at her back. "Detective Shoni Alexander. My mother has a place here."

The kid's terror leached away, replaced by false bravado. "You had a gun. I could've shot you."

Shoni laughed. "Right." She sobered. Even though the guard didn't appear to be the man after John, he hadn't followed procedure either. "Next time someone comes in here, make sure they're either on the tenant list or the approved guest list."

The kid drew back his unimpressive shoulders. "I check."

"You just let a man in without even looking at your list."

His face reddened. "He seemed like he'd been here before."

Shoni resisted the urge throttle the kid. Instead, she settled for a dressing down that Lieutenant Tyler would've been proud of.

HOURS later, Shoni placed her phone in its cradle and leaned back in her desk chair. Her spine cracked in two places, sounding like muted gunshots. She rubbed her gritty eyes and shoved her curly hair back from her face for the hundredth time that day. She'd forgotten to tie it back and didn't have any bands with her. Maybe she'd get it all cut off. Better yet, shave her head, like Bruce Willis . . .

Which made her think of John McClane. *Her* John McClane. Not that she needed much incentive to think about him. He hadn't strayed far from her thoughts all day. In a kind of scary, weird way, she envied his amnesia. What would it be like to start over with a clean slate? No trying to live up to a dead father's ideals and never knowing if she succeeded. No reaching for the phone to call a mother, then realizing she was gone. No obsessing about killing the man who took her mother's life.

She propped her elbows on her desk and pressed her throbbing forehead to her palms, thrusting her fingers into her curls. Just as she'd lose the painful memories, she'd also lose the happy ones. The family camping trips and the vacation at Disney World, where she'd gotten sick from the rides at Magic Kingdom and her father had rocked her in his lap even though she was ten years old.

No, the price was too steep, as John knew firsthand.

Her phone rang and she nabbed it, hoping it was Tasha with good news.

"Alexander," she said.

"This is the Norfolk PD ME."

Shoni shook her head in amusement at Dr. Pete Grady's standard phone greeting, as if nobody would know who he was if he simply gave his name. "What do you have, Doc?"

"A name to go with your burn victim."

She grabbed a pen. "Go ahead."

"William Markoff. According to the records, he was sixty-three years old."

"Do you have an address?"

The medical examiner read off a number and street name, which Shoni recognized as being in the affluent southeast waterfront area of the city. "Do you have cause of death yet?"

"Smoke inhalation."

Shoni frowned. "No sign of foul play?"

"There was no evidence of damage to the bones or deep tissues, so he wasn't shot or stabbed. No signs of blunt force trauma that might indicate he was knocked unconscious."

"So he just lay down and died?"

"It's possible he was unconscious before the fire started, but I can't determine anything specific."

"So we don't know if it was accidental, suicide, or murder."

"That's about it."

Shoni stifled a frustrated sigh. "Thanks, Doc."

"Just doing my job. You have a good day, Detective."

As soon as she hung up, she put William Markoff's name in the computer and a missing persons report popped up. The picture showed a man with thick white hair and a tanned, sun-lined face. He would've been a handsome man except for the scowl. But then, being the CEO of one of the biggest companies in Virginia, he probably had a right to frown.

As the detective in charge, Shoni had the responsibility to give the man's widow the news. She'd have questions to ask, too, and hoped Mrs. Markoff would be able to answer them.

A suited man entered the swinging doors of VCU. Mousy brown receding hair, brown eyes, midthirties, average build.

Shoni cursed under her breath.

Across the aisle, Raff followed her gaze. "Who's he?"

"I'm guessing fed. Profiling expert."

"Ahhh."

Shoni clenched her jaw. "Maybe if I ignore him, he'll go away."

Raff snorted. "Dream on, Alexander."

She shot him a glare.

The FBI agent stopped at the first occupied desk and the detective pointed toward Lieutenant Tyler's office.

Shoni swore and shut down her computer, then grabbed the arson file as well as the paper with Markoff's address.

As the VCU door swung shut behind her, she heard Tyler's familiar bellow. Her footsteps didn't falter.

SHONI followed the curvy tree-lined driveway up a gently sloping hill. As she rounded the last curve, the grounds opened to reveal a picturesque three-level Victorian home with a wraparound porch. Above the porch was a covered balcony that probably came out from the master bedroom.

She parked in the circular driveway and stepped out of her car. Her eight-year-old Camry appeared old and shabby beside a shiny new BMW. Tugging her coat around her to ward off the cool breeze coming off the Chesapeake Bay, she climbed the white stairs to the white porch with its white colonnades. Even the door was white.

Squinting, Shoni pressed the doorbell. Chimes rang through the house, not unlike the chimes of her mother's

Tellurium clock. Moments later the door swung open and a redhead around Shoni's age stood in the entrance.

"Can I help you?"

Shoni dipped into her jacket pocket and pulled out her badge. "Detective Alexander. Norfolk PD."

The redhead's complexion paled, making her faint freckles more apparent. "Is this about my husband?"

Shoni doubted she was Markoff's first wife. "May I come in?"

Without a word, Mrs. Markoff stepped back to allow Shoni inside.

The home was as immaculate on the inside as it was on the outside, with a polished hardwood floor and expensive rugs strategically scattered across it. The willowy redhead led Shoni to the front room with floor-to-ceiling windows that held a breathtaking view of the bay. However, the water looked angry and forbidding under the low-hanging gray clouds. Shoni sat on an overstuffed love seat with spindly legs while Markoff's wife perched on the edge of a matching chair.

"You found him."

It wasn't a question, but Shoni nodded. "Yes. I'm sorry."

The young woman's chin trembled; either she was a decent actress or she'd truly cared for her husband. Maybe both. "Where?"

"His body was found in an old warehouse down on the docks ten days ago."

Mrs. Markoff's eyes swam with moisture but fiery indignation burned through the tears. "Why did it take so long?"

Shoni sought the right words. "He was burned. It took time to match his dental records."

The woman's head dropped and she covered her face with trembling hands. Her wet sobs tore at Shoni, and she leaned forward to lay a hand on the woman's shaking shoulders.

"I'm sorry, Mrs. Markoff." The words were awkward

and inadequate, but they were all Shoni had to offer. She handed a box of tissues to the grieving woman.

"Thank you," the widow said quietly.

"You're welcome." Shoni gave the woman time to regain her composure.

When Mrs. Markoff raised her head, her eyes were red and puffy and her cheeks wan. "Where's his . . . his body?"

"The morgue."

The woman nodded and wiped away fresh tears.

"I know this is a difficult time for you, but I need to ask you some questions," Shoni said. "Do you know why your husband would've been in that warehouse?"

"If it wasn't one of the company's, then no. If they were looking to buy or rent more warehouse space, someone else would've been assigned the job. Bill didn't do that kind of thing."

"Is there anyone you can think of who'd want to harm your husband?"

Mrs. Markoff laughed, a harsh, brittle sound. "He's the CEO of a company that makes munitions. I'm sure there are more than a few nuts out there who'd want to kill him for that reason alone."

"Did he receive any death threats?"

"Occasionally, but they were usually from the same people. Bill had his own security people check them out. From what they learned, the letter writers were mostly harmless nutcases."

"What about those who weren't?"

"You'll have to talk to the head of security."

Shoni jotted down notes in her notebook. "Was there anyone else—maybe someone in his company or a business competitor—who might have a grudge against him?"

The redhead's eyes widened. "My husband might not have been the easiest man to work for, but he was fair."

"Do you know what company he had the majority of contracts with?"

"Eighty percent of his business was with the government. Department of Defense."

That didn't surprise Shoni, not with the Iraq war. "Your husband must've talked to you about his work."

A weak smile caught the widow's full lips. "I used to work for his company."

Office romance.

"Has there been any infighting within the company?"

Mrs. Markoff's brow creased and she continued to twist the tissue in her hands. "There was a new contract coming up, a big one. The board was pushing to bid on it, but Bill was fighting it."

Shoni tipped her head to the side. "Why would your husband not pursue a major contract?"

Mrs. Markoff rose and crossed to the spacious windows that faced the bay. "He has a son, from his first marriage. Billy." A watery laugh. "He likes to be called William now. He was in Iraq last year. He lost a leg. Bill was devastated. It's changed the way he thinks about things. In fact, he told me he was going to step down from his position after the first of the year." She turned and met Shoni's gaze. "After he made sure the company didn't get the new contract."

Shoni wrote Motive? in her notebook and underlined it.

Shoni stood. "Thank you, Mrs. Markoff. I know this was hard for you."

A tear rolled down the widow's cheek and she brushed it aside. "Do you think he was murdered?"

"There's no evidence of foul play, but it does seem odd that there was no reason for him to be in that warehouse." Shoni handed her a card. "If you think of anything else, please call me."

The woman stared down at the business card. "When can I have my husband's body?"

"Someone from the ME's office will call you as soon as the body is released." Shoni paused. "Is there someone you can call, someone who could come and stay with you?"

Mrs. Markoff lifted her chin. "When I filed the missing persons report, I started to prepare myself for this. I'll be all right."

Shoni admired her strength, but she also knew how grief could ambush a person. She squeezed Mrs. Markoff's cold hand. "I know you will, but sometimes it's easier to have someone you can talk to."

"I'll call my sister. She lives in Virginia Beach." The widow walked Shoni to the massive door. "Thank you, Detective." Her expression hardened. "And please find out why my husband died."

"I'll do my best."

Shoni hurried down the steps to her Camry. Inside her car, she opened her cell phone. Three missed calls. She put the phone to her ear and listened to the first message.

"The profiler from the FBI is here. Get back to the station."

Lieutenant Tyler didn't sound happy.

Second message.

"That wasn't a request, Alexander."

Definitely not happy.

Third message.

"Call me."

Pissed off.

Although Shoni had bent some rules in the last week or so, she'd never blatantly ignored an order. Taking a deep breath, she punched in her boss's number.

"Lieutenant Tyler is unavailable. Leave a message."

Shoni breathed a silent sigh of relief. "This is Alexander returning your call."

If Bob wanted to ream her out this evening instead of waiting until morning, he'd call her.

She glanced at her watch. Five fifteen. Too late to talk to Markoff's employees. She'd have to wait until tomorrow.

She could return to her desk, but after the lieutenant's messages, she didn't think that was such a good idea. Fortunately, she'd grabbed the arson file on her way out of the bullpen. She could study the reports at the condo as easily as at her desk in VCU.

As she drove away from the Victorian home, snow flurries began to filter down from the dull gray clouds.

A sound outside the condo's door caught John's attention. After the murder attempts and Shoni's odd call soon after he'd gotten into the apartment, he wasn't taking any chances. Without thought, he glided into the hidden alcove just inside the kitchen. The door whispered open and John sensed rather than saw Shoni enter.

He stepped into the foyer.

Shoni dropped a file to snatch the gun from the holster at her back. However, she quickly tilted the barrel up when recognition struck. She tucked the weapon away, her eyes sparking with anger. "Damn it, McClane, I nearly shot you."

John shrugged. "Impressive reflexes, Detective."

She scowled and squatted to gather up the papers that littered the floor. Although the bird's-eye view of her low neckline was appealing, John hunkered down to help her. He noticed enough phrases to figure out the reports were about the fires. "Bringing your work home?"

She snatched the papers from him and stuffed them in the file. "Some of us have to work for a living."

John gnashed his teeth. *I would, if I knew who I was.*

"Hear anything?" he asked, hoping he didn't sound as desperate as he felt.

"Not yet," Shoni replied.

She rose and set the fat file on the foyer table. As John climbed to his feet, she removed her jacket and shoes, tossing them in the foyer closet. She paused and sniffed. "What smells so good?"

"Just something I threw together," John replied offhandedly.

"And he cooks, too," Shoni said, a twinkle in her eyes.

"Apparently."

John lifted the cover off a pan on the stove and stirred the contents. Shoni raised herself on her tiptoes to see what was in the kettle. "Rice?"

"With a few added ingredients." He motioned to the frying pan. "I just have to cook up the shrimp and it'll be ready."

"Anything I can do?"

He shrugged. "Sit down and relax. You look tired."

Shoni didn't argue and planted herself on one of the stools at the breakfast counter. "We got a name on the John Doe that was found in the second fire."

He dropped a dab of butter into the pan and flicked on the burner beneath it. "Oh?"

"William Markoff."

John glanced at her. "Markoff?"

"That's right. Sound familiar?"

A sharp pain stabbed through his temples and he squeezed his eyes shut. "I'm not sure." He massaged his forehead with his fingertips. "I think so."

The butter sizzled in the frying pan, forcing John to open his eyes. He turned down the burner and added the shrimp, sautéing them in the melted butter.

"He was the CEO of a munitions company based in Norfolk," Shoni said. "He has a son who lost a leg in Iraq."

"A lot of men did," John remarked without thinking.

"You sound like you have firsthand experience."

Explosions.

Searing heat.

Screams.

Gunfire.

Blood.

John dropped the stirring spoon and clapped his hands over his ears. His mind was filled with visions of men in desert fatigues, faces covered with sand and sweat, and barking orders.

"John, are you all right? John?"

The frantic tone rather than the words themselves pulled John back to the present. He leaned against the counter, his legs shaking and a migraine threatening. Only Shoni's strong grip on his arms kept him from sliding to the floor.

"Are you back with me?" Her concerned expression negated her light tone.

He scrubbed a hand across his face. "Yeah, I think so."

"What happened? You looked like you were a million miles away."

"I was. The Middle East." He met her worried eyes. "If these visions mean what I think they do, then I was a soldier over there."

"Lieutenant Tyler thought you might've been in the military." She managed a wry grin. "He said it takes one to know one."

"That's why you told the fingerprint tech to check military records."

Shoni nodded.

The smell of scorched shrimp put an end to their discussion as John tried to salvage their dinner. It wasn't until they were both seated at the dining room table with plates full of rice and shrimp that Shoni picked up the conversation.

"Being a soldier would explain your fighting skills and those scars you don't know how you got."

John's pulse thrummed. "I might not be a criminal."

Shoni's genuine smile reflected in her sparkling green eyes. "I never thought you were."

Her confidence humbled him. She hadn't doubted him, even when he suspected the worst of himself. His emotions too near the surface, he kept his gaze aimed downward as he dug into his meal. The flavors sparked images in his battered memory, of the woman called Tiffany and the girl Chelle. There was laughter and teasing as they ate the same meal that John had just prepared.

Feelings crashed through him and he blinked against the

sting of moisture. Although he didn't actually remember them, he knew they were important to him; vital to him, like air or water.

He lifted his gaze to the woman across the table. The light from the chandelier gave her dark curls an auburn tint, and shaded her eyes the color of spring grass. Yet it was her strength and compassion that attracted him even more than her beauty. He wanted her more than he wanted the unknown Tiffany.

Suddenly the prospect of learning his identity lost its appeal.

Chapter Thirteen

SHONI noticed his mood shift. Although John seemed relieved that he was likely a soldier and not a criminal, he became melancholy and distant moments later. She had to bite her tongue to keep from asking him what was wrong. He was her witness, not her best friend. Except it didn't feel that way. She'd met him only two nights ago, and didn't know his real name or where he lived or what he did for a living . . . But it didn't matter. She knew all she needed to about him.

"Coffee?" she asked him.

He nodded, and she set two steaming cups on the table. She retrieved the file she'd brought home and opened it. She was aware of John's scrutiny and found it difficult to concentrate. "I'm sure there's something on TV that would be more interesting to watch," she said without looking up.

"Maybe I can help."

She lifted her gaze and propped her chin in her palm. "Theoretically, you shouldn't be within a mile of these reports since you're a suspect in the case."

"Then you shouldn't have opened up the file right in front of me."

Shoni's cheeks heated. Maybe subconsciously she wanted his help. With or without a memory, he had a sharp intellect and he might find a connection she missed. Still . . . "Sue me."

He laughed, and his eyes crinkled at the corners.

She tipped her head, enjoying the masculine sound. "That's the first time I've heard you laugh, John."

He glanced down and shifted uncomfortably. Shoni reached across the table and placed her hand on his wrist. "I'm sorry. I'm sure you haven't had a lot to laugh about lately."

He turned his hand over and clasped Shoni's. She fought the urge to tighten her fingers around his large, capable hands.

"Maybe not," he admitted. "But if it wasn't for you, I wouldn't have anything at all."

His heartfelt gratitude swelled her throat, but Shoni wasn't like her mother, who never had any trouble putting her feelings into words. "I did what any other cop would've done."

This time John's laugh was deep and rich, and filled some part of Shoni that she didn't even realize was lacking. "Estelle said pretty much the same thing. But I doubt many people would bring an injured, amnesiac stranger into their home. And no other cop would've invited me to stay with her."

Desire heated John's eyes, turning them to cobalt fire. Shoni's heart kicked against her ribs. This attraction went beyond anything she had ever felt before, beyond lust and need. If she believed her mother about soul mates, she might think John was hers.

Except John McClane probably already had a wife.

She eased her hand out of John's grasp and opened her mouth, but no words came.

"I know," John said, his voice gruff with strangled passion.

Shoni's cell phone jangled faintly from her bedroom, and she thanked the fates for the welcome interruption. She scrambled to her room to answer before it went to voice mail. The ID told her who it was and she took a deep, steadying breath. "Alexander."

"Where the hell have you been? You didn't log out or call in your location." Lieutenant Tyler's voice boomed through the small phone.

Shoni dropped onto her bed and planted her elbows on her thighs. "The ME called with the fire victim's name. I went to see the widow."

There was a startled pause at the other end. "Who was it?"

"William Markoff."

"CEO of Markoff Industries?"

"One and the same."

"So this wasn't some homeless person."

Shoni gnashed her teeth. "It wouldn't have mattered."

"I didn't say otherwise, Alexander," Tyler said impatiently. "But with a higher-profile victim, there's going to be more media attention. Did the ME have the cause of death?"

"It appears to be smoke inhalation."

"Why would Markoff have been in that building?"

"No idea, sir." Shoni paused. "Serial arsonists usually aren't murderers, unless the arsonist is a murderer using a fire to cover his crime."

"Then how do you explain the other fires?"

She pinched the bridge of her nose. "I can't."

"If you checked your voice mail," Tyler began in a dry tone. "You'd know the FBI profiler came in this afternoon. Seems you just missed him."

"Seems that way." Shoni held her breath. Tyler was a natural bullshit detector.

However, the lieutenant let it go. "He's coming back at

oh nine hundred tomorrow. I expect you to have your ass and the arson file in my office then. Do you understand me, Detective Alexander?"

"Yes, sir."

"Good." Tyler ended the call.

Cringing, Shoni pressed the End button. She left her phone on the nightstand and returned to the dining room table.

John's gaze followed her. "Another fire?"

Shoni dropped to her chair. "No, at least not that kind. My lieutenant. Wants me in his office at nine sharp tomorrow morning. He brought a federal agent in to help catch the arsonist."

John flinched. "Ouch."

"You're the first person not to say how lucky I am to get his help. But the truth is, I don't know where to go with this case, and maybe getting help from the FBI isn't such a bad deal." She shrugged. "Even if I don't like it."

She turned her attention to the report in front of her and tried to concentrate on the black-on-white words. Once she was finished, she picked it up to place it under the pile, but paused. She'd been a by-the-book cop. Always ensuring she followed regulations to the letter, not wanting to risk a criminal getting off on a technicality. Until her mother was killed.

She'd given John refuge in her mother's condo and provided personal security for him instead of following regulations. What was one more bent rule?

She slid the report across the table toward John.

"I thought—" he began, startled.

"I won't tell if you won't. Besides, maybe a fresh pair of eyes will see something we've all missed."

John's grateful smile sent a shiver down Shoni's spine and she quickly turned her attention back to her work.

She immersed herself in the details, wanting to put an end to the fires before anyone else was hurt or killed. However, she never lost her awareness of John sitting across from her. At some point he refilled their coffee cups and she murmured a thanks.

They'd been working silently for over an hour when Shoni felt a change in John. She glanced up at him and found his eyes narrowed as he scanned a report.

"What is it?" she asked.

"The first warehouse . . ."

Shoni waited, but John continued to stare at the paper. "What about the first warehouse?" she prompted.

"It's the only one that doesn't fit the pattern," he murmured.

Shoni leaned across the table. "What pattern?"

John blinked and rubbed his jaw, his evening whisker growth rasping against his hand. "I'm not sure. The warehouses were all owned by different companies. One had a fairly hefty insurance payoff. One had a dead body. And one took out both a warehouse and an apartment building." John lifted his gaze to meet Shoni's eyes. "Estelle told me that the only thing holding back a developer was a legality that wouldn't let him evict the apartments' tenants."

"And with the apartment building destroyed, he can go ahead with his plans."

John nodded, bemused. "Four fires related only by the burn method and their supposed randomness. Everyone would be looking for a serial arsonist rather than an organized crime spree."

Shoni hadn't even considered that angle. She'd been working under the assumption it was one person who had a jones for starting fires.

"That's a better theory than anybody else has come up with," she said, then teased, "Maybe you're a cop."

"Hate to tell you this, but cops aren't exactly on my top ten list." He shrugged. "More of a gut reaction than actually knowing."

Another thought, more sinister, struck her. "Maybe it was a cop who left you for dead."

John's forehead furrowed, but he didn't speak.

Shoni felt the blood leave her face. If a cop was involved in John's attack, had she endangered his life by taking him to the police station?

Clearing her throat, she said, "I think we've done enough for one night."

"I'll make sure everything is locked up," John said.

Shoni should've argued, should've told him she was the cop and he the protected witness, but she didn't. "Thanks. I'll see you in the morning."

Once in bed with her door closed, Shoni lay awake for a long time. John had brought up a valid theory and, if it was true, one that went beyond simple arson and into the shadowy world of criminals for hire.

JOHN'S eyes snapped open to darkness lit only by rheumy city lights behind the curtains. He lay there, disoriented, trying to determine what had awakened him. A sharp pain jabbed through his head and he pressed a hand to it. New images, of fire and scorching heat. More than likely a result of his evening reading material.

A barely heard click brought him to a sitting position. He rose soundlessly, pulled on his jeans and sweatshirt, and slid his feet into his tennis shoes. He stalked to the door and listened intently. Silence. But a sixth sense told him something was wrong.

He eased the French door open. A shadowy figure stood in the kitchen. John froze. The figure was too tall and broad to be Shoni. He glanced back in his bedroom, searching for a weapon, and remembered the scissors in the bathroom vanity's drawer. He peeked through the crack of the French doors and spotted the intruder treading stealthily across the living room, toward Shoni's bedroom. He didn't have any time.

Praying the door didn't squeak, he opened it far enough

that he could slip out into the dining room. John fell back on skills which, at some point in his life, had become incorporated into who and what he was. He glided across the carpet on the balls of his feet, his limbs loose but his muscles bunched, ready for action.

The stranger reached toward Shoni's door, his gloved fingers curving around the knob. John didn't know who the man was after, him or Shoni, but it didn't matter. He was an unknown, and John didn't waste time or opportunities with unknowns. He launched himself at the intruder. The force of John's tackle sent both men crashing into Shoni's bedroom.

John landed on top of the uninvited guest and looped his injured right arm around the man's neck. The trespasser rolled. John didn't have the leverage to hold him and was pitched sideways. His injured arm screamed in protest, but he bounced to his feet. The intruder rose quicker and kicked out at John, who evaded the blow by jumping backward. He swung a right hook that grazed John's jaw. Rage surged through John, and he used it to strike back. The intruder's head snapped back and he retreated.

Although the two men were close to the same height, John had less weight. And from what John could ascertain, the man's extra pounds were all muscle.

John moved in, hoping to end it with one more punch. But the intruder charged him and head-butted John's chin, snapping his head back. John staggered. This wasn't just some street tough like Jamar and his goons. This man knew how to fight.

"Police! Freeze!"

Over the ringing in his ears, John heard Shoni's barked command. He blinked, and for a moment he thought he was hallucinating. Clad only in a white camisole and bikini panties, she stood in the middle of her bed with her gun held between her hands.

A muttered curse, and John was shoved aside as the unwelcome guest dashed out of the bedroom. Shoni jumped off the bed, intent on following him. John didn't have a choice—he followed Shoni.

He ran through the living room and kitchen, flicking on the lights, and staggered to a stop in the hallway outside the condo. Seemingly unaware of her state of undress, Shoni stood looking down one end of the hallway, then the other.

"Damn it," she cursed. She went to place her weapon in the holster at her back but aborted the motion. Her face reddened and she dodged back into the condo. John barely had time to get out of her way.

"Did you recognize him?" she demanded.

Unable to resist a smile at her mad dash, John closed the door behind them. He shook his head and regretted the movement immediately. "I didn't get a good look at him. Too dark."

Despite his somewhat battered condition, John couldn't help but notice her slender body with just enough curves in all the right places. The white thin-strapped camisole and matching panties titillated more than hid her feminine charms. He couldn't help but chuckle at the incongruity of the gun with her attire.

She glared at him, obviously guessing his thoughts.

His gaze skimmed up and down her body. "It's actually kind of sexy."

She shook her head in exasperation and marched back to her room, but not before he noticed her nipples peaking beneath the nearly transparent top.

"Call the security desk downstairs and find out why they let that guy in," she called over her shoulder.

John punched in the security desk number and listened to the phone ring. And ring. And ring. He slammed the phone down just as Shoni came out of her room, now wearing low-cut jeans and a form-fitting blouse. Her holster and gun were snapped to her waistband at her back.

"No answer," he said to her.

Concern tightened her lips. "Let's get down there."

Shoni and John didn't speak until they were on the elevator.

"Anything broken?" she asked.

He swiped his wrist across his lips and idly noted the blood he wiped off. "No. Hurt my pride more than anything."

"Don't be too hard on yourself. He was good. Too good for a run-of-the-mill B&E perp."

"No, it wasn't a simple breaking and entering. He was out to get one or both of us." John shivered, trying not to think about what would've happened if he wasn't such a light sleeper.

The elevator doors slid open on the lobby level and John was gratified to see Shoni's caution. With her Glock in her hands, she motioned for John to stay behind her. Although he chafed at the notion of hiding behind a woman, she was the one with the weapon. She could also kick some serious ass.

John fell in behind her and they exited the elevator warily. Empty silence greeted them. There was nobody behind the security desk.

"Maybe he's in the restroom," John whispered.

Shoni grimaced, but didn't comment. She continued her cautious approach to the desk. The faint but unmistakable scent of blood intensified.

Once close enough, John peered over the counter and he spotted the source of the smell. "Guard's on the floor. Shot."

Shoni stepped closer and John moved around to her side. The young, pimply faced guard lay with unseeing eyes staring at the ceiling. Blood soaked his shirt and created a rivulet on the floor. John wondered why he wasn't sickened by the sight. Was he so used to death that it didn't even faze him?

They squatted on either side of the guard, and although John had no doubt the kid was dead, Shoni pressed two fingertips against his neck. After a few moments of concentration, she shook her head.

She sat back on her heels, and John suspected the exhaustion that lined her face had little to do with lack of sleep. "It looks like he didn't learn his lesson about letting strangers into the building," she said.

"What do you mean?"

"He was on duty when I brought you back here yesterday. He just let you in without checking your name on his sheet. I called him on it and thought I made an impression." She pushed herself to her feet as if it were a monumental struggle. "Obviously, I didn't."

As she used her cell phone to call 911, impotent rage filled John.

Three assassination attempts in three days. The killer was nothing if not relentless.

How long before an attempt became a success?

Chapter Fourteen

"THAT'S it. I want you and McClane in a safe house."

Shoni shoved away from the wall of the condo lobby that bustled with crime scene techs, detectives, and the coroner's crew, and met Tyler's granite eyes. "This guy's a professional. If he found John here, what's to say he won't find him in a safe house?"

"We'll have a two-officer protection detail with him at all times," Tyler said. "And increased patrols around the house."

"And what if a cop is involved?"

The lieutenant's eyes widened, then narrowed. "Why would you think that?"

"We don't know who's involved. Besides, who knew where John was staying besides you and me?" Shoni refused to believe Estelle might be involved.

Bob glared at her. "Are you insinuating that I told someone?"

Oh, hell . . . "No, but maybe someone at the station overheard us or saw John with me and put two and two together."

Bitter bile churned in her stomach. "My blowup over Mom's death wasn't exactly discreet, and someone could've figured out where Mom lived."

"You make this sound like a conspiracy."

Her temper flared anew. "Maybe it is. An arsonist usually doesn't go around trying to kill a witness, especially with a sniper rifle and a bomb." She motioned to the activity surrounding them. "And now this."

Bob's gaze sidled to John, who remained silent at his post near the wall, far from the front glass doors, watching them with a neutral expression. The lieutenant's attention returned to Shoni. "Have you considered that you're dealing with two different issues here? The arsonist and someone who's out to kill McClane?"

Shoni had considered it at some point, but it didn't make sense. The first attempt had been made while the fourth arson fire was being brought under control. John had seen the suspect, so it followed that it was the arsonist out to silence him. Still, considering John's amnesia, it was a possibility that he'd crossed someone in a big way and didn't remember it. But then it followed that he would have to have been involved in something that, at the least, was on the fringes of the law.

"It's possible," she replied reluctantly.

"You're running his fingerprints?"

"Yes. As soon as there's a hit, the lab will call me."

"You call me the second you hear."

John straightened and his steely eyes bored into the lieutenant. "*After* she calls me. With all due respect, sir, you're not the one who had his life stolen."

Tyler held John's gaze without flinching, although his flinty features lost some of their sharp edges. "I understand, son, but you have to understand that we're looking for a possible murderer. Your identity might somehow be tied to all of this."

Unable to curb her defensiveness, Shoni said, "You don't know that, sir."

"That's right. We don't, which is why we need to know who McClane really is."

Shoni wanted to stomp her foot in protest, but John's touch on her arm stayed her angry words.

"Your lieutenant has a point," John said. He turned to Tyler. "And as soon as *we* know, you'll know, sir."

Tyler's impatience gave way to grudging acceptance. "All right." He tipped his head to the side. "How did you come up with John McClane, anyway?"

The corners of John's lips tugged upward. "A seven-year-old girl gave it to me. McClane is one of her favorite heroes."

Tyler stared at him a moment, than harrumphed. "Better than Bambi or Peter Pan." He strode away to talk to Raff and Delon, who were assigned the security guard's murder investigation.

Shoni laughed at John's disgruntled expression, one that said he didn't know if he should be insulted by the lieutenant's comment. "I don't know," she said. "I always liked Bambi."

He shot her a disgusted look, which made her grin. A yawn caught her by surprise, and she glanced at the clock on the wall. Four thirty A.M. She doubted they'd get any more sleep tonight.

After Tyler left, Delon joined them, his green and gold shirt slightly less flamboyant than his usual attire. He rubbed his eyes. "Couldn't you have waited until we weren't on call?"

"Next time some goon breaks in, we'll politely ask him to come back another night," John said, his sarcasm rapier sharp. "That is, if we aren't killed first."

Delon's shoulders stiffened, and Shoni held up her hands.

"We're all tired and cranky, but going at each other's throats isn't going to help," she said. "Ask your questions, Delon."

For the next twenty minutes they answered the standard questions, but ended up with little information that would assist in finding the suspect.

"Was there anything on the surveillance footage?" Shoni asked, motioning toward the screen behind the security desk.

Delon's dark complexion grew dusky. "Nothing we can use. Black clothing, hat, mask, and gloves. Not a single solitary inch of skin showing."

"He knew about the cameras," John said.

Delon swung his gaze to him. "Yep. More than likely a professional."

"You'll keep me in the loop on this?" Shoni asked her colleague.

Delon nodded, then rejoined his partner.

By the time the young security guard was rolled away in a body bag and Raff and Delon had left, it was almost five thirty. With only the crime scene techs who were still collecting physical evidence remaining, Shoni figured they could return to her mother's condo.

Once inside the apartment, Shoni made a beeline for the coffeepot. John wisely stayed out of her way as she readied the coffee.

He leaned against the counter with his arms crossed. "Do you think someone in the police department is involved?"

"At this point, I don't know who to suspect. We just don't have enough evidence." Dark crescents shadowed her eyes and frustration bled into her words.

John curled his fingers into his palms to keep from drawing Shoni into his arms. He didn't doubt her strength, but everybody had a breaking point. And Shoni, with the recent death of her mother, the arson case, and a deadly mystery with a man with no memory in the center of it, was close to hitting that mark.

"Why didn't you tell your lieutenant about the theory we came up with last night?"

Shoni poured water into the coffeemaker and set the glass carafe on the hot plate. She turned and mirrored John's stance. "It didn't seem like the right place. Besides, it's only hypothetical at this point."

"Do you think Tyler is right, about this being two separate cases?"

"Maybe. But it seems a little too coincidental."

John stared over her shoulder. "What if—" He broke off and his eyes squinched shut, his lips stretched thin. John dropped his head into his hands.

Shoni took hold of his arms. "What's wrong?"

She barely felt the shake of his head. Ducking, she tried to see his face, but his hands kept it hidden from view. "I'm taking you to the hospital." She tried to tug him forward, but he was as solid as a boulder. "John, please, this could be something serious."

"N-no," he stammered. "Visions."

"Of what?"

"People. Places." His voice was hoarse and his muscles quivered beneath her hands. "M-memories."

Shoni forced back the panic that clawed at her. "Maybe you're right and they're only memories starting to come back, but maybe it's something else. Please, John, let me take you to the hospital."

Some of the tension melted from his muscles. "No." He eased his hands away from his head. Sweat sheened his brow and two droplets tracked down the side of his face. Although his eyes were pain-filled, they were clear and focused. The weak smile he managed to paste on was both comforting and alarming. "I'm all right."

Shoni understood his aversion to hospitals—they weren't her favorite vacation spot either—but she didn't like his pale face and the vicious trembling. "For now. What about next time? It seems they're getting progressively worse."

"If it gets so bad that I can't stand it, then you can take me to the hospital."

"By then, it might be too late," she muttered in irritation.

She spun away, but John caught her shoulders and turned her toward him. His tender expression startled her, momentarily making her forget she was annoyed with him. "Don't worry about me. I'll be fine."

"Famous last words." But the punch was lost when it came out more frightened than sarcastic.

John studied her, his warm gaze binding her more than his powerful hands clasping her arms. Then he lifted one hand and brushed a wispy curl from her forehead. The warmth in his eyes heated to something more volatile, but his touch was gentle as he brushed his fingertips down her cheek to rest on her jaw.

Shoni's heart slid into her throat and her chest tightened until she could barely draw in a breath of air. She leaned into him, flattening her palms to his chest to feel the steady beat of his heart. The heat of his hard body sparked an answering fire in her own.

His gaze fastened on her lips and, so slowly she almost thought she imagined it, John lowered his head. It was a gentle, almost chaste kiss.

Knowing this was a very bad idea didn't stop her from kissing him back. Darting out her tongue, she traced the firm contours of John's lips. A small moan escaped him and she grew bolder, teasing the seam of his sensuous mouth. When he invited her in, she didn't waste any time. She slipped her tongue into his warm moisture. John reciprocated, mating his tongue with hers.

She felt the throb of his erection against her belly. Her body answered and she grew damp with desire. She slid her hands down his chest and under his sweatshirt. His skin burned as she skimmed up and down his muscled flanks. Suddenly all she could think of was feeling his bare skin against hers. She whimpered into his mouth and worked the sweatshirt upward, to remove the hindrance to her goal.

John grabbed her hands and drew away from her mouth. "No." His denial came out breathy and needy.

Shoni glared at his kiss-swollen lips. "Yes."

"No," John said more firmly. "We can't. Not until . . ."

Not until I know who I am.

If I'm married.

Even though he didn't say the words, she nonetheless heard them. Fighting the tide of passion that threatened to drown her, Shoni retreated. Her nerves hummed with arousal and she ached for John's touch. But he was right. Damn him.

"I'm going to take a shower," she said, backing out of the kitchen.

"A cold one," she heard John mutter as she made her escape.

"You and me both," she said low enough that John wouldn't hear.

The cold water did its job, freezing her libido and bringing sanity back to her desire-clouded brain. She quickly dressed and, with damp curly hair, returned to the kitchen, surprised that she'd finished before John. After pouring a cup of coffee for herself, she pulled out the carton of eggs and scrambled five. By the time the eggs were done and the bread toasted and buttered, John still hadn't come out of his room.

A niggle of alarm crawled up Shoni's neck and she knocked on the French doors. "John?"

No answer.

She pounded harder, but there was still no sound from behind the closed doors. The niggle graduated to a full-blown klaxon. Shoni shoved open the doors, and before she even checked the bathroom, she knew John was gone—his battered backpack wasn't in its place by the bed.

Panic vied with anger as she raced to the front door and threw it open. Dashing into the hallway, she nearly tripped on a scruffy green pack. Glancing down, she saw John hunkered down with his back against the wall.

"What the hell are you doing?" she demanded, worry making her tone curt.

Only his eyes moved as he met her gaze. "Thinking."

"You couldn't think in the apartment?"

"No."

There was something in John's voice she'd never heard before—resignation. Dread dropped like a lead ball in her gut and she lowered herself to the floor across from him, her legs crossed beneath her. She braced her elbows on her thighs and tried to keep her voice steady and calm. "Talk to me, John."

He took a deep breath. "If your lieutenant is right and someone is after me, then I'm only endangering you by hanging around."

The misery in his voice was the only thing that kept Shoni's temper from erupting. "First off, we don't know if he's right. Second, I'm a cop, John. I took a vow to serve and protect the citizens of this city. I'm perfectly capable of taking care of myself." She paused and eyed him more closely. "What's the real reason you were going to run?"

He stared at the wall above her right shoulder. "What if I find out who I am and I don't like that person?"

Shoni's heart thudded heavily in her breast at his desolate tone. She wanted nothing more than to wrap her arms around him, like she'd done with frightened children during her time in the Special Crimes Unit. But a hug wouldn't dispel John's monsters.

"You've lost your memories, John, but not those basic qualities that make you who you are. From what I've seen of that man, he's kind and gentle with those he cares about, and will protect them no matter the cost to himself. He's intelligent and strong, and able to survive against incredible odds." Her throat grew thick. "And he's a man that a woman could easily fall in love with."

His gaze shifted and focused on Shoni. She fought the urge to lower her eyes, to hide what was too close to the truth. But John needed to know she was sincere.

A smile quirked his lips. "I think you might be a little biased."

She shrugged, his lightening mood buoying her. "Only because I know you, and no matter what John McClane's real name is, he's still a hero in my book."

John's cheeks grew ruddy as he grinned wryly. "I don't know about that hero stuff, but I hope you're right about the rest."

"I am." Shoni had never been more certain of anything. She rose and extended a hand. "Let's eat before the eggs grow feathers and fly away."

John chuckled. "Now that's an appetizing picture."

"Not so much," Shoni shot back.

Shaking his head in amusement, he placed his hand in hers. Shoni drew him to his feet, feeling the warm connection flowing between their clasped hands. Before it could graduate into something more fiery, she released him. John grabbed his pack and followed Shoni into the condo. After reheating the scrambled eggs in the microwave, they ate breakfast in companionable silence.

SHONI and John were stopped by the two guards at the front desk as they walked through the empty lobby. The security company obviously wasn't taking any chances with one of their own murdered.

A cold breeze whipped down the street that ran between the condo and the entrance to the fenced parking area. A patrol car stood near the entrance. The two officers got out of the front seat.

"Hop in, Detective, Mr. McClane," the older of the two said.

Shoni sighed. "C'mon, Renovitz, can't you just follow my car to the station?"

Renovitz drew his bushy eyebrows downward. "Sorry, Alexander, but the lieutenant will have my ass in a sling if I let you do that."

The younger cop, whom Shoni didn't recognize, said, "Just following orders, ma'am."

Ma'am. Either the academy was now allowing children in its hallowed halls, or Shoni was getting older. She didn't much like either option.

She glanced at John, who stood beside her with his backpack over a broad shoulder. "Looks like we have our own personal escort."

John merely grunted.

Renovitz and his rookie partner dropped her and John off at the entrance of the station. She hustled John into the building and got his visitors pass in record time.

"Coffee?" John asked once they were at her desk.

With as little sleep as she had last night, even Delon's coffee would be welcome to keep her awake. "Thanks."

She watched John move with now familiar animal grace.

"Eyes off the man's ass, Alexander."

Startled, she noticed Raff standing by her desk, a smirk on his classically handsome face. He must've been in the lieutenant's office. Her cheeks heated, but she glared at the well-dressed detective. "You catch the guy who broke into the condo yet?"

Raff grinned, obviously not willing to be sidetracked. "Careful, Alexander, wouldn't want to get involved with a witness. Against regulations, you know."

"Gee, I didn't know that. Thanks for the warning." If

sarcasm was a weapon, Raff would be on his way to the morgue.

Instead of the expected laughter, Raff's expression sobered. "Be careful, Shoni. You don't even know who he is."

She bit her tongue and counted to ten. "He's my witness and he's the target of a killer. That's all I need to know."

Raff's hazel eyes held a hint of impatience. "Keep telling yourself that, Alexander." He returned to his desk.

Although Shoni understood, and even appreciated, her friend's concern, she was too tired and too wound up to acknowledge it.

John returned with their coffee and took the chair at the side of her desk.

Even before Shoni took a sip, she knew Delon had made it. However, she'd risk her stomach lining and drink it, knowing she needed the caffeine. Didn't mean she had to like it, though.

"I think we should tell the lieutenant your theory," Shoni said after her grimace faded. "If he thinks it's plausible, he might cancel the appointment with the BAU agent."

"It's your ass on the line."

Despite his comment, Shoni knew he'd risk his own ass, if for no reason other than to assist her. "Come with me."

John seemed taken aback, but didn't balk. He followed her to her boss's office.

"You beat me to it. I was just going to call you in," Tyler said.

Shoni instantly went on the defensive. "Why?"

"I've got a safe house arranged for you and McClane."

"*I* don't need the protection."

Bob shook his head, his bald pate catching and reflecting the light. "We don't know that. Your apartment was booby-trapped and it was your bedroom the perp was entering this morning. I'm not taking any more chances."

Tension crackled in the office. Bob finally sighed. "Coffee?"

Even though Shoni knew he was bribing her, she was too weak to turn down a cup of his private stock. He handed John and Shoni two heavenly smelling cups.

Shoni forced herself to take only a sip and savor the robust taste. "New flavor?"

A dreamy look came over the lieutenant's characteristically uncompromising features. "Yirgacheffe. From Ethiopia. It has an almost sweet, floral scent, but a rich flavor."

Out of her peripheral vision, she noticed John gaping. She kicked his ankle and he snapped his mouth shut.

Shoni closed her eyes and allowed the Yirgacheffe to wash away the foul aftertaste of Delon's coffee.

"I put a rush on McClane's fingerprints, so we should be hearing something soon," Tyler said, his voice all business again.

"Thank you, sir," John said, surprised.

"I don't like someone coming after my people. It gets personal and makes me mad. I've given both the sniper and the bomber cases to Raff and Smith. I'm going under the assumption the same person that busted into your mother's condo and murdered the security guard is also behind those."

"But I'm still primary on the arson case?" Shoni hated that it came out more a plea than a statement.

"Yes, but there's going to be a lot more media attention on it since Markoff's name was released." Tyler grimaced. "But I'll take the media heat. I want you to find out who is starting those fires and why."

"John came up with a theory," Shoni began.

Tyler's eyes narrowed, but he made a circular motion with his hand for her to continue.

"Only one of the four fires doesn't include a possible motive. Fire number two was to kill Markoff. Fire number three was for the insurance payoff. And fire number four, to get rid of the apartment building so the developer could begin his billion-dollar project."

"Arson for hire?" Tyler asked.

Shoni shrugged. "If we factor out the first fire, it fits."

"Are you certain all four fires were started by the same person?"

"Ian is ninety-nine percent certain, and he's been in the business long enough to know."

Tyler's eyes darted to John. "So McClane came up with it." The lieutenant's sharp gaze returned to pierce Shoni. "McClane, go wait at Alexander's desk. I want a word with my detective. Alone."

Chapter Fifteen

As soon as the door closed behind John, Mount Tyler erupted. "Do you realize you've compromised the entire investigation? If McClane is involved, you've given him the ammunition any decent defense attorney can use to get the charges thrown out."

The moment she'd allowed John to see the arson files, she knew the risk she'd taken. "He's not involved."

Bob's face reddened. "Because he told you? Damn it, Alexander, I thought you were smarter than that."

Her own anger blossomed and she leaned forward, perching on the edge of her chair. "You used to trust my instincts. Why don't you trust me now?"

"Because the detective I knew before has been AWOL ever since Iris Alexander was killed. This arson case was your chance to prove to me you could still handle it." Bob threw himself back in his chair. "And as of right now, you're doing a piss poor job of it."

Shame blunted Shoni's temper but pride took up the

slack. "No other detective could've done better with this case. I've done everything I should have."

"As well as things you shouldn't have." Bob took a deep breath and exhaled slowly. Both his expression and his tone gentled. "I'll grant you that I don't think McClane is the arsonist either. But you have to admit he's not exactly your typical eyewitness. He gave a concise description of the arsonist, and hasn't even flinched at the attempts on his life. This morning he didn't seem bothered by a dead body covered with blood."

Shoni's defense of John was immediate. "Being a soldier who's seen action would explain his reaction to both the murder attempts and the body."

Bob nodded reluctantly. "True."

"Then why does it matter if he saw the reports? He even came up with a theory that no one else even considered."

Bob stared down at his desktop, his brow creased. Finally, when the silence grew oppressive, he lifted his head and met Shoni's gaze. "It's obvious you're attracted to McClane." She opened her mouth to deny it, but he held up his hand. "Don't. We both know it's true. What if McClane is using you like Mack St. Clare did? Only instead of a scoop on a story, McClane gets to live in an upper-level condo with three meals a day."

"He'd be getting a roof over his head and food if he was in a safe house." Even as she argued, she knew her justification was a shaky one.

Bob's slight smile held too much pity. "Where would you rather stay?" He paused deliberately. "And with who?"

She was the one who convinced him to stay at the condo. She'd bought him new clothes without him asking. In fact, he'd seemed embarrassed by her gift. But wasn't that what a good con man did, let the mark think that it was all his or her idea?

Were his visions—memories—part of the act, too?

She recalled the paleness of his face and the pain in his eyes. No, no one could fake that.

"You're wrong, Bob. He's not lying and he's not using me."

He studied her solemnly. "You're staking your career on a man you don't even know. Hell, a man who doesn't even know himself."

Her resolve strengthened. "I know what I'm doing." She stood and gazed down at her boss and friend. "I appreciate your concern more than you know, but I'm not wrong on this one, Bob. You used to trust me." She blinked against the unexpected and unwelcome sting of moisture. "Trust me again."

"Find the arsonist."

The moisture dissipated before it graduated to tears. "Yes, sir."

She spun around to leave.

"Oh nine hundred. I expect you to be in here with the arson file," Bob said.

Her stomach clenched. "I'll be here, sir."

"See that you are."

Shoni escaped his office, feeling as if she'd just survived a category five hurricane. Her gaze sought her desk, and she breathed an involuntary sigh of relief to find John sitting beside it. It wouldn't look very promising if he'd disappeared while she'd been defending him.

"Reamed you a new one?" John asked in a low voice.

His eyes slid over her, feeling too much like a caress.

She dropped into her desk chair and ran a tired hand through her hair. "Isn't that what bosses do when their people screw up?"

John grimaced. "He figured out that you let me read the reports."

Shoni shrugged. "Not hard to figure. You had to have seen the file to come up with your theory."

"So what happened?"

"I convinced him you could be trusted." So it wasn't exactly the truth, but it was all she was willing to give him.

Worry flitted across John's well-sculpted face. "What if I can't be?"

She couldn't let his doubt sway her own certainty about his character. Besides, she was laying her career on the line for him. "Believe in yourself, John."

"Hard to do that when I don't even know who I am."

"We'll know soon."

He huffed a laugh. "For having been woken up by a possible assassin, you're awfully optimistic."

"We're still alive, aren't we?"

He shook his head in part amusement and part worry.

"Do you want to be taken to the safe house now?" she asked. "Might be more comfortable than hanging around here all day."

"With two cops I don't know looking over my shoulder every minute?" He snorted. "I'd rather stay here. Besides, the fingerprint results should come in soon."

Shoni nodded, then turned away to call Markoff Industries and made an appointment to speak to a vice president. As she set the phone back in its cradle, she spotted the same suited man she'd managed to escape yesterday.

"FBI?" John asked.

"I'm hoping this won't take too long. You have something to do?"

He held up a newspaper. "Found this on a desk. Figured I'd borrow it."

Shoni noticed one of the lower page headlines. *Markoff Industries CEO Victim of Serial Arsonist.* She grabbed the paper from John's hand and read the byline. "Son of a bitch."

John peered over her forearm and his lips thinned to a grim line. "Your old boyfriend."

"How did he get this?"

"So you've seen it."

Shoni jerked her head up to see Ian Convers standing in front of her desk. "Who gave this to him?" she asked.

"Don't look at me. I thought since you and him . . ." Ian said, his meaning clear.

She glared at the arson inspector. "Your rumor mill's behind the times. By about six months. And even when I was seeing him, I never gave him anything off the record. Despite what people might've thought."

Ian didn't look convinced, but he was wise enough to remain silent.

"Why are you here?" Shoni asked. "Did you find something new?"

Ian shook his head. "Your lieutenant called me yesterday. Wanted me here to talk with the FBI. You should've been the one to call me," he said, his disapproval obvious.

Shoni's cheeks heated with embarrassment. "You're right. I'm sorry."

Tyler's door opened and Shoni looked over to see her boss waving her inside.

At least he didn't bellow.

Shoni gathered up a pile of freshly printed reports and jammed them into a folder. "If you need anything, ask Raff or Delon," she said to John.

Shoni and Ian entered the office and the lieutenant made the introductions. Shoni gave Special Agent Leonard an overview of the fires and the little evidence they'd come up with as the man took notes on a yellow pad. He asked a number of questions, and Shoni was gratified by the agent's businesslike tone, as well as his thoroughness.

"Since the targets are deserted warehouses owned by unrelated companies," Leonard said, "I think we can rule out an extremist. The same with someone trying to commit fraud, since only one building had a sizable insurance payoff.

"I'd like to get a copy of everything you have. I'll take it back to Quantico and have the Criminal Investigative Analysis team look it over. There are a couple of ATF agents assigned to the center who specialize in arson. We'll check for other fires with similar MO's, too."

"I was hoping you'd say that," Shoni said.

"How long will it take?" Tyler asked.

Leonard shrugged. "Hopefully we can have something for you by next Friday."

That was over a week away—too damned long.

"How many arsonists are also skilled with rifles and in bomb-making?" Shoni asked bluntly.

Leonard's plain face creased in puzzlement. "I haven't run across any. Why?"

Shoni described the attempts on their lives. When she was done, Leonard shook his head. "I think you have something more going on here than a simple fire starter."

"Or not," Tyler interjected, scowling. "We could have two separate cases."

Shoni's cell phone buzzed and she rose, stepping away before answering it. "Alexander."

"Detective, Tasha down in the lab. I've got a name."

Shoni's heart jumped into her throat, but she kept her expression blank. "I'll be down as soon as I can. Thanks."

She tucked the phone back in her pocket and rejoined the meeting. Tyler glanced questioningly at her, but she shook her head. She'd promised John he'd be the first to know.

"Have you interviewed everyone in the area who's been convicted of fire starting?" Leonard asked her.

Irritation surged, and she barely managed to stifle it. Any rookie detective would've known to question habitual fire starters. "Everyone we've been able to find. They all have alibis for at least one of the fires."

"Have you considered the possibility of a criminal ring that uses arson as a means to an end?"

Shoni glanced at Tyler, but he only stared back at her. "The possibility has come up." She handed Leonard the file in her hand. "Here's all we have on the four arsons. I printed it up this morning."

Leonard seemed surprised by her efficiency. "Thanks. I made a note to bring up the shooter and bomber issues. I have to say, though, that I tend to agree with your lieutenant. You're probably dealing with two separate cases."

Shoni kept her mouth shut and shook the agent's hand, thanking him for his assistance. Although he hadn't given her anything new, his questions and comments convinced her she was on the right track. And despite her earlier fears, he didn't seem inclined to take the lead on the case. Of course, that might change if the four fires were tied to others outside Virginia.

Ian had a meeting and followed Leonard out of the lieutenant's office. Shoni glanced at her watch. She had a couple of hours before her own meeting at Markoff Industries, and she needed to see Tash before leaving.

Shoni started toward the door. "I have an ap—"

Tyler held up the *Virginian Pilot*. "Can you explain this?"

Dismay was quickly usurped by anger. "Do you think I had something to do with that?"

"So you didn't talk to St. Clare about the case?" The tone of his voice implied that he wouldn't believe a denial.

Shoni hung on to her temper by a thread. "He left messages to call him numerous times. I didn't. And even if I had, I wouldn't have told him anything. Just like I never told him anything while we were seeing each other." She paused and forced her fingers to uncurl. "But it looks like he got a hold of someone else who's involved in the investigation."

"What about McClane?"

She stiffened, her defensiveness boomeranging back. "What about him?"

"He knew all about the fires. Maybe he gave St. Clare the scoop."

"Why would he do that?"

"Money."

"Why are you so determined to make John the bad guy?"

"I'm only doing what a good cop should be doing—drawing conclusions from the evidence."

His implication that she wasn't being a good cop rankled her even further. "I thought we worked this out earlier." She took a deep breath to allay some of her fury. "Look, if you don't want me on this case, assign it to someone else."

As much as she hated to surrender the case, she was tired of defending herself—and now John—at every turn.

Bob took a deep breath, and the tense silence was broken only by the drumming of his fingers on his desk. Finally he raised his head and his gaze was somber. "I'm going to hand it over to Robinson, but leave you as secondary."

Shoni's heart plummeted. Her shiny record, already tarnished by her outburst against the cop who allowed her mother's killer to get off, would get another blemish. Yet what difference did it make? She no longer believed the law was sacrosanct. How could she, when she planned to shoot down Tony Durkett with an illegally obtained gun?

Shoni stiffened her spine and set her gaze over the lieutenant's shoulder. "I'll give him the file, sir."

"So that's it. You're not even going to fight for your case?" Tyler asked incredulously.

"Why should I? You obviously feel I can't handle it."

Tyler swore under his breath. "The Detective Alexander I knew would have fought me tooth and nail to hold on to her case. What the hell happened to her?"

Shoni's anger disappeared like a puff of air on a breezy day and exhaustion dropped on her shoulders. She locked her knees to hold herself upright. "She's tired, Lieutenant. Tired of patching one hole in the dam only to have ten more show up."

"That's the way it's always been, Shoni. What's changed?"

She crossed to the window and watched tiny raindrops hit the glass. "Me. I've changed."

She heard the creak of Bob's chair and the slight movement of air as he came to stand beside her, his arms crossed as he, too, stared out into the gray dreariness.

"Losing a parent, especially one as close as your mother was, is a difficult thing," Bob said, his usually gruff voice gentle. "It was even more horrible because of the suddenness of her death. You have to grieve in order to let her go and move on, Shoni. You know as well as I do that she wouldn't want you to throw away your career."

Shoni swallowed the growing lump in her throat. "If Dad hadn't been a cop, he would still be alive. And if I wasn't a cop, Mom would still be alive."

"You don't know that."

She whirled to face him. "Yes, I do. I was the reason Mom was on that street. I was working the Parsons case and couldn't take the time to pick up my own dry cleaning. I asked Mom to do it." Her voice broke and she cleared her throat. "If I'd only taken some time from my precious job, she'd still be alive."

"You don't know that."

The compassion in Bob's face nearly undid Shoni's precarious control, and she allowed her anger to fill the empty place within her. "Yes, I do. Maybe I don't believe in the job anymore."

"I don't believe that. I heard stories about your father, about how good a cop he was. You're just like him."

Remembering all those evenings spent in front of Durkett's home and imagining squeezing the trigger . . . Her laugh was short and bitter. "Not so much."

Bob drew away and his boss persona returned. "Robinson is off until Monday. The case is yours until he comes back."

"Yes, sir. I have a meeting at Markoff Industries. That is, unless you think someone else should do the interview."

Tyler's entire head reddened and Shoni almost expected to see steam erupting from his ears. "I think you can handle it."

"Thank you, sir." She tried to keep her tone professional rather than sarcastic, but suspected she didn't succeed. She spun around to leave, but Tyler's voice stopped her.

"She's gone, Shoni, and there's nothing you can do to bring her back. You have to let her go."

She didn't turn to look at him, but found herself frozen, her throat constricting and her eyes burning with unshed tears. She couldn't do this. Not here. Not now. Maybe not ever.

Without acknowledging his words, Shoni strode back to her desk. And remembered that John had a real name waiting for him.

John looked up as she approached and his expression turned to concern. "Are you all right?"

She must look as terrible as she felt, but the fact that John cared chased away some of the darkness. She gave him a weak smile. "Lieutenant Tyler decided to give the arson case to another detective. Someone more objective."

"It's my fault, isn't it?"

"No," she replied without hesitation. "There's a lot more to it than that, John."

"Like what?"

Despite aching to wallow in John's solicitude, she'd already given too much of herself to him, whether he knew it or not. Besides, her troubles were minor compared to his, and she now had the key to help him unlock his past.

"Are you ready to find out who you are?" she asked.

Chapter Sixteen

JOHN'S blood roared in his ears and vertigo washed through him.

Am I ready?

A part of him wanted the answer this moment, while another part didn't know if he'd ever be ready. But he'd been stuck in this void for nearly a month, unable to build a life without a foundation. There were so many questions he wanted—needed—answered.

"Did she tell you?" he asked, shocked by the huskiness of his voice.

"No. I figured we'd go down to the lab together."

Shoni led the way out of the bullpen and to the elevator. John's knees trembled, and it was only by sheer force of will that he remained upright. The elevators were busy, and it took longer than usual before one stopped at their floor. They boarded it and rode down to the lab. John appreciated Shoni's silence. He doubted he could've held a semi-coherent conversation about the weather, thanks to all the fears and doubts bombarding him.

Before John knew it, they were standing by Tasha's computer. He wiped his sweat-slicked palms on his jeans.

The lab tech handed the paper to Shoni, who kept it flipped over so they couldn't see the results of the search.

Shoni extended the paper to John. "It's your name and your identity.

Despite the almost physical ache of needing to learn about the man he'd been—who he was—John refused to take it. "I wouldn't have gotten it without your help." He took a deep breath. "Turn it over."

The sheet trembled slightly as Shoni flipped the paper so both she and John could read it. On it was a copy of a driver's license with a familiar picture of a clean-shaven man and an unfamiliar name.

"Zeke Monroe," Shoni read.

John expected a cascade of memories to go with the name. However, there wasn't even a blip. Nothing. Nada. Zilch. For all the name meant to him, Zeke Monroe could've been a stranger he just met on the street. He fought down the desperation that clawed at his entrails and mocked his childish belief that all would fall into place when he learned his name.

Shoni lifted her gaze and smiled. "It's nice to finally meet you, Zeke."

Tasha gazed up at him with something akin to awe. "His name popped up when I was running military records. Former Navy SEAL. Awards for bravery and skill under fire. You're a real hero."

"A hero, not a criminal," Shoni said softly.

He gazed into her eyes, the summer-grass green brilliant behind a sheen of moisture. He wanted to give her something, some piece of Zeke Monroe. She deserved it. She'd believed in him even when he didn't. But he had nothing to give her. "It's still a blank," he whispered.

Her expression fell, and John almost wished he could've lied.

"But you have a name now. We'll be able to find more pieces of your life Joh—Zeke," she reassured him, obviously forcing the smile and upbeat tone. "As soon as I interview the VP at Markoff Industries, I'll take you to the address on your driver's license. Maybe seeing your place will spark something."

He nodded numbly. He had a home, a real address. Not an anonymous warehouse with cold water and a lumpy sofa. Of course, after the fire, he didn't even have that.

After taking some time alone in the restroom to gather his composure, John found himself sitting in the front seat of a sedan that Shoni had checked out of the police motor pool.

She kept shooting him concerned looks that only irritated him. He'd been so certain that once he knew his name, the floodgates would open and his memories would return. But despite having a name, he still thought of himself as John McClane.

"Come up with me. I'm sure they have a waiting room you can hang out in," Shoni said.

John blinked and realized they'd parked in a large asphalt lot that fronted a multistory glass building. An image of the same contemporary facade flashed through his mind. Had he been here before?

The comforting weight of Shoni's hand on his arm brought his attention back to her.

"Try not to worry, Joh—" She shook her head, a wry smile on her lips. "It'll take some time to get used to Zeke." She tilted her head and he was hit with her intense green eyes and the keen intelligence behind them. "But I have to admit Zeke fits you."

Uncertain how to respond, since he didn't feel like Zeke Monroe, John shrugged and asked, "Did you let Tyler know about my name?"

Shoni's gaze slid away as she nodded. "He wasn't surprised you were ex-military."

She was holding something back, but he was too drained to play Twenty Questions.

"So this is Markoff Industries?" he asked, not really caring but wanting to get back on firmer ground.

"The corporate offices occupy one of the floors."

John slid out of the car and followed Shoni across the asphalt lot, hunching his shoulders against the cold rain.

"Aren't we supposed to have some sort of protection detail?" he asked.

"You're looking at it."

In spite of his bleak thoughts, John's lips quirked upward. He'd be willing to bet his backpack that she'd bent the rules again.

Shoni immediately went to the bank of elevators tucked in an alcove off the lobby. Before she pushed the floor button, John *knew* it would be seventeen. Her finger punched seventeen. As they rode upward, John's sense of déjà vu intensified.

When the doors opened, they faced a massive reception desk some twenty feet away. A petite blonde spoke on the phone and typed on a computer keyboard. There was something about her, something familiar . . . Frustrated, John clenched his hands into fists.

He followed Shoni to the desk, his gaze on the receptionist. The nameplate on her desk read *Sandra.*

"I'll ensure he gets your message today. Thank you." The woman put the phone back in its place and lifted her head. Her friendly, welcoming expression and her styled hair, manicure, and smart violet jacket and lavender blouse made her the perfect receptionist.

"May I help you?" she asked Shoni.

"I have an app—"

"Zeke?"

It took a moment for John to realize the receptionist was talking to him.

"It is you." Sandra's eyes raked up and down his body,

making him feel like a bull on the auction block. "I haven't seen you for a while."

John's heart raced as he tried to remember her, but his memory remained frustratingly blank.

"Do you know this man?" Shoni asked.

Sandra tore her gaze away from John. "Who are you?"

Shoni dug her badge out of her coat pocket and held it up. "Detective Alexander. Norfolk PD. I have an appointment."

The receptionist relaxed slightly. "Yes. Eleven thirty with Mr. Gardner."

"You know Zeke Monroe?" Shoni reiterated.

Sandra appeared both irritated and puzzled by the question. "Of course."

"Did he come here often?"

"A few times. He usually came with Mr. Jensen."

"Who?"

"Mr. Jensen. With Paladin Security." Sandra's voice had lost much of its pleasantness.

Did he work at Paladin Security? It sounded like a rent-a-cop company.

"Is Paladin Security one of your customers?" Shoni asked.

Sandra motioned with her chin toward John. "Ask him. Or Mr. Gardner."

"I'll do that. Where's his office?"

She held up her hand. "I'll see if he's ready to see you."

The phone conversation was short, and Shoni was directed to an office down one of the long hallways. John ignored Sandra's affronted expression and crossed to the waiting area. He sank into a buttery-soft leather sofa, his back to the receptionist.

He had the distinct impression he and Sandra had either gone out, or he'd stood her up after he'd lost his memory. Either way, it meant he wasn't married. Or he was a two-timing bastard.

The Tiffany in his fractured memory was small, too, and

had light-colored hair. Were petite blondes Zeke Monroe's idea of the ideal woman?

He pictured Shoni: dark-haired, tall, and muscular, yet soft in all the right places. Her knit tops, hip-hugging jeans, and scuffed boots were a far cry from Sandra's classy clothing and pumps. Did that mean that once John's memories returned, he wouldn't lust after Shoni?

He huffed a silent laugh. Only if he were dead.

John picked up a magazine from the neat pile on the end table. He leafed through it, simply to keep his mind occupied until Shoni returned.

The soft thud of heels on carpet and nose-numbing perfume alerted him to the approaching receptionist. Slender legs made more attractive with three-inch heels filled John's field of vision. He lifted his head to find a skirt hem that hit a few inches above her knees and a fitted jacket that followed barely-there curves on her model-thin body. She was probably pretty enough—short wispy blonde hair, a pug nose, and full lips—but if Zeke Monroe had been attracted to her, John McClane sure didn't share the attraction.

"Why didn't you call me?" she asked, her voice pitched low.

Although startled, hadn't he expected something like this? "I got busy. Sorry."

It was a lame excuse, and both he and the mysterious receptionist knew it. But he wasn't about to spill his guts about his amnesia.

"I didn't think dinner was too much to ask after the favor I did for you," she said.

John stiffened. "What did you do for me?"

With a deep scowl and narrowed eyes, Sandra certainly didn't look cute now. "Funny that you should forget both dinner and the favor." She shook her head in disgust, but curiosity got the better of her. "Why are you with the detective? Don't tell me you decided to quit Paladin and join the police force."

"Okay, I won't." Yet for all he knew, maybe he had.

A phone buzzed and Sandra glared at him. "Don't bother about dinner. And don't ever ask for another favor."

Muttering expletives that almost scalded John's ears, she marched back to her desk. However, when she answered the phone, her tone was honey sweet.

Before he could start wondering what kind of favor she'd done for him, he spotted Shoni coming back down the hall. Her long legs ate up the distance between them and her entire body moved with confidence and grace. Her jacket flapped open, revealing the swell of her breasts and her slender waist that flared to rounded hips and thighs. She had a woman's body, with ripe curves made to fill a man's hands.

John's nerves hummed with awareness and arousal struck below his gut. He curled his fingers into his palms, willing away the urge to shove her up against a wall and kiss her until she was gasping his name.

"Ready?" she asked, her tone flat.

He pushed himself up from the depths of the couch, ignoring the twinge of hard flesh behind his zipper. Without waiting for him, Shoni strode to the elevator. John caught up with her just as the car stopped on their floor. The elevator was filled with lunchgoers, so John couldn't ask Shoni about the interview, or her impatience.

The rain had intensified and the temperature had fallen in the hour they'd been in the building. Ice pellets struck John's face and plopped against his coat. Shoni punched the remote button to unlock the car doors and they quickly dived into the shelter against the icy moisture.

She started the car and cranked up the heat.

"Did you find out anything?" John asked.

"Nothing new." She pressed her lips together and her nostrils flared slightly. "What were you and Sandra talking about?"

Although he sensed Shoni's underlying current of annoyance, he didn't understand it. "She basically said I was a pig for not calling her."

"You were supposed to call her? What? For a date?"

Definitely pissed off.

"Dinner, I guess. She said it was for some favor she did for me."

Shoni gave him her full attention, her expression now entirely professional. "Do you remember anything about her or this favor?"

"No, not a glimmer. But ever since we got here, I've had the feeling I'd been here before." He shrugged. "Seems I was right."

"Does Paladin Security ring a bell?"

"No." John swallowed. "But it sounds like I work for them. What are they?"

"One of the many security companies that popped up after the Iraq War started. They usually hire ex-military, preferably those with specialized training in covert ops, like Rangers and—"

"SEALS," John said, feeling something shift within his fractured memories. "Mercenaries."

Shoni nodded. "With your background, you'd be the perfect recruit."

"So why didn't they miss me? Wouldn't they have realized something was wrong if I didn't show up for work?"

"You'd think so." Shoni shrugged. "The only way to find out is to talk to them. But first, let's go take a look at your home."

It took a moment for John to remember that Zeke Monroe had a residential address. Again the cross between excitement and terror skittered through him. Unable to speak, he merely nodded.

SHONI slowed her driving as the rain-ice mix turned the roads into skating rinks. Within ten minutes of leaving

Markoff Industries she saw two fender benders and a car nose-to-nose with a traffic light pole.

The address on Zeke Monroe's license was on Lake Cavalier, a fairly upscale part of the city. With the weather against them, the drive was going to be a long one with too much time to think. About John—Zeke—and his connection to Paladin Security and Markoff Industries.

"I'm involved somehow, aren't I?" Zeke asked.

Shoni had ceased being surprised when their thoughts ran parallel. "We don't know that."

Zeke snorted. "So you believe it's only a coincidence that I was at Markoff Industries not long before Markoff died in that warehouse? Torched by the same arsonist who burned down the warehouse where I was living. Hell, maybe I'm faking my memory loss, and I'm the fire starter." His voice rose with his frustration.

"You didn't kill anyone," she reassured him, keeping her temper tamped down. "Gardner told me that Paladin Security has had a couple of small contracts for automatic weapons and body armor with Markoff Industries." She took her foot off the gas and tapped the brake gently as the traffic light a block ahead turned yellow. "You were accompanying your employer when you went there. Besides, Gardner told me that Markoff dealt only with the largest contractors, so it's doubtful you even met the man. Gardner handles the contracts with Paladin Security."

As Shoni came to the red light, the tires slid a few yards, but she'd slowed enough that there was still a good ten feet between her and the SUV in front of them. Ice droplets tap-danced on the roof of the car, creating a gentle percussive symphony inside.

"Don't you think it's strange that there hasn't been a fire since I've been at your mother's condo?" Zeke asked, his low voice a counterpoint to the ice's beat against the car.

Although she hadn't considered that angle, she shook

her head. "I've never met a man more determined to take the blame for something he didn't do."

"You keep saying I'm not a criminal." He paused, his gaze capturing Shoni. "So why is it that I feel so damned guilty?"

Shoni took her eyes off the slick road long enough to cast him a compassionate glance. "Only you can answer that, Zeke."

She took the freeway entrance ramp her GPS indicated and kept to less than half the speed limit. Most of the other drivers did the same, although there were a few who didn't seem to care if their cars turned into out-of-control Zambonis. By the time they arrived at the exit for the road leading to Zeke's home, she'd counted a dozen cars in the median and ditches.

At the exit's stop sign, Shoni's cell phone buzzed and she eased the car off to the side to answer it. "Alexander."

"Where the hell are you?"

She flinched at Tyler's explosive question. "A couple miles from John's—Zeke's home."

Shoni ignored Tyler's descriptive muttering. She'd known he'd be angry, but Zeke needed this. He deserved to know who he was and who might be missing him.

"Look, Lieutenant, Zeke has helped us with the arson case. The least I can do is help him get his life back."

"Do you realize that the entire city has been put on alert? The department is pulling every available body to work traffic accidents."

"I'm not surprised," Shoni said.

More creative muttering.

"Once you get to McClane's place, stay there. Don't move. Is that understood?"

"Yes, sir. And it's Zeke Monroe's place."

"Whatever. Stay there." It was obvious that Tyler spoke through clenched teeth before ending the call.

"Your lieutenant didn't sound happy," Zeke said.

Shoni huffed a laugh. "Try pissed off." She pulled back onto the road, the tires spinning before catching some gravel and getting her back on the street-sized skating rink.

Through the sleet, she spotted the correct street sign and made a left turn. The car continued sliding forward. Shoni took her foot off the gas and twisted the steering wheel the opposite direction. A massive tree loomed and she turned the wheel again. The front bumper missed the trunk by inches. The sedan stuttered to a stop after making a full three-sixty.

Her heart double-timed and Shoni took a few deep breaths before speaking. "Well, that was fun."

"Not." Zeke eased his hand off the dash, leaving a lingering imprint of his fingers.

With adrenaline-induced trembling, Shoni turned the key in the ignition and put the car back into gear. The tires found purchase on some loose rocks and the car crept forward. The houses were few and farther apart, with lush growths of trees separating each place from its neighbors. Zeke's was the last one and it was set back a hundred feet from the road. Through the bare trees, she could see a beautiful log cabin with a covered porch that ran the length of the front of the house.

She turned onto the gravel driveway and immediately felt the firmer grip of the tire treads. As she neared the cabin, she took in more details, including a breezeway that led to a double garage. The cabin was a story and a half, telling her it probably had a loft. It also had a massive chimney for a fireplace.

After pulling the key out of the ignition, she looked at Zeke, who was gazing at the cabin, his forehead creased.

"Does it look familiar?" she asked softly.

Chapter Seventeen

He stared at the cabin, and the interior crystallized in his mind. "There's a fireplace made of field rock that takes up half the wall. The floors are hardwood—a bitch to keep buffed, but beautiful," he said, almost as if seeing the rooms in a dreamscape. "There's a covered balcony off the loft that overlooks the lake." The memory of his home snapped back and a giddy thrill raced through him. "You'll like the sunsets over the water."

"You remember?"

"More or less." He got out of the car. Shoni followed him up the porch steps to the front door. Mail overflowed from a box attached to the house. Zeke plucked an envelope from the mailbox and held it up.

Shoni read the name on the front. "I guess we have the right place."

Zeke nodded and tried the door. Locked.

"Now what?" Shoni asked, raising her collar around her neck.

He stepped off the porch and walked to one of the many

rocks that outlined the flower beds fronting the porch. The extra door key was under it. He wiped the dirt from the key on his jeans and inserted it into the lock. He froze, and for a moment, he felt split into two persons—John McClane and Zeke Monroe. Their visions overlapping, seeing things both familiar and foreign. Then the identities converged and Zeke Monroe emerged, not complete yet, but more Zeke than John.

A cold hand touched his and he followed the arm to Shoni's face, seeing her through Zeke's eyes with John's memories. A shudder passed through him, and he didn't know if it was from the freezing rain or desire.

"Let's get inside before we turn into icicles," Shoni said. Her hands were filled with the envelopes, magazines, and catalogs from the mailbox.

Zeke blinked and pushed the door open. He stepped across the threshold and was acutely aware of Shoni at his back. Reaching to the side, he flicked on a light.

Disbelief washed through him, swiftly followed by outrage.

"It's beautiful," Shoni said in a low, awe-filled voice. "But I hope this isn't your usual level of neatness," she added with a dry tone.

"I didn't leave it like this." His gaze tracked across the high-ceilinged living and dining area, noting the overturned rustic furniture and items thrown on the floor. A large braided rug in the middle of the room was bunched up and broken glass littered the shiny hardwood floors.

Shoni donned her somber cop mask. "I don't think this was a simple B&E. This looks more like someone was trying to find something. I'm going to call it in, but I doubt we'll get anyone out here, not with the icy roads."

Zeke wandered into the home he'd forgotten for nearly a month. He leaned over to set a dining room chair upright, but Shoni's voice stopped him.

"Don't touch anything. I'll get the camera and fingerprinting kit out of the car."

Zeke jammed his hands into his jeans pockets. He heard Shoni's low voice on her cell phone then the sound of the front door opening and closing.

He remembered buying the solid oak dining room set and matching hutch, as well as the leather sofa set in the living room. As a military enlisted man, he'd never made much money, but he'd stayed in because he'd loved his country and believed he was protecting it and all the people who lived here. It wasn't up to him to make foreign policy; it was his duty to follow orders. So he'd risked his ass for a couple grand a month.

When he'd gotten out and joined Paladin Security, his income had increased to ten thousand a month, and he could afford to buy solid wood furniture and Italian leather living room sets. As well as his dream cabin with five acres of wooded land and a waterfront view.

Was it only the money that had tempted him out of the Navy to become a mercenary for Paladin Security? Pain arrowed through his head and he rubbed his forehead. No, something was missing. Something important. Something more that severed his loyalty to the U.S. military and his fellow SEALs.

Sick with the ravaging of his home, Zeke climbed the stairs that led to the loft master bedroom. At the top of the stairs was a large balcony with a sliding glass door that led to the covered deck where he liked to watch the sun set. The inside balcony held two bookshelves, a comfortable reading chair, an end table, and a lamp. Now, however, the books were strewn across the floor and the lamp tipped over, surprisingly in one piece.

The master bedroom door was to his left and it was wide open, revealing what appeared to be the site of a tornado touchdown. His bed was torn apart, pillows and blankets thrown helter-skelter about the room. Every dresser drawer had been yanked out and his clothing dumped on the floor. His stomach ached with both rage and helplessness. While he'd been surviving on the street, someone had violated his home.

A picture frame on the floor by the nightstand caught his attention, and he hunkered down to pick it up. Careful of the broken glass, he turned it over and stared at a younger version of himself with the woman called Tiffany, the girl named Chelle, and a black-and-white dog named Sarge.

Like a waterfall, the memories of laughter, love, and joy cascaded through him. His wedding day; Tiffany giving birth to their daughter; Chelle's first steps; the addition of a rambunctious puppy to the household; a rare family trip to Sea World while he was stationed in San Diego.

Then the other memories came, these like a tsunami ripping through him, stealing the air from his lungs. Called into the captain's office; the horrific words; Tiffany and Chelle dead; the closed caskets at the funeral.

The weight of grief forced him to his knees and he bent over, his forehead touching the cold floor. The pain, though nearly three years old, was as stark as if he was hearing about the fire for the first time. Paralyzing cold seeped through his limbs and deep shudders wracked his body. He heard a moan, and somewhere within him, he knew he was making the anguished, heartrending sound.

A patch of warmth settled between his shoulder blades and a gentle tone coaxed him to listen, to hear.

"Shhhh, it's all right, Zeke. You're home now. You're safe. No one can hurt you."

Zeke didn't believe the words, but the soothing voice beckoned him and he curled into the soft warmth. Arms surrounded him, rocked him like he used to rock Chelle when she was hurt or upset. The voice continued, soothing and tender.

Finally, after an eternity, Zeke's anguish lost its torturous edge. Sorrow remained, but it was dulled with acceptance and the acknowledgment of the passage of time. Tiffany and Chelle had been gone for nearly three years now, long enough that the heart-wrenching despair had receded to a deep-seated grief.

He unfolded his body and drew away from Shoni. His face felt hot, and when he put a hand to his cheek, he felt dampness. Embarrassed, he wiped his sleeve across his face.

Shoni shifted, stretching out her legs and leaning back against the foot of the rustic log bed. "Want to talk about it?" she asked, her tone gentle.

Zeke shook his head, but eased over to sit beside her, their shoulders brushing and their outstretched legs only inches apart. The memories were still too much, his nerves raw and bloody.

He expected Shoni to press him for answers or leave him alone, but she did neither. Instead, she remained sitting beside him, silent, giving him her presence, her willingness to listen if he wanted to talk. For a long time, there was only the sound of ice particles hitting the windows.

"My wife's name was Tiffany. We had a daughter, Chelle. She would've been nine." That Zeke spoke was a surprise to both himself and Shoni.

"SEALs aren't home much, but Tiffany didn't complain." He paused, remembering, and smiled wryly. "Not too much, anyhow. I was one of the lucky ones. I was home when Chelle was born. I'll never forget that night."

More memories, of Tiffany screaming at him while she labored to bring their daughter into the world; Chelle looking nothing like those neat, clean babies on TV, but Zeke falling in love with her the moment the nurse put the red, wrinkled newborn in his arms.

"We lived in apartments, but always wanted our own house. While we were stationed in Florida, we bought our first house." Zeke's smile faded. "It was what Realtors called a fixer-upper. But Tiffany loved the location and it was all we could afford on an E-6's income. Whenever I wasn't on an assignment, I'd be working on the house. Tiffany and even Chelle would help." He laughed, but it was filled with bittersweetness. "My team had just finished an extraction when my CO called me into his office." Zeke fought back the encroaching pain. "There was a gas leak. It was an old furnace. We couldn't afford to replace it right away."

Zeke lifted his head and blinked back the stinging moisture in his eyes. "The explosion leveled the house. They said it was fast, that they didn't suffer."

Shoni's hand crept into his and she folded her warm fingers around his cold ones. "I'm sorry, Zeke."

Her simple declaration of sympathy nearly undid his precarious control. "It happened three years ago."

"But regaining your memories, I'm sure it feels like it just happened again."

Zeke couldn't deny it, but already the throbbing ache was growing more tolerable. "Not long after they died, I got out of the Navy and joined Paladin Security. If we'd been able to afford a decent house, Tiffany and Chelle would still be alive."

"So money was the reason you upped with Paladin?"

"Yes." His smile felt brittle. "I made more money than I knew what to do with, but I would've traded it all to have my family back."

Shoni's grip tightened.

Zeke wasn't so wrapped in his own grief that he missed her reaction. "Your mother, she was the only family you had?"

"It was just her and I after Dad died."

"You said your father was a cop?"

Shoni nodded, a small smile playing on her lips. "A hero. He was killed during a domestic disturbance call. Saved a child, but not himself."

"If I'd been home, maybe I could've saved Tiffany and Chelle," Zeke said softly.

"Life is full of what ifs, Zeke. If you dwell on them too long, they'll drive you crazy. Tiffany probably wouldn't want you locked away in a straitjacket the rest of your life."

Again, Zeke was struck with the knowledge that Shoni truly did understand his loss and pain. He found his own lips curling into a smile. "You're right. She wouldn't."

He looked around as if seeing his room for the first time. "Have you taken pictures yet?"

"Not up here, but I have in the rest of the cabin."

Suddenly anxious to put his house back in order, both literally and figuratively, Zeke stood. He extended a hand to Shoni and pulled her to her feet, noticing a camera sitting on the bed. "Get your pictures taken. I'll start cleaning downstairs."

Zeke descended the stairs and made the living room his first area of operations. He set to work, picking up things and righting furniture. With everything he touched, a forgotten memory would emerge. While he was sweeping up the last of the broken glass, Shoni joined him.

"How did the perp get in here?" Shoni asked, her brow furrowed. "No broken windows, doors aren't busted."

"Must've picked the lock."

"A professional?"

Zeke dumped a dustpan of glass pieces into the kitchen trash can. "You have another explanation?"

"What did he steal?"

Zeke shrugged, glancing around at the plasma TV on a wood stand and the movie theater system connected to it. "He wasn't wanting big items to unload and I don't have expensive jewelry. There wasn't any money lying around either."

Shoni stared at him, but her green eyes weren't seeing him. "A professional. Like the sniper and the bomber."

Zeke's mind spun. "He's after me."

"Or something you have." She motioned around the room. "He was obviously searching for something."

"But what?"

Shoni eliminated the distance between them and gazed up at him. "What's the last thing you remember before waking up with amnesia?"

Zeke frowned and poked through his newfound memories. "Getting up and going to work."

"What happened at work that day?"

"There was a meeting in the morning. One of Paladin's government contracts had run out and it hadn't been renewed. They were talking about laying off some employees."

"Were you one of them?"

The day was blurry and indistinct in his mind. "I don't think so."

"What about after the meeting?"

He shook his head. "I can't remember."

Shoni lifted a hand to brush back a strand of hair that had fallen across his forehead then jerked her hand back, as if just realizing what she'd done. Despite the brief contact, Zeke's heart picked up its pace. He stared down at her, devouring the brush of her eyelashes against the gentle curve of her soft cheeks; the slight upturn of her delicate nose. She was so near, all he had to do was duck his head and press his lips to hers.

Shoni abruptly turned away. "The lieutenant might be right," she said. "We could be dealing with two separate perps. The arsonist and whoever is after you."

It took a moment for Zeke's upper brain to wrest command from his lower brain. He sucked in a deep breath of stale air. "Why would someone want me dead?"

"The same reason they searched your house." Shoni shrugged. "There's nothing we can do right now except straighten up the place. Maybe something will jog your memory."

Although most of his memories were back in the right place, Zeke was still left with an annoying itch that couldn't be satisfied. A vital piece of the puzzle remained missing.

What was the favor Sandra at Markoff Industries had done for him?

SHONI wiped the last countertop and rinsed the dishcloth. She leaned against the kitchen island and surveyed her work. Every last speck of food and debris had been picked up, wiped up, or swept up. Pots, pans, dishes, and glasses were washed and back in what she hoped were the right cupboards. She'd volunteered to do the kitchen while Zeke took care of the rest of the house. At the time she thought she'd taken the easy assignment.

Not so much.

The cop inside her was reluctant to tamper with the crime scene, but a simple B&E didn't have the clout to bring out the crime scene techs when driving was deemed hazardous at best. However, she'd taken pictures and dusted for fingerprints, but suspected that if it was the same person who'd been taking potshots at Zeke, the intruder had been professional enough not to leave any prints.

Zeke had finished his share of the straightening and had taken the pile of mail to the dining room table to sort through the mess. There were some bottles of a decent micro brew in the fridge and, after a glance out the window at the damp dreariness, she carried two beers into the dining room.

Zeke looked up from the papers scattered across the table and impatiently shoved his hair off his forehead. "Finished?" he asked.

"Yep." Shoni dropped into a chair and set a beer in front of him. "Thought you could use one."

He tilted his head in acknowledgment. "Thanks."

With a twist of his wrist, he removed the bottle top but held on to it, rolling it around and around between his fingers. He took a few swallows, and Shoni found herself fascinated by the glide of his Adam's apple. She cleared her throat and quickly looked away to take a deep draught of her own beer.

"This is pretty good." She glanced at the label. "I don't think I've heard of it."

"Had a friend, another SEAL, from Montana. He got me hooked on it." Zeke's gaze took on a faraway cast. "He's dead, too. Died in, uh, a training mission."

Shoni nodded, understanding. It was odd to see the man she'd known as John McClane in his own niche. No longer a man without a past, but someone who'd endured tragedies most people couldn't even imagine. She'd been attracted to John McClane—the core essence of Zeke Monroe. However, Zeke's experiences gave him more layers, more vulnerabilities—and more defenses.

She'd been surprised when he'd opened up to her about his wife and daughter. She'd also felt his grief, an echo of her own.

"Do you blame the military for your family's deaths?" she asked before she could censor her mouth.

Zeke froze momentarily, then continued to riffle through the stack of mail. "I used to."

"What changed your mind?"

Zeke dropped the envelopes onto the table and leaned back in his chair. "Time. I realized that I was the one who made the decision to become a SEAL. The Navy didn't hold a gun to my head. I knew what kind of pay I got for the risks I took, and I accepted that." His fingers curved around the beer bottle but he didn't raise it. "I just didn't realize I was risking their lives, too."

"No one has a crystal ball, Zeke." If she'd had one, she never would have asked her mother to pick up her dry cleaning that day.

His probing gaze searched her face. "Why do you blame yourself for your mother's death?"

The unexpected question shook her and she stood, suddenly eager to escape the intensity of his blue eyes. She walked into the living room, running her fingers along the cool surface of the stones that made up the fireplace. "If we had some dry wood, a fire would feel nice."

Zeke rose and joined her, crowding into her personal space. She backed up against the fireplace. Zeke loomed over her. "She was hit by a car. Why do you blame yourself?"

A fist clenched her stomach and her lungs couldn't find enough air. "Why did you blame yourself for your wife's and daughter's deaths? You were on a mission."

Frustration shadowed Zeke's features. "That's exactly why I blame myself. I should've been there with them."

"Then you'd be dead, too." Shoni almost didn't recognize the husky voice as her own.

"Maybe that would've been better."

"No!" The word was shouted before she even realized it was coming.

Zeke pressed closer, one hand going to the mantel beside Shoni's head. "Why? Why wouldn't that have been better?" he whispered.

His masculine scent made her dizzy, made thinking nearly impossible. She fought to bring reason back, to find an answer to his question that wouldn't cut her open, expose her innermost feelings. "I wouldn't have a witness for the arson case."

He struck the mantel with his palm. Shoni jumped at the thunderous thump. Zeke whirled around and paced the living room.

Despite everything, Shoni couldn't help but notice the generic jeans she'd bought him had been exchanged for a pair of faded Levis that molded to his backside and long, muscular thighs and calves. A faded blue sweatshirt with a diver and the phrase *The Only Easy Day Was Yesterday* stitched on the front left side covered his torso and accented the breadth of his shoulders and chest. This was the real Zeke Monroe, the ex-SEAL, the widower.

And the man I'm falling in love with.

Chapter Eighteen

ZEKE halted his pacing by the window that looked out across the front yard. "All I could think about while I was on the street was regaining my memory, but now that I have, I wish I hadn't."

Moisture burned Shoni's eyes and she crossed the room to stand by his side. She kept her arms folded across her waist, holding in her emotions so they wouldn't escape.

"Then you wouldn't have the happy memories, either," she said softly.

"But that's what makes the bad ones so much worse." His voice cracked.

Shoni surrendered to the need to comfort and stepped in front of him, wrapping her arms around his waist and resting her head against his shoulder. "I'm sorry, Zeke. No person should have to relive a loved one's death."

Zeke eased his arms around Shoni and pulled her closer. His head rested against hers and she could feel his warm breath on her neck, smell his sweat and his own masculine scent. They were so close she felt the pulse of his heart against her breast. Despite the fact she was supposed to be watching over him, she felt safe and protected in his embrace. Only when her father had held her as a young girl had she felt as secure.

But the similarities ended there. Zeke's muscled body against hers was reminding her how long it had been since she'd been with a man. Yet those past sexual encounters paled beside her attraction to Zeke.

She slid her trembling hands beneath his sweatshirt, her fingers encountering hot skin and hard muscle, and glided up his spine. Zeke moaned and shifted so Shoni stood between his legs, her belly pressed against his hardening flesh. Fire answered fire, and she felt the growing dampness between her thighs.

Zeke cupped her left cheek in one hand and angled his mouth downward, kissing her with an urgency that Shoni understood all too well. With his other hand, he palmed her neck, then drifted downward, dipping beneath her shirt. He fanned his strong, blunt-nailed fingers over her collarbone, beneath her bra strap, and pushed both her shirt and her strap down her arm, baring her shoulder.

Zeke's lips deserted her mouth, kissing a trail that followed the sweep of his hand. Heady desire quickened her breath and she tipped her head back. The alternating tickling and sucking of his lips against her neck and shoulder made her gasp. Her fingers scrabbled for something to cling to, to keep her from overloading on the sensual pleasure. She found his arms and grasped iron biceps.

Cool air eddied across her chest, and she was shocked to find Zeke had lowered the other side of her shirt and unhooked her bra. Zeke pressed the lacy material aside and his mouth settled on her breast, drew in the turgid nipple. She almost didn't recognize her own needy moan and tried to raise her arms, but found herself trapped by her clothing. She jerked her arms free of sleeves and bra straps, leaving the shirt around her waist. White satin and lace lay on the floor by their feet.

While Zeke's mouth was busy paying each breast a personal visit, his hands unbuttoned and unzipped her jeans. One large hand massaged her belly in lazy circles, expanding in larger and larger circles until his fingers dipped beneath her panties. At his first touch of her heated center, Shoni stifled a shout that emerged as a whimper.

"You want it, Shoni. I can feel how ready you are," Zeke murmured in a passion-husky voice.

Her brain cells were shutting down, exchanging thought for sensation. "I want *you*, Zeke."

She scrambled to undo his jeans, felt his erection throb against her wrist as she lowered his zipper. Before she could take him in hand, Zeke pressed one finger inside her. Her breath quickened and the scent of her own arousal only made her more slick, eager for more than Zeke's fingers.

Although trapped in a vortex of pleasure, Shoni didn't forget her objective. She traced Zeke's length with her fingernails, his briefs doing little to hide his arousal. This time the deep moan wasn't hers. She wanted to hear it again. She slid her hand beneath the elastic waistband. Smooth silky skin covered his firm, steely erection. As she ran her fingers over him, he throbbed within her loose grip.

Zeke moaned again and sought her lips with his. Their mouths clashed, lips separated and tongues dueled. There was no gentleness in their kiss, only frantic need.

Zeke removed his finger and she wanted to cry out at the loss. But then he cupped her mound and found her sensitive nub. Shoni stroked him with a firmer grip as Zeke massaged her flesh with his thumb and forefinger.

Her belly grew taut, her climax only a hairsbreadth away. She was close, so close to the edge, but fought the final step. She wanted to take Zeke with her.

He suddenly nipped her lower lip and the tremors running

through her exploded into pleasure. She caught the scream in her throat. Zeke threw back his head and shoved forward into her hand. She felt him pulse, and warmth coated her hand.

Her knees trembled, threatening to dump her on the floor, but Zeke held her upright. Shoni had no idea how he managed to do so after his own explosive release. With her head against his chest, she felt the rapid rise and fall as he regained his breath. When his began to slow, she found her own breathing had returned to normal, though her legs still wobbled like gelatin.

The gentle vibrations of his body brought her head up sharply, only to find amusement dancing in his eyes. "It's a good thing nobody's out in this weather."

She turned her head. They stood directly in front of the uncurtained window. For the first time in years, Shoni giggled. "I can see the headlines now, 'Cop arrested for indecent exposure.' "

Zeke's eyes turned smoky. "There's nothing indecent about you."

Her cheeks flamed and she forced levity into her tone. "I doubt your neighbors would feel the same way." She glanced down at their disheveled clothing. "Uh, I think we should clean up."

"My shower is big enough for two."

Desire flared anew. Passion vied with duty. She looked out the window again, seeing the same mixture of ice and snow raining down. She doubted anyone, even a professional killer, would be out in the inclement weather.

Her heart pounding, Shoni smiled. "I'll wash your back if you wash mine."

Zeke led the way to the master bathroom with its monstrous shower. At the time he bought the house, he'd thought it was a stupid waste of space . . .

After he started the water for the two showerheads, he returned to the bedroom to find Shoni standing in the middle of the room. She'd tugged her shirt back up over her breasts and zipped her jeans. If they hadn't just streaked past third base like a couple of hormone-driven teenagers, he'd think she was a virgin.

Instead of asking her what was wrong, Zeke took matters into his own hands. He stepped up to her and grasped the hem of her shirt, but waited a moment before lifting it upward. If she was having second thoughts, he wanted to give her a chance to stop him.

She met his gaze, and although there was a reticence in her eyes that hadn't been there earlier, he couldn't see any sign that she wanted him to stop. He eased the shirt upward and over her head, then tossed it onto the dresser. With the first heady flash of lust satisfied, Zeke took his time to admire her ivory skin, small breasts, and tan nipples.

"You're beautiful," he said, voice hoarse with renewed passion.

Her flesh pinkened and her nipples pebbled beneath his gaze. She lifted her arms as if to cover herself, but Zeke clasped her wrists and his thumbs caressed her forearms.

"When I first met you, I wanted to find out what you were hiding underneath that tough cop exterior." His gaze lingered on her chest and heated blood moved toward his groin.

She lifted her chin, but there was a hint of shyness in her eyes. "When I first met you, I wondered why a homeless man with a scruffy beard and shaggy hair made me think things I had no business thinking."

Surprised warmth flowed through Zeke. "What kind of things?"

She caught his sweatshirt and tugged it off him. Her palms pressed flat against his smooth chest, hot and arousing as hell.

"Things like this." She pressed her lips to the center of his chest. "And this." His right nipple. "And definitely this." His left.

Zeke clung to his control but his voice grew husky. "Funny, I wondered the same things." He leaned down and circled his tongue around one pebbled breast, then the other.

Shoni's breath hitched and Zeke couldn't conceal a grin of smug satisfaction. Besides recalling his past, he also remembered how he loved to make a woman come apart in his arms, his name on her lips as she shuddered through a quaking orgasm. Although he'd basically lived as a monk since Tiffany died, he couldn't forget the thrill of making love to a woman he cared for . . . and loved.

Do I love Shoni?

John McClane did, but what about Zeke Monroe?

"Zeke?"

Shoni's concerned voice brought him out of his too-serious musings. He peered into her eyes and his reassuring smile was genuine. "I'm right here, Shoni." He settled one hand on the curve of her bare waist and kissed her, not with the fiery frenzy of lust, but with the tenderness of a lover.

They undressed one another and Zeke took her hand. He led her into the steam-filled bathroom and, for the first time, appreciated the size of his shower.

AN obnoxious buzzing woke Shoni and she blinked in the unfamiliar surroundings. A heavy weight across her waist and cozy warmth along her back brought back the past few hours in instant clarity. Despite the urge to ignore her cell phone, Shoni eased out from under Zeke's arm and searched for her jeans. She found them on the floor, where they'd been tossed before she'd showered with Zeke. A smile curved her lips. Showering was the least of what they did.

She found her phone, tiptoed out of the loft bedroom and down the stairs as she answered it. "Hello. Alexander."

"Do you want a protection detail?"

It took a few moments for her fuzzy mind to recognize

the lieutenant's voice, then more time to process what he was asking. She gazed out the same window where she and Zeke had stood earlier. The dusky light didn't allow her to see if there was still freezing rain mixed with snow. "Um, I don't think we need it. I doubt whoever ransacked his place will be back."

"Has he told you anything?"

"About?"

"Why someone searched his place and why someone would want to kill him."

Shoni pulled an afghan off the back of the sofa and wrapped it around her nude body. She considered telling him about the receptionist at Markoff Industries who recognized Zeke, but decided against it. The lieutenant would think the worst since he didn't trust Zeke. "He doesn't remember most of what happened the day he was assaulted. I don't think it's that uncommon for a person who suffered a concussion."

He grunted. "What do you know about Monroe?"

Shoni doubted her boss was asking about Zeke's sexual prowess. Shifting to less pleasant thoughts, she sat on the couch, tucking her legs beneath her and keeping the afghan snug. "He's a former Navy SEAL, now works for Paladin Security."

"Isn't that the company that's been accused of killing Iraqi citizens?"

Shoni frowned. "Is it?"

"Paladin is contracted to secure the supply caravans moving around Iraq. About six weeks ago some of their people allegedly opened fire on innocent Iraqis when they got too close to the trucks. They lost a big government contract because of the incident."

"How do you know that?"

"Don't you watch the news?"

She leaned back against the couch. "Haven't kept up with it since Mom died."

"Oh." Bob seemed uncomfortable with her confession. "I have a friend who works for the company. He told me about it the other day, right before it hit the national news."

"He didn't mention an employee being absent, did he?"

"No." Silence. "You're wondering why no one missed Monroe at Paladin."

"Aren't you?"

"Not really. Once they send someone out on a job, their employees are fairly autonomous," Bob explained. "That's what got them in hot water in Iraq. They weren't policing their own."

"Something doesn't seem right."

"Maybe not, but I can't believe Paladin Security condones murder."

She sighed. "You're still handing Williams my arson case on Monday?"

"It needs a pair of fresh eyes, Shoni." Bob's tone was weary. "Besides, I think you've gotten too personally involved with your witness to be objective."

For a frantic moment, she wondered how he'd found out about her and Zeke. Then she realized he hadn't, but even growing friendly with a witness was a no-no. Objectivity was the name of the game, and she'd been a champ at the game. Until Zeke.

"What else did you find out about Monroe?"

"Not much. His wife and daughter died in a house fire while he was still in the Navy."

"Isn't that damned coincidental?"

"What?" Shoni asked, puzzled.

"His family dies in a fire and he's in the middle of an arson investigation?"

Angered by his callousness, she shot back, "He was on an assignment when his home burned down."

"We both know how psychological trauma can make

people do things they never would have otherwise. Maybe that's what happened with Monroe."

Shoni tipped her head back on the couch and stared up at the beamed ceiling, not wanting to believe Zeke could be guilty, no matter the reason. "Look, Lieutenant, you've been determined to distrust Zeke since the beginning. Is it cop instinct or something else?"

"I've been a cop for over twenty years. I guess suspicion becomes a hard habit to break." He paused, and when he spoke again, his tone gentled. "You remind me of our daughter, Shoni. I don't want you getting hurt."

His paternal concern made Shoni blink back tears. Her mother had loved her, but since Shoni's father died, Iris Alexander had been the one who needed reassuring. Bob had taken to Shoni almost right away, and he and his wife, Helen, had had her over for dinner a few times.

"I'll be careful, Bob. I promise," she said, her voice thick with emotion.

"I'm holding you to that promise, Alexander," he said with gruff affection. "If you see or hear anything suspicious, call it in immediately. Don't take any chances."

"Yes, sir."

Bob ended the call and Shoni set her phone on the end table.

Although Shoni didn't believe Zeke was involved in the arson, Bob had planted a seed of doubt. Maybe having had his family die in a fire had unbalanced Zeke. Maybe something had occurred that shattered his fragile psyche and brought on the amnesia.

Maybe Shoni was falling in love with a man who was mentally unstable, as well as an arsonist and a murderer.

ZEKE woke from his nap and raised his head to find an empty place where Shoni had lain. Frowning, he glanced toward the bathroom, but the door was ajar and the room empty. He rose and snagged his jeans from the floor. Shoni's clothes still lay scattered where they'd fallen earlier, so she couldn't be far.

Raking a hand through his hair, he flinched at the length. One of the first things on his to-do list was a haircut. His bare feet were silent on the cool wood floor as he walked out the bedroom door to the railing along the upper-level walkway. He looked down into the living room. Wrapped in an afghan, Shoni sat motionless on the sofa. He had a view of her back and couldn't tell if she was awake or asleep. Her rigid posture suggested she was awake . . . and upset.

Did she regret what happened between them? He had thought he might regret it. Although he'd been alone for a long time, sharing what he did with Shoni felt like a betrayal of Tiffany. However, his wife wouldn't want him to be alone and grieving the rest of his life. Tiffany would want him to be happy.

And Shoni made him happy. Happier than he'd been since before he'd received the horrific news of Tiffany and Chelle's deaths.

He continued downstairs, his gaze never leaving Shoni's head with its dark, wild hair. Earlier he'd buried his hands in those soft, silky curls just as he'd buried himself within her welcoming body. He suspected he'd never tire of touching her, tasting her, and hearing her passionate cries.

Zeke rounded the sofa and Shoni jerked her head up, her eyes wide and her lips parted slightly. She hadn't heard him coming. That wasn't like the vigilant detective.

"Hey," he said quietly.

She replaced her surprise with a smile that didn't reach her eyes. "Hey, yourself. You didn't have to get up."

He shrugged, his gaze roaming over the afghan as his memory recalled what lay hidden beneath. "My stomach was growling."

Her cheeks pinkened, but that didn't stop her from looking at his bare chest with greedy eyes. "Finding something to eat might be a little difficult."

"I've been trained to survive in a desert without food or water. I'm sure I can come up with something."

"As long as it's not beetles or worms, I'm game."

"So the June bug casserole and earthworm salad are out?"

She wrinkled her nose. "Definitely." She stood, keeping a tight hold on the blanket. "I think I'll go upstairs and dress."

He waggled his eyebrows. "You don't have to on my account." One step placed him directly in front of her and he clasped her slim hips. "In fact, I prefer you this way."

She kept one hand clutched to the afghan but dipped her fingers of the other into his waistband and gave a quick tug. He stumbled against her and the lower halves of their bodies pressed together. "I hope you're not one of those men who prefer a woman barefoot and in the kitchen."

"Only if it involves chocolate sauce and whipped cream."

"Only if I get first dibs."

Zeke grinned. "That can be arranged."

He felt Shoni shudder, and her eyes were bright with desire. With a moan of surrender, he plunged his fingers into her hair and clutched the riotous curls in his fists. Angling her head, he kissed her and she opened for him, her tongue unfurling against his. Despite having made love twice in the past few hours, he was ready for round three.

Shoni leaned back and he followed, unwilling to put an end to their kiss. Flattening her palms on his chest, she pushed.

"Slow down, Lothario," she said in a breathy voice. "I thought you said you were hungry."

"I did. And I am." He attempted to show her how hungry, but she ducked under his arms and dashed across the room.

She stopped at the foot of the stairs leading to the loft.

"Why don't you do your magic in the kitchen while I get dressed?"

Her gaze bounced around, as if she was afraid of something. His passion ebbed, and he wanted to ask her if she regretted what they'd done. But he wasn't certain he wanted to hear the answer.

"Could you toss my sweatshirt down?"

She nodded and flew up the stairs, the afghan slipping down her back. A few moments later his shirt sailed over the railing and he caught it one-handed. He heard Shoni moving around in the bedroom and tried not to remember how she'd looked in his bed. Face flushed, lips swollen, body eager.

Shaking the tantalizing visions aside, he concentrated on throwing together a meal. He opened the pantry door and stared at the cans and packages of food. How often had he eaten at the soup kitchen and scrounged in Dumpsters these past few weeks? And the entire time his home was here, waiting for him.

By the time Shoni returned, hamburger browned on the stove as noodles boiled.

"Smells good," she commented, leaning against a counter.

He glanced at her and his breath caught in his throat. She'd borrowed one of his button-down shirts to wear over her jeans. Although it was baggy and hid her figure, a primal possessiveness swept through him.

"I hope you don't mind," she said. "I didn't have any spare clothes with me."

Zeke cleared his throat and turned back to the stove, afraid he'd turn into a complete Neanderthal and drag her up to his bedroom. "That's fine. Besides, I owe you for the things you bought me."

"You don't owe me anything."

He forced a chuckle as he stirred the burger. "It's not like I can't pay you back."

She remained silent behind him, and he wondered if he'd hurt her feelings. Aware of Shoni on a level he didn't understand, Zeke sensed her movement then felt a brush against his elbow.

"Tell me about your work at Paladin Security," she said.

Alarms clanged through Zeke, the same alarms that had saved his life more than once.

Chapter Nineteen

"Why?"

Her gaze flicked downward, but not before he noticed something akin to guilt in her eyes.

"I'm curious," she replied.

"Cop curious or friend curious?"

She lifted her chin and met his gaze this time. "Both."

The timer beeped and Zeke turned off the burner beneath the noodles. After draining and rinsing them, he added condensed soup, burger, and peas, and mixed them together.

"After my initial training with Paladin, I was sent overseas, working with a security detail for some high-level government officials. When that assignment was over, I rode shotgun on supply convoys." He shrugged. "Basic mercenary stuff."

Her eyes narrowed. "Supply convoys, huh? Were you involved in the shooting of the Iraqi citizens?"

Grimacing, he shook his head as he turned off the burner. "I was in the States when it happened. If I hadn't been, maybe I could've stopped it."

They ate at the dining room table, gazing out the floor-to-ceiling windows that faced the monochromatic gray lake behind the cabin.

"You wouldn't have been able to afford a place like this on a military salary," Shoni commented.

Zeke's appetite dwindled and he set his fork on his plate. "I loved the Navy," he began softly. "In fact, there were times Tiffany joked that I loved my job more than her." He paused. "Sometimes I think I did. I was an adrenaline junkie. I loved the danger, the action, the camaraderie."

He chuckled without humor. "God knows, I didn't do it for the pay. And that's what killed Tiffany and Chelle." His lungs constricted and he felt the familiar sting of tears, but though the grief remained, he could manage it now. "Steve Paridot, a former SEAL I knew, came to the funeral. He worked for Paladin. He gave me his card and told me to call him. A week later I did. A month later I was out of the Navy and working at Paladin, doing the same job I'd been doing in the military, but for a hell of a lot more money. When I came back to the States after my first assignment with Paladin, my bank account was unbelievable. I'd never seen that much money. I bought this place and went on a spending spree for furniture, buying the kind Tiffany and I had dreamed about."

After a few minutes of silence, Shoni asked, "Was it common for you to accompany your boss on business meetings?"

"Like going with Jensen to Markoff?"

She nodded.

He shrugged. "Not usually, but I was back in the States and Paladin had just lost a contract, so there wasn't anything else for me to do."

"Why was Jensen doing business with Markoff if Paladin just lost a contract?"

Zeke rummaged through his memories. "A couple of weeks earlier Paladin had signed a contract with Markoff for more weapons and body armor. Paladin was so certain their contract with the government would be renewed. When it wasn't, Jensen was trying to find a way out of the contract with Markoff."

"Did he?"

Pain stabbed through his brain and he pressed his hands to his head.

"What's wrong?" Shoni's concerned voice cut through the agony.

Zeke fought to bring the arrowing pain down to a dull throbbing and he spoke through clenched teeth. "Headache."

"Maybe you know something about Markoff's murder."

The pain eased. "Like what? There's no reason Paladin would want Markoff dead."

Shoni tapped her fingers on the table in a steady rhythm. "No reason we know of. Do you know the Paladin employees allegedly involved in the Iraqi shootings?"

"Yes. It's not that big of a company. What has this got to do with your arson case?"

"Probably nothing. Or maybe something." She rose and carried their empty plates into the kitchen.

Unwilling to leave her enigmatic statement alone, he followed her. "What do you mean?"

"I don't see a connection, but in my line of work, coincidences aren't usually simple coincidences." She leaned against the counter and crossed her arms. Wearing his shirt, she resembled a girl playing grown-up. "You're right in the middle of all this, Zeke. The fires and Markoff Industries."

Irritation sharpened his words. "You're the one who was so certain I wasn't involved."

Her lips thinned and she glanced away. "You said it yourself. The fires didn't start until after you ended up on the street."

"How do you explain the man starting the fire in the warehouse where I was living? A subconscious illusion?" He took a deep, calming breath. "When was the first fire?"

"Three weeks ago yesterday. About eleven o'clock at night."

Zeke thought back to that night, his memories coming from John McClane. He smiled, relieved he could give her an answer she could verify. "I was at Estelle's. You can ask her."

Her shoulders slumped with relief. She hadn't been able to totally dismiss Tyler's theory.

"Speaking of Estelle, you should probably let her know you've figured out who you are," Shoni said.

Zeke's eyes widened. "She's going to have my hide for not telling her right away."

Shoni laughed, feeling a lightness that had been missing since Tyler's call.

Zeke looked up the number of the motel where Estelle was staying. "Do you want to confirm my alibi?" he asked, his finger poised to punch in the number.

She shook her head. "I'll do it later. Just let her know you're all right." She tipped her head to the side and her green eyes glittered. "I'll be waiting for you upstairs."

She could feel Zeke's gaze on her backside as she crossed to the loft stairs and put an extra swing in her hips.

"Call her," Shoni said over her shoulder, laughter in her voice.

"Right. Calling."

Shoni stepped into the loft bedroom with excitement sparking her nerves. For the first time since she was eleven years old and decided she wanted to be a police officer like her father, she didn't care about her job. Those sacred rules and regulations she'd followed with blind allegiance for eight years seemed unimportant. Nowhere in those rules and regulations did they allow a cop to fall in love with a witness in an active investigation. Nor did they tolerate vigilantes who took justice into their own hands.

Shoni was guilty of the first, and on the road to becoming the second.

ZEKE opened his eyes to the rosy hue of sunrise. It took him only a few moments to recall where he was, as well as the events of the past month. A soft snuffle beside him caught his attention and he smiled down at the halo of dark curls against the snow white pillow. He shifted to his side and propped his head on his hand to gaze down at Shoni. Careful not to wake her, he brushed a strand of hair from her cheek. Her warm skin beckoned, but instead of touching her, he simply caressed her with his gaze.

The last time he'd woken with a woman in his bed was the morning before he left for yet another mission. There'd been nothing different about that morning, nothing that hinted it would be the last time he'd kiss Tiffany; the last time he'd share some overly sweet cereal with Chelle; the last time he'd let the dog out. The last time he'd see his family alive.

For the first time he considered sharing his life with someone else. Someone like Shoni. He didn't resist the impulse to kiss her brow, but kept his lips feather-light so he wouldn't wake her. He'd noticed the dark circles beneath her eyes before, but last night he couldn't ignore them any longer. He knew it was sorrow that put the shadows there. Shoni had lost her mother, the only family she'd had, only two months ago. Zeke understood that kind of pain, understood how it took over your life, coloring every thought, every emotion, every decision. He'd survived his loss and he'd help Shoni move past hers.

The police composite of the arsonist flashed in his mind, bringing a jab of pain. He rolled onto his back and pressed his skull into his pillow, his eyes squinched shut.

I recognize the arsonist.

Why would Steve Paridot torch the warehouse? Steve had seen him, but maybe he hadn't recognized him with the beard and secondhand clothing.

A sober possibility iced Zeke's gut. Steve, like most other Paladin employees, was skilled with rifles and bombs. Had he been the one behind the sniper's gun? And the sophisticated bomb at Shoni's apartment? What about the condo break-in and the murder of the security guard?

Why would Steve do those things?

The answer flitted just beyond Zeke's consciousness, but it was there. Somewhere.

Unwilling to risk Shoni's life to find the answers, Zeke silently rose and grabbed some clothes from his closet. He used the downstairs bathroom to shower.

His SUV's keys were hanging in their normal place. But he'd driven the vehicle to work the day before he'd been struck with amnesia. Had he driven it home, too?

After plucking the keys from their peg, Zeke sent a longing—and apologetic glance—toward the loft where Shoni continued to sleep. He thought about leaving a note, but it would only anger her. And she was going to be pissed as hell anyhow. No, it was better just to talk to her later.

Surprised and grateful, Zeke found the SUV in the garage. Its motor turned over on the first try. While he let it run, he checked the glove box and found his wallet. He looked through it. Nothing was missing. Zeke slid it into his pocket. What had happened that last day?

The roads proved to be more slushy than icy due to the rising temperatures and the chemicals spread by the city maintenance trucks. The morning rush hour traffic moved slower than usual, and it took nearly an hour to arrive at the Paladin Security offices.

He parked and turned the ignition off, but remained in the vehicle, staring at the entrance. Unease trickled down his spine and he didn't understand why. He'd worked at

Paladin two and a half years. He'd been getting tired of the job, but he had no real complaints. He was paid well for his work and his employers treated him decently. So why did he feel like a fly caught in a web?

Shaking aside his apprehension, Zeke stepped out of the SUV and strode across the lot. He didn't see anyone he recognized until he arrived at the front desk.

"Zeke," the woman—Brenda—greeted him with a friendly smile. "We didn't expect you back for another month."

He managed a smile, even as he wondered where she thought he'd been. "Got back yesterday," he replied. "Is Mark Jensen in?"

"You're in luck. He came in early this morning. I'll buzz him."

Zeke stopped her with a hand to her wrist. "I'd like to surprise him."

Although Brenda appeared puzzled, she nodded. "All right."

He turned to walk to his boss's office, but paused. "Whatever happened with the contract with Markoff?"

She grinned. "Mr. Jensen managed to get them to cancel it with a nominal penalty. That's why I still have a job."

Although that was good news, it made his nape tingle. He smiled and injected a note of enthusiasm into his voice. "Great."

He continued down the hall that was both familiar and foreign. At Jensen's door, he knocked once, then opened it. Jensen looked up, and his face passed through a gamut of expressions. It settled on wary. "Zeke, what're you doing back so soon?"

First Brenda, now his boss. Zeke closed the door and noticed Jensen's shoulders stiffen. Zeke's soldier instincts pealed an alarm.

He settled in a chair in front of the desk, assuming a relaxed pose. "Where was I supposed to be?" he asked, keeping his tone at a normal conversation level.

"South America. Protection detail."

Zeke didn't believe the too-fast response. "Never made it there. I must've been in an accident. I've spent the last few weeks living on the street with no memory."

"What?"

"I just regained my memory yesterday. Didn't you miss me?"

Jensen's gaze slid away, then returned to Zeke's face. It was enough to confirm Zeke's instincts.

"No one at the other end told us you didn't show up." Jensen leaned back in his chair, but he appeared anything but relaxed. "So what do you remember?"

"Not much. The last thing I remember is coming to work. I think it was Wednesday, the fifteenth. And today's what, the fourteenth of November?"

"You were supposed to fly out on the sixteenth."

"Obviously I didn't."

"I'm sorry, Zeke. We had no idea you were missing."

If—and it was a big if—Jensen was telling the truth, then that was the reason there was no missing persons report filed. Zeke glanced out the window. It was a sad commentary on his life that nobody, not even the company he worked for, missed him.

"Does Steve Paridot still work here?" Zeke asked, keeping his voice casual.

The tension that had drained from Jensen returned. "Yes. Why wouldn't he?"

"I saw him when I was living on the street." He paused, his gaze intent on his boss. "He started the fire that burned down the warehouse I was living in."

Jensen's eyes widened. "Why would Steve do something like that?"

Zeke shrugged. "Got me."

"You said you had amnesia during that time?" Zeke nodded. "How did you recognize him?"

"I didn't. Not until this morning."

"It couldn't have been him. He's been out of the country for a couple of weeks now."

For a split second, Zeke doubted his own memory. But no, it had been Steve, the same man who'd come to Tiffany and Chelle's funerals, and given him a Paladin Security business card. The friend who'd changed the course of Zeke's life.

Zeke stood, placed his knuckles on Jensen's desk, and leaned forward. He took a moment of satisfaction when Jensen drew back. "Something is going on here. Something involving you, Paridot, me, and Markoff Industries. I don't know what it is. Not yet. But I'll figure it out. I promise you that."

Zeke spun on his heel and marched out. As he neared Brenda's desk, he slowed and gave the petite redhead a charming smile. "I have a favor to ask. Could you tell me the date my assignment to South America was issued?"

Brenda frowned. "It should be on your paperwork."

A wry, boyish grin. "I lost it."

It took only seconds for the information to come up on her computer screen. "October fifteenth."

The last day he remembered. Their work was usually assigned a week or more in advance. Funny how the assignment was issued only the day before he was to leave. Someone was covering his tracks. He glanced down the hallway.

And he knew who.

He just didn't know why.

Yet.

SHONI rolled over and blinked open her eyes. Sunlight streamed in long, narrow windows, illuminating the bedroom with its slanted ceiling and rustic furniture. It was a room she could easily get used to waking in every morning. As long as Zeke came with the bed.

She extended her arm behind her but found only empty space. She sat up, holding the sheet over her breasts, and surveyed the room. No Zeke. Tipping her head to the side, she listened, but there was only hollow silence.

Shoni climbed out of bed and donned Zeke's shirt. The hardwood floor was cool beneath her soles and she hurried out to the railing. No sign of Zeke confirmed the empty silence. He'd probably gone out to buy something for breakfast.

Willing herself not to worry, Shoni took a long, hot shower. She told herself Zeke would be downstairs in the kitchen when she was done.

He wasn't.

Dressed in the same clothes she'd worn yesterday, Shoni paced the living room, barely noticing the dramatic view of the lake outside the floor-to-ceiling windows.

Where was he?

Was Tyler right? Had Zeke lied to her last night? Was his amnesia all a lie, a ploy used to gain sympathy and take the suspicion off him? The composite of their suspect could've been another ruse.

If he was innocent, why had he left without waking her or leaving a note? What was so urgent that he couldn't wait?

Worry and anger in equal measures pulsed through her, upsetting her stomach and giving her a headache. How could she have been such a gullible idiot? From the beginning, she'd gone against police regulations for Zeke. She'd allowed her emotions to influence her decisions—she'd listened to her heart. Her mother would've been proud; her father, disappointed.

She pressed her fingertips to her throbbing temples. She'd managed to mess up everything. If her career had been in jeopardy earlier, it was now on the verge of collapse. Her witness, whom she had slept with, was gone.

Shoni dropped her hands from her face and pulled back her shoulders. She couldn't hide here forever.

On her way to the station, she stopped by her apartment to change clothes, and was relieved to see the police tape gone from her door.

Half an hour later, Shoni entered the bustling bullpen. Detectives were busy with phone calls, witness statements, and the dreaded paperwork. Typical noises for a typical day. Yet for Shoni, it felt anything but typical.

She dropped into her chair and simply stared at the files and papers tossed onto her desk. Stalling, she glanced through them and found most were follow-ups on the arson case.

"'Bout time you got your ass in to work, Alexander," Raff said with a smile to temper his words.

She glanced across the aisle that separated their desks. "Bite me."

He grinned. "My pleasure."

She glared. "I wouldn't bet on it."

He chuckled. *The bastard.*

"So, where's your shadow?" he asked.

Shoni's cheeks flamed. "Not here."

"I'm a detective. I figured that one out all by myself."

"First case you've solved in months."

Before Raff could retort, Tyler stuck his head out the door. His gaze immediately netted her, and he motioned for her to come to his office.

"That's not good," Raff said in an undertone.

A typical Tyler summons involved a bellow. The hand wave could instill terror in the most seasoned detective.

Shoni swallowed and crossed to the lieutenant's office, ignoring the sympathetic glances aimed her way. She knocked on the door frame and entered without waiting for a reply. Closing the door behind her, she met Tyler's stern expression.

"Yes, sir?"

"Where is he?"

Shoni's heart thudded against her breast. "Who, sir?"

"You know damn good and well who I'm talking about. McClane. Monroe."

Shoni focused on a spot on the wall behind her boss. "I lost him, sir."

"How the hell did you do that?"

"He took off while I was sleeping."

"How long ago?" Tyler's quiet voice alarmed Shoni more than his roaring.

"I'm not sure, sir. When I woke up, he was gone."

"And when did you plan on telling me?" Even softer.

"That's why I'm here."

Tyler slammed a fist on his desk and she jumped, startled.

"You're in here because I called you in here," Tyler shouted.

Shoni wasn't going to remind him that he'd gestured her in rather than called. "Yes, sir."

"Your job was to watch him. What the hell happened?"

She didn't think he wanted to know that because of her and Zeke's bedtime activities she'd fallen into an exhausted slumber. "I screwed up, sir."

"Damned right you did, Alexander." Tyler breathed deeply and his anger shifted to something akin to concern. "The detective I knew wouldn't have let herself get mixed up with a witness during an active investigation. Ever since your mother died, you've been a loose cannon. I thought maybe this case would give you something to focus on, something to get your mind back in the game. But all you've done is lose a witness who could very well turn out to be the prime suspect."

Shoni clamped her teeth together. Even after Zeke

disappeared without an explanation, she felt the urge to defend him.

"Give me a reason why I shouldn't suspend your ass right now," Tyler said.

Anger leaped through her defensive wall. "You seem to have your mind made up, sir."

"Damn it, Shoni, I don't want to lose one of my best detectives." He paused. "And a friend."

Shoni's throat tightened. It would've been easier if Tyler had kept it impersonal. "Zeke Monroe is the key to the case," she said with a husky voice. "Give me a chance to find him and bring him in."

Tyler's expression gave nothing away as he studied her. "And if you don't bring him in?"

"You can suspend my ass." Shoni paused. "And I'll buy you a case of your favorite coffee."

A corner of the lieutenant's mouth twitched. "You realize that'll run you close to five hundred dollars."

Shoni resisted the urge to pump her fist in a victory gesture. "Yes, sir."

Tyler lowered his gaze and remained silent for a full minute. Finally, he raised his head. "I'll give you twenty-four hours. You haven't found him by then, we'll put out an APB."

Shoni nodded and some of the tension flowed away. "Thanks, Bob. I won't let you down."

"Go on, get out of here and find McClane."

"Monroe."

"Whatever. Just find him and get his ass back here."

"Yes, sir." She turned toward the door but stopped and looked over her shoulder at Tyler. "You said you have a friend at Paladin Security. Would you be willing to give me his name?"

"Mark Jensen."

Shoni's breath faltered. Jensen. The man Zeke had accompanied to Markoff. Another coincidence?

Filled with apprehension, Shoni threaded her way back to her desk.

"You made it out with your head attached," Raff commented.

Shoni made a face, but her attention was on a report from Raff and Delon. "Is this all you have on the murder and break-in at the condo?"

The well-dressed detective grimaced. "All we have so far. We're still talking to people, trying to find anyone who might have seen something that night."

"Nothing from ballistics or the lab?"

"Not yet."

"Damn it! Who is after Zeke? And why?"

"Maybe it's you they're after. It was your apartment that was wired," Raff said almost apologetically.

Shoni thought for a moment, then shook her head. "No, the shooter was after Zeke. Then he somehow learned that Zeke was staying with me. He got my address and booby-trapped my apartment. Only we were staying at Mom's condo."

"So how did he find that out?" Raff asked.

"Myself, Zeke, and the lieutenant are the only ones who knew."

"If you and the lieutenant didn't tell anyone, then it had to be your buddy."

"I was always with him. . . ." *Except for when he went to see Estelle.*

Shoni shoved back her chair and jumped to her feet.

"Where you going?" Raff asked.

"To visit a friend of a friend." She headed toward the door.

"Did you see the ballistics report from the shooter's rifle?" Raff called out.

Shoni halted. "No. What did they find?"

"A .338 Lapua Magnum."

She frowned and shook her head. "I'm not familiar with it."

"No reason you should be since you've not ex-military. It's a cartridge used for long-range sniper rifles. Been used in Afghanistan and Iraq."

Shoni's mouth grew dry. "And Paladin Security employs ex-soldiers who've had tours of duty in those countries."

Chapter Twenty

"Where'd you pull Paladin Security from?" Raff asked.

Instead of answering, Shoni said, "Do me a favor and find out everything you can about them. See if there's any connection between them and the torched warehouses."

"Why?"

"Just do it, Raff. Please. Any connection at all."

Annoyance flashed across Raff's face, but he nodded.

"Thanks." Shoni dashed out of the bullpen.

As Shoni drove across town to Estelle's temporary residence, her mind raced. Paladin Security was popping up too many times in the investigation to be merely a coincidence. But what would be their motive for killing Markoff? The death of a CEO wouldn't negate a contract with his company. And why would they want Zeke dead? Or was there a rogue firebug in Paladin Security? What about Tyler's connection to Jensen at Paladin? Was it merely, as he said, that of old friends? She couldn't believe Bob would be involved in murder, but the lines were becoming blurred. Her head ached with all the unanswered questions.

She parked in front of Estelle's unit and jumped out of the police-issued sedan. She knocked on the door.

There was the sound of a chain being slid free, then the door opened. The squat, white-haired woman smiled. "Detective. Come on in."

Shoni stepped inside.

Estelle toddled to a nearby easy chair and sank into it. "Sit down, so I don't get no crimp in my neck."

Shoni perched on the sagging sofa. "I'm looking for Zeke." At Estelle's blank look, she clarified. "John McClane."

"Why didn't you say so in the first place?" The woman shook her head. "Gonna be hard callin' him Zeke. Got used to him bein' John."

"I know what you mean. Have you seen him today? Or maybe heard from him?"

Estelle tipped her head to the side, her dark eyes shrewd. "You lose him?"

Shoni gave up her pretense of calm. "He slipped out this morning while I was sleeping. No note, no explanation about where he was going."

"Seems to me the man can take care of himself."

"Normally I'd agree with you, but somebody's out to get him. A professional."

"He told me. Said he seen the arsonist." She pursed her lips. "Also said he had police protection."

Shoni's face heated under her subtle reprimand. "I was his police protection until he skipped out." She clasped her hands, her fingers pressed tight against her knuckles. "We think there's more going on than we originally suspected."

"And John's smack dab in the middle of it?"

"I'm afraid so."

"John wouldn't be party to arson."

Estelle's faith in him was admirable, but Shoni had just

been burned by the man. She couldn't afford to blindly trust him again.

"Maybe not, but that doesn't change the fact that he disappeared."

"Maybe he was kidnapped."

"Zeke would've put up a fight and I would've heard something. But I didn't."

"The last time I heard from John was yesterday. Called to tell me he got his memory back."

"So you haven't seen him today?"

Irritation sharpened Estelle's tone. "Ain't that what I just said? Cops," she muttered and shook her head.

Fighting her own annoyance, Shoni asked, "Did Zeke tell you he was staying with me?"

"Said you was at your momma's condo."

"That's right. Did you tell anybody?"

"Course I never told no one."

"What about Lainey?"

"She was in bed."

Movement out of the corner of her eye caught Shoni's attention. She turned to see Mishon stumble out of one of the bedrooms and into the bathroom. "Did Mishon know?"

"She works at ni—" Estelle stumbled, then scowled. "She come home early that night. High, as usual. So even if she heard, she wouldn't have remembered."

"Somebody found out about the condo and killed the security guard on duty, then came up to my mother's place to get rid of Zeke. So either you, Mishon, or Lainey let it slip to someone."

"Lainey wouldn'ta done it even if she'd a heard. Mishon . . ." Estelle's dark face grew troubled. "If there was somethin' in it for her, she'd do it."

The bathroom door opened and Mishon, her hand along the wall, shuffled back to her room. Shoni jumped to her feet and went after her. The bedroom was dim and stank of stale sweat and cheap perfume.

Shoni grabbed Mishon's arm and spun the prostitute around. "Who did you tell?"

Mishon's eyelids did a slow roll. "Don't know what you're talkin' 'bout."

"Zeke. John McClane. Who wanted to know where he was?"

Mishon's pupils nearly covered the brown irises. Her head drooped, like it was too heavy for her neck. "N'body."

Shoni shook the skinny woman. "Tell me who you told."

Mishon struggled ineffectually. "Just some guy. Was askin' ev'ryone. Had a picture."

"What did he look like?"

Mishon's head lolled back. "J'st some guy. Gave me a hundred bucks."

No wonder she couldn't remember what he looked like. Her eyes were on the money and her mind was on what the money would get her.

Although frustrated, Shoni kept from shoving the girl aside in disgust. She'd known too many hookers and addicts like Mishon. It was easy to blame the girls for being weak, but too often circumstances beyond their control had forced them into their sordid lives. But there were places to get help, to get off the drugs and find a legitimate job.

"If you don't get some help, you won't be around to see your daughter graduate from grade school," Shoni said.

Mishon stared at her with blank eyes. Maybe it was already too late for her. Pity rolled through Shoni and she released the girl.

After saying good-bye to Estelle and promising she'd call when she found Zeke, Shoni left. Once in her car, she used her cell phone to touch base with Raff.

"Have a couple uniforms show Zeke Monroe's picture around in the downtown district. Find out who was looking for him," Shoni told the detective.

"You got it."

"Have you found any connection between Paladin and the fires?"

"Not yet."

"Call me if you do."

"Will do."

Shoni ended the call and checked her voice mail. Nothing.

Damn it, Zeke. Where the hell are you?

ZEKE rode the sleek, state-of-the-art elevator up to the seventeenth floor. Although it had been only yesterday that he'd been here with Shoni, it felt like years. Not surprising, considering that after they'd left Markoff Industries, he'd gone home and his newfound memories had nearly crushed him. Years of them, hundreds of them, descending upon him like a flock of vultures, picking him apart and peeling back protective layers. He'd been laid bare by the barrage, forced to remember with crystal clarity the most horrendous and excruciating days of his life.

The doors slid open and Sandra, the blond receptionist, glanced up. Her lips turned downward. Zeke had his work cut out for him. Pouring on the charm, he sauntered over to her desk and smiled down at her. "Hello, Sandra."

She tipped her head to the side, her pixie features wary. "Where's your cop friend?"

Zeke shrugged. "Don't know. Don't care. I came here to apologize."

"It didn't work yesterday."

"Yesterday I still had amnesia."

Her eyes widened, then she laughed. "I thought I'd heard all the lame-ass excuses, but that's a new one."

"It's true. For the past month, I didn't know who I was. I lived on the street."

Sandra searched his face. "You aren't jerking me around?"

He shook his head. "Scout's honor."

The phone rang. Sandra held up one hand and answered it with the other. Zeke tried not to fidget. Sandra held a missing piece to the puzzle. Once she put the call through to the correct office, she returned her attention to Zeke.

"I believe you," she said. "And I accept your apology."

Zeke breathed a sigh of relief.

"Provided you buy me that dinner you promised," Sandra added.

All Zeke had to say was yes, but he wouldn't lie. Not even to learn the truth.

"The only reason I didn't take you out to dinner last time was because of the memory loss," Zeke said. "This time I won't make that promise because I know I won't keep it."

Sandra seemed taken aback. "Either you're an honest man, or a hell of a con man."

Zeke kept silent, knowing nothing he could say would convince her.

"I always thought you were too much of a Boy Scout," Sandra said with a wry shake of her head.

Zeke took a deep breath. "I'm still missing some memories. You said that you did a favor for me. What was it?"

"It wasn't that big of a deal. Just copies of some e-mails between Mr. Gardner and Mr. Jensen concerning the Paladin contract."

"I take it you gave them to me."

She nodded. "The last time I saw you."

"Did I say why I wanted them?"

"I asked, but you wouldn't tell me."

Frustration gnawed at Zeke's gut, but he managed a smile for the woman. "Thanks, Sandra. I appreciate your help."

"Do you think it had anything to do with Mr. Markoff's death?" she asked.

"I don't know," he replied honestly. "Why would you think that?"

Sandra glanced away. "Before Mr. Markoff disappeared, it was tense around here. He didn't want to place a bid on a lucrative government contract. He was the only one opposed to it."

Zeke frowned. "Why?"

"His son lost a leg over in Iraq. It changed Mr. Markoff."

"So after he disappeared, things were less tense?"

Sandra shifted uncomfortably. "Yes and no. Everyone was worried about him, but the vote went through since he wasn't here to veto it. The bid was submitted three days ago."

Zeke was on the right trail. He could feel it. "Thanks for your help, Sandra. I really mean it."

"Funny thing is, I believe you."

Zeke headed back to the elevator. More puzzle pieces. His home had been searched, quite possibly for those papers Sandra had given him. Why? What was in those e-mails? Was it something that someone would kill for?

What if his amnesia was the result of a first murder attempt? Then why wait so long before trying again? While he'd lived on the street, he would've been an easy target.

Or maybe they'd thought he was already dead. When Steve Paridot saw him in the warehouse, they realized he was still alive. And now, thanks to his visit to Paladin, they knew his memory was back, too. Except one part of Zeke's memory still remained AWOL. The part that couldn't figure out why they would try to kill him.

Only they didn't know that.

They—Paladin Security—who had the finest trained soldiers at their disposal.

SHONI had two reasons to visit Paladin Security. The main one was to find Zeke. The other was to try to discover why Paladin Security seemed to be in the middle of her investigation.

The chair behind the reception desk was empty. Shoni glanced at the clock on the wall. Three thirty. Maybe the receptionist had already gone home.

"Can I help you?"

Shoni spun around to find a man wearing suit pants with a white dress shirt and tie. His hair was dark, but there were a few telltale signs of gray above his ears. "I was wondering if I could speak to Mr. Jensen."

"And you are?"

Shoni showed her badge. "Detective Alexander."

"In that case, I'm Mark Jensen. You wouldn't happen to know Bob Tyler, would you?"

"He's my boss."

Jensen smiled widely. "It's a small world."

"Have you known Lieutenant Tyler long?"

"Over twenty years. We met in the Marines. He got out and became a cop. I turned it into a career."

"When you retired, you started Paladin Security?"

"With another friend. Larry Wren. What can I help you with?"

"I'm looking for a Paladin employee. Zeke Monroe."

"He's in South America on an assignment. I haven't seen him in over a month."

The man's answer was too practiced. He didn't even ask what the police wanted with Zeke. "He's been living on the street with amnesia for the past month."

"What?" Jensen might have the good looks of a Hollywood star, but he lacked the acting abilities.

"He just regained his memory yesterday. That's why I thought he might've shown up here."

"No. I haven't seen him."

Shoni motioned to the desk. "Maybe the receptionist saw him."

"She's gone home."

"Then I'll just have to come back tomorrow."

"Can you tell me why the police are looking for Zeke?"

He finally remembered to ask. "He's a witness in an active investigation."

"So he's not accused of any crime?"

Shoni thought he sounded almost disappointed. "None we're aware of. Can you tell me what your relationship was with William Markoff?"

Jensen's lips tightened and his gaze darted past Shoni, but his voice was steady. "I'd met the man only once. I was sorry to hear about his death. We've done business with Markoff Industries, but worked with a VP named Gardner."

"Do you handle the negotiations with Gardner?"

Jensen nodded. "We're a fairly small company. Most of our employees are scattered around the world. Here in the office, we have eighteen people to take care of the administrative and management details."

"Why did Zeke Monroe accompany you to Markoff Industries?"

"We're considering grooming him for a management position, and since he was between overseas jobs, I had him come with me."

It made sense, but Zeke hadn't mentioned anything about moving into the managerial side of the company. Or was that something else he was hiding from her?

"Do you conduct psychological screenings on potential employees?"

Jensen crossed his arms and a hint of impatience touched his features. "No. Everyone who works here was in a branch of the military. We figure the military would've drummed them out if there'd been problems. Why do you ask?"

Shoni hated to ask the next question, but it was her job. "Did Zeke Monroe ever exhibit any behaviors that might lead you to believe he could be a fire starter?"

Jensen remained quiet, his expression thoughtful. "We never saw anything to suggest he might have that tendency. However, it's a possibility, considering how his family died."

Shoni hadn't wanted to hear that answer. It too closely

paralleled her own suspicions. However, if Jensen was involved in some cover-up, he'd encourage anything that took the heat off him. "Thank you, Mr. Jensen. I appreciate you taking the time to talk to me."

She stuck out her hand and Jensen shook it, his grip firm but not overpowering.

"If there's anything else I can help you with, don't hesitate to call or stop by," Jensen said.

"I'll do that."

Shoni left Paladin Security with even more questions and fewer answers. Before driving away, she dug out Zeke's phone number from her pocket and called him, but his voice mail picked up. Just as she ended that call, her phone buzzed.

"Alexander."

"Delon. I was helping Raff with the Paladin Security angle. I found a connection."

Excitement thrummed through her. "What is it?"

"The third warehouse that burned was owned by a small company run by Keith Hadsen."

"And?" Shoni prompted impatiently.

"His sister is married to a man named Steve Paridot. A Paladin Security employee."

No way in hell was it another coincidence. "This was the warehouse that had the hefty insurance payoff?"

"Yep," Delon said.

"So we have two fires that have a connection to Paladin Security. What about the other two?"

"Nothing, but Raff and I are still looking."

"Check to see if any of the building owners were ever in the military."

"Will do."

"Thanks, Delon."

Adrenaline surged through Shoni's blood. She was getting close. She could feel it. Every instinct told her Paladin Security was behind the four fires. However, she had no proof, and only gossamer threads connected Paladin to two of the fires.

What about Zeke? Where did he fit into all this? If Paladin was involved, did that mean Zeke was, too?

One thing was clear. Zeke held the key. The attempts on his life and the condition of his ransacked home pointed to his possessing knowledge someone didn't want him to share.

She had to find him. Her future as a cop rested on it.

However, for the first time in her life, her job wasn't her number-one priority. Zeke Monroe was.

Chapter Twenty-one

SHONI paced in the limned darkness of Zeke's cabin. After deciding she'd only be wasting time by driving all over the city to search for Zeke, she'd returned to his place. There was no sign that he'd been there since he'd left that morning.

She poured herself another cup of coffee and sat on the couch in the living room, lit only by the moon's glow coming in the massive windows. Removing her Glock from the holster on her belt, she set it on the end table within easy reach. As much as it hurt to admit, she couldn't afford to trust Zeke again.

Although Zeke's betrayal burned like acid, she couldn't help but recall his heat and passion when they'd made love. She thought it had meant more to him than a one-night stand, but obviously it hadn't. She was grateful she hadn't uttered the three words that had been so close to her lips. If she had, her humiliation would've been complete. At least this way, she could salvage some of her pride.

It was close to eight o'clock when Shoni heard tires

crunching over the freezing slush. Either it was Zeke or someone looking for Zeke. She curled her fingers around the Glock and waited in the darkness. Her heart pounded and sweat slicked her palms, but it wasn't fear. Instead, it was a baffling array of anger, concern, deceit, and desire. She concentrated on the anger.

Footsteps pounded on the porch and the door swung open. The dark figure stepped inside and closed the door. He flicked on the light switch and froze when he spotted her, the Glock aimed at his chest.

"Shoni."

Even after Zeke had betrayed her, she wanted him with an overwhelming need that made her tremble. Which only made her more furious. She stood but remained by the sofa, keeping some distance between them. Although she wasn't a lightweight when it came to self-defense, she knew he far outclassed her fighting abilities.

"Monroe." Ice was warmer than her tone.

"I can explain." He took a step toward her.

Shoni raised her weapon. "Don't."

He halted, his gaze on the gun. "You don't need that."

"Because I can trust you?"

Zeke had the grace to glance away. "I'm sorry."

Her heart fracturing, she said, "Save it, Monroe. Down on your knees, hands behind your head."

Anger overcame his remorse. "Am I under arrest?"

"I'm taking you in for questioning."

"Why can't we do that here?"

Shoni wanted nothing more than to keep the questioning unofficial, but he'd given her no choice. She had to go by the book this time. "On your knees, Monroe. Now!"

He stared at her a moment longer, then knelt and cupped the back of his head. The position drew his coat taut against his chest and shoulders. She fought the urge to kneel in front of him, press herself against him, and place her hands on his firm flesh. . . .

"You're making a mistake," he said, more disappointed than mad.

"You made the mistake." Shoni moved around him cautiously, keeping her weapon trained on him. However, she knew it was a hollow gesture. No matter how hurt and angry she was, she could never shoot him.

She cuffed one wrist, then the other, and was surprised when he didn't try to escape.

"Why are you doing this?"

And just like that, his question released the dam holding back her emotions. She sidestepped so she stood directly in front of him, glaring down at him. "Why the hell did you leave this morning? No note, no explanation. Nothing!"

"I remembered something," he said.

Disbelief fed her rage. "So why didn't you just wake me up and tell me?"

"Because I needed to find out for myself first."

"Find out what? How to cover your ass?"

His eyes widened and his mouth gaped. "I had nothing to do with those fires."

"Save it for someone who gives a shit."

"What's wrong with you?"

She laughed and it came out even more bitter than she anticipated. "Me? What's wrong with me? Oh, that's rich, Monroe."

"I was trying to protect you."

"*I'm* the one who was assigned to protect you. Try again."

Zeke rolled his head as if trying to loosen neck muscles, but his jaw clenched. "The arsonist. I recognized him. Steve Paridot."

Shoni started. This was the second time she'd heard that name today. "What about him?"

"He works for Paladin Security. In fact, he recruited me. I've known him for nearly ten years."

Was this simply another ploy to throw her off the track? "Why would he be starting fires?"

Zeke shook his head in frustration. "I don't know."

Shoni wanted to believe him, wanted to more than she'd wanted anything in a very long time. But he'd already tricked her once. "Maybe the two of you decided to make some extra money on the side. Paridot's brother-in-law was probably fairly generous with his insurance payoff. But why Markoff? Why kill him?"

"What the hell are you talking about?"

Shoni wanted to close her eyes, wanted to sleep and wake up and find out this was all a nightmare. Except for the making love with Zeke part. "The third fire. The warehouse it destroyed was owned by Paridot's brother-in-law. There was a hefty payoff."

"I didn't even recognize Paridot when that fire happened."

"So you say."

"My word was good enough when I was John McClane."

The reminder of how fully she'd been sucked in fed her temper. "Well, I know better now, don't I? Get up."

Zeke stared at her a moment longer, then struggled to his feet. Shoni's grip tightened on her weapon to keep from helping him. She motioned toward the door with the gun barrel. "Let's go."

"Where?"

"The police station."

"But—"

"Now, Monroe."

"You're making a mistake."

"The only mistake I made was trusting you. Move it."

Zeke crossed to the door, but with his hands cuffed behind him, he couldn't open it. Shoni carefully reached out to turn the knob and swing the door inward. Zeke moved through the doorway onto the porch and halted. Shoni followed him outside into the cold evening air.

"My coat," she said, impatient with herself.

Zeke sighed and turned at the same moment a rifle cracked. A bullet thunked into the door.

Instinct sent Shoni diving to the porch. She slammed into Zeke, who'd done the same. Zeke rolled onto his knees. "Into the house," he shouted.

Shoni followed the command without hesitation and scuttled back inside. Another shot sent wood splinters flying in her face. Zeke rolled in behind her and sprang to his feet with surprising skill, considering his hands were at his back. He used a shoulder to slam the door and pressed himself against the wall to the left of it.

"You all right?" he asked Shoni.

She glanced up at him and her breath was sucked from her chest at the concern in his face. "Yeah. Fine."

"Your face is bleeding."

A tickling sensation down her cheek brought her hand to her face. On her fingers was blood. "It's nothing. Probably from a wood splinter." She raked her gaze across him. "You?"

He grimaced. "Other than skinned knees, I'll live."

Another shot shattered the window above Shoni and she dropped down, covering her head.

Zeke slid down the wall to the floor beside her. "Get these off me."

Indecision froze her.

"Shoni, you have to let me go."

"Why?"

"Gee, maybe because a sniper is shooting at us."

His sarcasm snapped Shoni out of her indecisiveness. "How do I know that isn't your buddy Paridot out there? That you and he didn't plan this?"

Zeke rolled his eyes. "Why would I do that? If I wanted

to get rid of you, I could've done it while you were sleeping in my bed."

Her face burned. Shoni had been so certain he had played her for a fool that she was ignoring reason. She stuck her hand in her jeans pocket and tugged out the key. "It's probably the same person who shot at you the night you saw the arsonist."

"Steve Paridot."

She nodded and fumbled with the cuffs. "So did he burn the warehouses because Paladin ordered him to, or did he do it on his own?"

Zeke rubbed his now-bare wrists. "That's the ten million dollar question."

"Is Paridot trying to kill you because you saw him?"

"Probably. But I have this feeling there's more to it than that." Frustration edged his voice.

Another shot rang out and Zeke lunged at Shoni, covering her body with his. For a split second, she thought he was attacking her, but the protective shell he formed over her quickly dispelled the notion. His weight and scent surrounded her. She should've been pissed by his Neanderthal move, but her reaction wasn't even in the same ballpark as anger. Before she could figure out what she was feeling, he eased himself off her.

"I'm thinking my amnesia wasn't accidental," Zeke said.

It didn't take long for Shoni to connect the dots. "Someone was out to get you before any of the warehouses were torched."

Zeke nodded grimly. "You gonna call 911?"

Shoni blinked and her face warmed with chagrin. That should've been her immediate thought when the shots began. She quickly punched in the three numbers on her cell phone. As she explained the situation to the operator, Zeke scrambled across the room and up the stairs to the loft. He returned just as she was ending the call. In his hand was a pistol. She didn't know if she should be angry or relieved.

"Do you think he's still out there?" she asked, tabling her confusion for now.

Zeke shrugged, but his jaw muscle clenched. "If he is, I'll find him."

Crouched low, he started to move toward the back door. She grabbed his sleeve, halting his progress. "The police are on the way. Wait for them."

"By the time they get here, he'll be long gone."

Shoni knew he was right, but damned if she was going to let him risk his life alone. "I'll go with you."

Zeke grabbed her shoulders and brought his face within inches of hers. The intensity of his gaze held her captive. "No. You stay here and stay down. This is my problem, not yours."

"The hell it is. The person out there tried to kill me, too. Not to mention he's clearly a suspect in *my* arson case."

"I'm trained for this kind of thing. And if I'm worried about you, I'm going to get one or both of us killed." The steely passion in his eyes softened, melted to warm concern. "I don't want you getting hurt or worse."

She wanted to argue, wanted to tell him the same held true for him. But the determination chiseled in his granite features told her it would be a pointless argument. Besides, he was right, damn it. A SEAL's training trumped a cop's any day.

His gaze searched her face, the look in his eyes feeling like a tender caress. Without warning, he pressed his lips to hers, a savage, possessive kiss. Then, just as quickly, he was gone.

Shoni stared after him, her mind hazed and her body keyed. A rifle shot snapped her out of the moment and she crab-walked back to the wall and pressed her back firmly against it.

"Be careful," she whispered, the words both a prayer and an order.

* * *

HUNDREDS of training sessions and countless assignments had honed Zeke's skills as a predator. He moved through the darkness with the advantage of being on home ground. However, the numerous trees afforded too many possible perches for a sniper.

Just as he came to the corner of the cabin, another shot rang out. He spotted a flash of light. It wasn't enough to pinpoint an exact location, but it gave him a starting point.

Keeping low, he crawled along the ground. His clothing soaked up the moisture, and before long, he shivered from the cold dampness against his skin. But he'd survived far worse conditions with far less important outcomes. This time he was fighting to save Shoni's life, and that alone gave him the impetus to win this battle.

Once in the dark shelter of the trees, Zeke rose, his back against an oak trunk to camouflage his movements. Uncertain which direction to continue, he remained motionless, bending his knees slightly so they weren't locked in place. He listened and heard the familiar hum of far-off traffic and the crackle of dead leaves shifting with the wind's whims. But nothing from the sniper.

A few minutes later Zeke's patience was rewarded with the almost inaudible slide of metal over metal, followed by a familiar click. A rifle's bolt-action mechanism. Although his eyes had adjusted to the lack of light, he could see only degrees of darkness. He'd give a month's wages for a pair of night vision goggles.

The next rifle shot blasted, and only Zeke's experience kept him from shutting his eyes against the sharp explosion. The light burst wasn't far away, maybe fifteen yards to his right. He ducked low and used the same shadows he'd cursed earlier to hide his approach. A breeze carried the scent of gun oil and Zeke knew he was close.

From twenty feet away, he spotted his quarry. Not in a

tree, but on a slight rise with a clear view of Zeke's cabin. The sniper was prone on the ground, the rifle barrel propped on a tripod.

Zeke took a deep breath and began a stealthy advance toward his target. A flare of light out of the corner of his vision brought his head up. While Zeke had been coming after the sniper, a second person had been moving in to torch his cabin.

With Shoni inside it.

A siren wailed, the volume rising as it neared. The sniper jumped to his feet, grabbed his rifle, and ran. Propelled by ingrained training, Zeke took two long strides after the shooter, but fear for Shoni stopped him. He spun around and crashed through the underbrush, branches and thorns tugging at his clothing and slapping his face, but he didn't slow. His toe caught a root and he stumbled, curling into a protective roll. Desperation brought him to his feet immediately and he kept running.

The front of the cabin was in flames by the time he made it to the driveway. The stench of gasoline struck him, and he flashed back to the night he'd seen the arsonist. "Shoni," he shouted frantically.

Unable to get close to the porch, he raced around to the side, to the door that led to the breezeway. The fire's heat drove him back. Acrid smoke clogged his throat and he coughed as his heart thundered in his chest. He'd already lost two loved ones to fire; he wasn't going to lose another.

Skirting around the burning cabin, he saw more flames. They hadn't reached the back entrance yet. With his forearm up to protect his face, he plunged through the smoke and shoved open the door. Heavy gray smoke billowed through the kitchen.

"Shoni," he hollered, ignoring the burn in his throat and chest. "Shoni, where are you?"

Only the rumbling rush of the fire, spreading and devouring everything in its path.

Zeke held out an arm, feeling his way through the dangerous cloud. "Shoni!"

"Over here."

Her voice, though faint, nearly sent Zeke to his knees. "Where are you?"

"Living room." *Cough.* "Coming t-to kitchen." Another round of coughing.

The smoke grew heavier, and this time Zeke voluntarily dropped to his knees and crawled toward the living room. He spotted Shoni, also on her knees, moving toward him. Her head was down and it was obvious she was struggling to breathe.

Zeke scrambled over to her. She lifted her head and tears trailed down her cheeks. She opened her mouth as if to speak, but a spate of coughing came out instead.

"Don't try to talk. Just breathe," Zeke said, fighting the urge to cough. Flames filled the room behind her. He grabbed her hand. "When I say go, stand up and run like hell."

Shoni gave him a weak nod.

"Go!" Zeke rose and pulled Shoni up. She stumbled along behind him. Roiling smoke covered the back door. As they drew nearer, flames engulfed one side. No time to waste.

He dived through the doorway, drawing Shoni with him. Out in the cool, fresh air, Zeke collapsed to his knees and Shoni went down beside him. For the next couple of minutes, they did nothing but struggle to drag in untainted air.

Regaining his breath first, Zeke framed Shoni's face in his hands and raised it. Her cheeks were damp and sooty, with blood trailing down her left one, and her hair was a tangle of curls, but she'd never looked more beautiful. "Are you all right?"

She nodded. "I'll live."

Although the raspy words were meant to reassure him, they only served to remind him how close he'd come to losing her. The fierce need to protect her overwhelmed him, and he wrapped his arms around her, as if his embrace would stop any harm from coming to her.

Her arms came around his waist. "I'm right here," she whispered hoarsely, as if reading his thoughts.

He laid his chin on the crown of her head, smelling the acrid smoke in her hair and remembering anew her close call. He faced the cabin and watched the fire engulf his home.

They destroyed his home and nearly killed Shoni. They took away his memories. They—

A uniformed police officer approached them warily, his hand on his holstered weapon. "Are you two all right?"

Shoni raised her head, but Zeke answered. "Yeah, we're fine."

"What happened here?"

Zeke and Shoni pushed themselves to their feet. "Detective Alexander, Norfolk PD," she said with a smoke-bruised voice.

Since this was Shoni's venue, he hung back and let her take the lead. They followed the patrolman around to the front just as the fire truck arrived.

An EMT cleaned and bandaged the cut beneath Shoni's eye. Zeke leaned against the patrol car, half listening to Shoni give the police a sanitized version of what happened, leaving out the part about him in handcuffs, as well as the probable connection to the arsonist.

She leaned against the car beside him, her arm pressed to his. "I'm sorry, Zeke," she said softly.

He shrugged. "It's only a house. I can rebuild. I wasn't around to save Tiffany and Chelle, and I would've traded a thousand houses just to have them back. This time, I was able to save you, and losing my house is a damned small price to pay."

Shoni's gaze dropped to her feet. "I'd better call my lieutenant and let him know what's happening."

Once she was away from the spray and hiss of water, the

firemen's shouts, and the crackle of radios, she punched in her boss's cell phone number. He answered on the fourth ring.

"Shoni Alexander, sir." After Tyler's harsh words earlier that day, it was better to keep things strictly professional. "I found Zeke. The sniper came after us. He got away, but he or an accomplice set fire to Zeke's home."

Tyler cussed loudly and creatively. "Are you and Monroe all right?"

"Some smoke inhalation. It could've been a lot worse. The police and fire department are here now. We've given our statements to the police and it looks like Zeke's home is a complete loss."

"I'll send Raff and Delon out there, since this attack is probably related to the murder at the condo complex," Tyler said. "Is Ian Convers on his way? We'll need to know if this fire was started by the same arsonist."

Shoni assumed the fires were related, but assumptions held no sway in a court of law. "I'll call him when I hang up."

"After you do that, you get yourself and Monroe back to the station, where you'll both be safe. Monroe probably isn't involved with the fires, but he's your only witness and somebody obviously wants him dead. Would help if he'd tell us who."

Shoni stifled a wave of annoyance. "I need an arrest warrant issued for Steve Paridot, an employee of Paladin Security."

"Why?"

"Zeke remembered why the arsonist looked familiar. He worked with him." She decided not to tell him that Paridot was also a friend of Zeke's and arouse Tyler's suspicions once more.

"Is he certain?"

"Are you afraid your buddy at Paladin will be pissed?" She must be more exhausted than she thought to be baiting her lieutenant. But what did she have to lose? Her job was already on the bubble.

The long silence made her wonder if she'd lost cell phone reception.

"I'm going to forget you asked me that," Tyler said, his voice low. "I'll have the warrant issued. But if Monroe is lying, it'll be your ass."

"It always has been, Lieutenant."

"Get yourself and Monroe back to the station now."

"Yes, sir."

A long pause. "I'm glad you're all right, Shoni." Tyler hung up.

Shoni stared at her phone. She disliked being thrown off balance, but couldn't deny she appreciated his concern. It had to be difficult for Bob to straddle the line between boss and friend.

She called Ian, then told the fire chief that the arson inspector was on his way. She also let the patrolmen know two detectives would be arriving.

Shoni paused to study Zeke before returning to him. He leaned against a black-and-white, his arms crossed over his chest as he stared at the fire that encompassed his home. There were ripples of John McClane in his deceptively relaxed stance and guarded expression. And just like John McClane, Zeke Monroe now had no home.

Taking a deep, shaky breath, she joined him. "Come on. Let's go."

He dragged his gaze from the fire. "Where?"

"The station. For protection."

He turned his attention back to the flames. "I want them, Shoni."

It took her a few moments to figure out who he meant. "We'll get them. We have a name now."

"That's all you have. Paridot won't talk."

Shoni suspected he was right. "Come on."

She headed to the police-issued car and Zeke followed

her silently. Once in the car, she checked her watch. Ten twenty. It felt later. Much later.

She drove away, the orange glow fading in her rearview mirror until it disappeared completely.

"Thanks," she said.

Oncoming headlights illuminated the confusion in his expression. "For what?"

"Saving my life. I don't think I would've found a way out of there on my own."

Zeke shrugged and turned away.

"Did you get a look at the shooter?" Shoni asked, suddenly realizing she'd forgotten about the sniper.

"No. I got within about twenty feet, but couldn't make out any details. As soon as he heard the sirens, he ran off." He paused. "The fire was started by a second person."

"How can you be sure?"

"I saw the sniper when the fire was started. He was nowhere near the house."

Anger pulsed through her. "Why didn't you tell the cops?"

He shrugged. "Same reason you didn't mention the other attempts on our lives, and the other fires."

Shoni's cell phone buzzed and annoyance flushed her features. She snatched the phone from the dashboard where she'd tossed it. "Alexander," she said curtly.

"Lainey's missin'."

Chapter Twenty-two

SHONI'S irritation fled at the sound of Estelle's worried voice, and she pulled over to the side of the road. "How long has she been gone?"

"Over an hour."

"She's probably out with friends."

"No. Mishon sent her to the store. It's only a block away. She shoulda been back by now."

She glanced at Zeke, who was gazing at her in confusion. "I'm sure she's fine."

"Is Johnny there?"

Shoni handed the phone to Zeke.

As he talked to Estelle, Shoni got back on the road. She listened to Zeke's side of the conversation, which wasn't much more than a grunt or two every once in a while. Clearly Estelle was doing most of the talking. Finally Zeke finished the call.

"Drive to Estelle's motel," he said.

"We're going to the station."

"Not until I know Lainey is all right."

"She hasn't been missing long. She's probably with friends."

"Or her mother's pimp snatched her."

Startled, Shoni glanced at Zeke and, despite the darkness, spotted his furrows of worry. "Where did that come from?"

Zeke scrubbed a hand across his face, his palm rasping his evening whiskers. "The night we met, in the alley. Those three men were Mishon's pimp and two of his goons. They were trying to take Lainey."

"Why?" As soon as she asked the question, she knew. Her blood iced. "Son of a bitch."

"Yeah." Zeke stared straight ahead but his fists pressed against his thighs. "You know what'll happen to her if he gets her."

Shoni wished she didn't, but she'd seen too many pictures of lost and found little girls. The found pictures usually told a horror story. She kept her gaze aimed out the windshield as she drove. What if Zeke used Lainey's disappearance to make his own getaway? Zeke had told her the sniper had run off. Or had Zeke let him escape? For all she knew, Zeke had started the fire that destroyed his cabin.

Shoni's first impression of Zeke—John McClane—had been that of a protector. He protected Lainey, Estelle, and Mishon. He'd even protected Shoni. Could a man like that be a murderer?

"Mishon came home early tonight," Zeke began. "It's a Friday night. Jamar wouldn't have let her take the night off without a very good reason. Estelle said Mishon sent Lainey to the store as soon as she got home, then disappeared into her room. When Estelle checked on her, Mishon was higher than a kite."

If she and Zeke went after Jamar, she could very well be throwing her job away. She'd joined the police force to help people, to make sure the guilty were punished, but lately it seemed only the innocent suffered. Innocent people like her mother. And now maybe Lainey.

No, she couldn't let another innocent life be lost.

"Don't make me regret this."

Zeke grasped her hand and squeezed it gently. "Thank you."

When they arrived at the motel, Estelle answered the door immediately. Her expression was drawn, her eyes haunted. She grabbed hold of Zeke's arm. "You have to find her."

Zeke patted the woman's shoulder. He wasn't accustomed to reassuring the tough-as-nails woman, but it was clear Estelle was scared. "We will. Where's Mishon?"

Estelle pointed to a closed door. "In there."

"Stay here."

Estelle nodded, but appeared lost and uncertain.

Shoni took her arm and helped her to a chair. "We'll find Lainey. You just sit here and try to relax."

Zeke led the way to the bedroom door. The knob turned in his hand and he pushed the door open.

Fully dressed, Mishon lay on the bed. Zeke crossed to her and checked her pupils, while Shoni set two fingers against the girl's wrist.

"Slow but steady," she said.

"She's so out of it, she probably doesn't know where she is," Zeke said in disgust. He patted Mishon's cheeks, slapping them a little harder until the girl's eyelids flickered open.

She attempted to bat away Zeke's hands, but her coordination was nonexistent. "Wh-what?"

"Where's Lainey?" he asked.

Mishon's eyes drifted shut. Zeke slapped her again, not hard enough to hurt but enough to grab her attention. "Leave me 'lone."

"Not until you tell us where Lainey is."

"Who?"

"Your daughter. Lainey."

Mishon stared past Zeke, and he had no idea if she was lost in a drug-induced haze again or trying to answer him. A tear trickled from the corner of her eye and disappeared into her hair. "Gone."

"Lainey's gone?"

"N-needed . . ."

Zeke grabbed her skinny shoulders and shook her. "Needed what?"

"S-sick. C-couldn't work."

"You needed a fix?" Shoni asked, her voice surprisingly gentle.

Another tear leaked from Mishon's eyes. "J-Jamar. P-promised he'd t-take care of her."

"So you sent Lainey out so Jamar could grab her?" Zeke could barely speak past his rage.

Mishon closed her eyes and buried her head in the pillow. "Had t-to."

Zeke clung precariously to his control as he spoke in a low, shaking voice. "She traded her own daughter for drugs."

Shoni's hand settled on his arm, her fingers long and slender, capable, strong. "It's not the first time it's happened, and it won't be the last." Her grip tightened. "But this child won't end up on a Missing poster."

Zeke released Mishon, absently noticing that his hands trembled.

"Do you know where Jamar hangs out?" Shoni asked him.

Zeke took a deep breath, tried to think, to remember those nights when he couldn't sleep and had wandered the streets. Because Mishon was Estelle's granddaughter, he'd watched out for her as much as he could. He'd drawn the line at standing outside doors of cheap motels while Mishon did her job, but knew her favorite corner and where she met Jamar.

"Bar called Neons. Not far from the rattrap hotel where Mishon usually does her business," Zeke replied.

"We'll check out the store first, see if anyone saw Lainey, then Neons," Shoni said.

Worried about Lainey and livid at Mishon, Zeke was grateful for Shoni's steadiness.

Back in the motel's living room, they went to Estelle. The older woman's eyes were red and puffy.

"What store did Lainey go to?" Shoni asked.

"The gas station on the corner," Estelle replied, then said in disgust, "Mishon wanted a candy bar. I shoulda known somethin' wasn't right."

Zeke laid a hand on her shoulder. "We'll find Lainey. I promise."

Estelle patted his hand. "I know you'll do your best, Johnny."

But Zeke hadn't done his best to protect them. Once he learned who he was, he'd abandoned them. Shoni was the one who'd reminded him to call Estelle, to let her know he'd gotten his memory back.

Feeling ashamed and guilty, Zeke headed to the door. Shoni followed, and they strode down the sidewalk toward the convenience store. Zeke slipped into soldier mode, his senses alert and his footsteps stealthy. However, neither he nor Shoni spotted any sign of Lainey.

Once in the store, Shoni walked up to the counter, pulling out her badge. Zeke let her interview the clerk while he checked each aisle and the bathroom for Lainey. Nothing.

"Thank you," Shoni was saying to the slack-jowled man behind the counter.

"Anything?" he asked as they exited the store.

Shoni shook her head, and even in the dim streetlight, he spied the pinched creases around her mouth. "He did notice three men loitering in front of the place an hour or two ago. Drove a new black Lexus."

"That's what Jamar has."

With muscles stretched taut, he and Shoni jogged down the block to her car. He'd barely sat down before Shoni swung out into the late night traffic.

"A lot can happen to a little girl in two hours," Zeke said, his voice husky.

"They aren't going to hurt her," Shoni said firmly. "The men interested in Lainey will want her untouched."

Zeke swallowed back a rise of bile. "I don't know if that's reassuring or not."

Shoni spared him a glance. "Hang on to it, Zeke. It's all we have until we find her."

Zeke ground a fist into his thigh and stared out the side window.

The traffic was sparse enough that Shoni didn't have to use the siren, but she did break all the speed limits on her way to Neons. On one side of the bar was an adult store advertising everything XXX-rated, and on the other, a tattoo and piercing parlor. On a late Friday night, the area buzzed with young and old, as well as prostitutes for whatever side of the fence you leaned.

All the parking slots were full in the block radius around the bar, and Shoni ended up parking near the Ecstasy Hotel, where they'd found Mishon the night the apartment burned. Shoni checked her Glock and ensured she had an extra clip in her coat pocket.

Shoni's breath misted in the cool night air. As she and Zeke neared Neons, the number of pedestrians increased, many of them either drunk or high, or both. It was nothing Shoni hadn't seen a hundred times during her police career, but unlike many of her colleagues, she never got used to it.

Zeke stuck his arm out, halting her before she could enter Neons. "I should go in alone. I've been around here. Some people might recognize me. They'll trust me."

As the cop, Shoni should insist she do it. But he was right. A woman dressed as she was would be singled out immediately as the police. Nothing clammed up these people faster than a cop.

She nodded reluctantly. "All right, but you get in any kind of trouble, and I'm coming in."

"Once I know something, I'll come out and get you."

"You damned well better," she said, her gaze moving across his determined features.

A smile eased his granite expression and touched his eyes. "Yes, ma'am."

Shoni grabbed two fistfuls of his jacket and stood on her tiptoes to press her lips to his. After a moment of surprised hesitation, Zeke kissed her back, his tongue sweeping into her mouth.

Shoni forgot about the thumping music and the cackle of voices and laughter spilling out from Neons. She forgot about Lainey and Jamar. She forgot everything but the taste and feel of Zeke.

He drew back, and the rush of cold air against her face slapped her back to the present. With a stifled moan, she pressed her forehead against his chest. Zeke was dangerous, but not because of his military background. Instead, it was because of what he did to her. If she let herself go, she'd bury herself so completely within Zeke Monroe, she'd never want to come out. And Shoni Alexander had never, ever allowed herself to surrender that much to a man.

A finger under her chin brought her head up and her gaze met Zeke's eyes, which appeared a dark, mesmerizing blue.

"Once Lainey is safe, and the arson case is tied up, you and I are going to take some time off. The two of us. Together," Zeke said, his voice rumbling through her and leaving pockets of heat deep within her.

Shoni didn't argue. She was in way over her head already.

"Wait here," Zeke said softly. He continued to stare at her lips, then abruptly released her and strode into Neons.

Shoni shoved her hands into her pockets as a chill chased through her. However, she had no idea if it came from the inside or the outside. Leaning against the building didn't seem to be a smart plan, so she walked past the XXX-rated store and down the alley. Behind the building was a parking area large enough for a dozen cars. All the spaces were taken.

Shoni turned to go back to the street when she spotted a shiny black car on the far end of the parking area. She glanced around. No one but herself lurked in the shadows. Slipping between the building and the cars, she crept down to get a better look at the vehicle. A new black Lexus.

Jamar.

And Zeke was inside alone.

Shoni didn't bother with stealth as she dashed out of the alley. As she approached Neons, intent on charging into the bar, Zeke stepped out. She stumbled, and he caught her arms.

"What is it?" he demanded, his gaze sweeping across her.

"Did you see Jamar?"

Zeke's concern changed to disgust. "He's not in there."

"Yes, he is. I saw his car parked in the back."

"He wasn't at his usual table and the bartender hadn't seen him."

"He probably came in the back. Didn't want to draw attention to himself with Lainey. He's more than likely in some back room."

Zeke was a welcome presence beside her as they jogged around to Neons' back door. Bass drum beats pulsed through the walls. Shoni found the door slightly ajar. The last person must not have pulled it shut. Lucky break. She held her Glock between her palms.

Zeke stepped past her to enter first and Shoni yanked him back. "You're not a cop, Zeke. Stay behind me."

He muttered something that Shoni suspected she didn't want to hear, but let her take the lead. She swung open the door and stepped into the dim interior. Pressing herself against the wall, she felt Zeke beside her do the same. A closed door ahead on the right caught her eye. She pointed to it and Zeke nodded.

As they crept down the hallway, the noise from the bar crowd increased. Fortunately, the band had taken a break. They reached the door and Shoni shifted to the other side of it. She pressed her ear to the wood and heard a man's voice, but she was unable to distinguish the words or his identity. Then a childish, high-pitched tone rang out. Lainey.

Shoni caught Zeke's gaze and grimly nodded. "She's in there. One man for sure."

"Let's get her out." Zeke's voice was quiet but intense.

"No," she said firmly. "I call for backup. We can't afford to have these guys get off on a technicality."

Zeke's eyes flashed with impatience. "The most important thing is to save Lainey."

Shoni understood, but she'd been a cop trying to see justice meted out for too long. Although she hated that her mother's killer fell through the cracks, justice was ingrained too deeply within her.

She gripped Zeke's wrist. "Listen to me. If we do that and Jamar gets off, he'll just try again. Either with Lainey or some other innocent girl."

Zeke's glare gradually softened and his shoulders slumped. He nodded. Breathing a silent sigh of relief, Shoni reached for her phone.

An angry bellow erupted behind the door. Zeke didn't hesitate. He kicked in the door. Cursing his macho ass, Shoni jumped into the office behind him.

Jamar had his hands pressed to his groin, and it was obvious Lainey had inflicted the blow. It might have been funny if his two hired guards—who were reaching for their guns—weren't with him.

"Freeze! Norfolk PD," Shoni commanded.

One obeyed; the other didn't. His hand dipped into his coat, and as his arm came forward, Zeke kicked his wrist, sending the gun flying. Zeke swung his leg around, faster than Shoni could follow, and his heel snapped the man's head back. He collapsed to the floor without a sound.

Shoni trained her weapon on the remaining guard and Jamar. "On your knees, hands on your head. Both of you," she ordered.

Jamar glared at her, but did as she said, as did the hired muscle. She nodded to Zeke, who frisked them both, removing a gun from each of them. He set the guns near Shoni, who gave him her set of regulation handcuffs and another set of PlastiCuffs. Zeke used the plastic ties on Jamar and the metal cuffs on the thug.

Once the two men were restrained, Zeke went over to Lainey, who launched herself into his arms. He caught her and hugged her close as her skinny arms wound around his neck.

Shoni's heart skipped a beat. The picture of Lainey and Zeke was like a reprint of the one from the night she'd met John McClane.

"Did they hurt you?" Zeke asked.

Lainey leaned back slightly and shook her head. "No. They talked about bad things, though." Her face lit with a huge smile. "I knew you'd come, John, just like in the movies." She hugged him again, burying her face in the crook of his neck.

Shoni's throat tightened at the relief and affection in Zeke's face. "Hey, I hate to break up the reunion, but someone should probably call the police."

"You don't have anything on me," Jamar stated with a sneer. "I just found Lainey and was trying to help her get back home."

"You're a liar," Lainey said, her dark eyes fierce. "You were going to let bad-ass men do things to me."

Shoni flinched at Lainey's language, but figured the girl had heard far worse in her young life.

"We've got you for kidnapping," Shoni said to the pimp.

"And assault. These were the men who attacked me in the alley five nights ago," Zeke said.

Had it been only five nights ago? It felt like she'd known Zeke for much longer. Her mother might say in another lifetime.

Shoni shook away both the thoughts of her mother and the preposterous notion of past lives. She took out her cell phone and called for assistance.

It was less than ten minutes later when the cacophony in the bar was interrupted by the arrival of two squad cars and an ambulance.

The man Zeke had taken out regained consciousness before the ambulance arrived, but was taken to the hospital, accompanied by one of the patrol cars. Shoni told the two remaining officers what had happened and, after ensuring the arrested men had their rights read to them, she had the patrolmen take the suspects and book them at the police station.

It was nearly two A.M. when she rejoined Zeke, who held a sleeping Lainey in his lap. "I'm jealous," Shoni said in a low voice so she wouldn't wake the girl.

A gentle smile curved Zeke's lips. "Don't be. You'll be sleeping in my arms soon enough."

Despite her bone-deep exhaustion, a shiver of desire quivered through her. "Sleeping is about all I'm up to," she admitted.

Zeke brushed his thumb across her cheek. "It's been a hell of a long day. Let's get Lainey back to Estelle's. Then we can get some rest."

Estelle was waiting for them when they arrived and led Zeke, who carried the slumbering girl in his arms, to one of the bedrooms. Shoni dropped onto the sagging sofa and laid her head back against the cushion. Although beyond tired, satisfaction teemed through her.

No matter what she'd told Tyler earlier, she didn't want to lose her job. As much as she cared for Zeke—might even love him—she couldn't imagine not being a cop. But what she'd done—getting personally involved with a witness and basic insubordination—were definite grounds for suspension, or worse. And after her stunt with the patrol cop who didn't read the Miranda rights to her mother's killer, she was already on shaky ground.

Her future as a cop hinged on the arson case. Thanks to Zeke, they now knew the arsonist was a Paladin Security employee, which made the suspect a professional instead of a simple fire starter. So why had he used gasoline instead of an incendiary device?

The reason was brilliant in its simplicity. To throw off the investigation. The deception would've worked, too, if not for Zeke seeing him.

She felt more than heard Zeke return to the living room, and opened her eyes. He lifted his arm and wrapped it around her shoulders, tugging her close. She snuggled into his side and smelled the acrid scent of smoke in his clothing. Was it only a few hours ago that his place had been set afire?

"Estelle is tucking her in." He yawned and his jaw cracked. "I could fall asleep right here."

"I'm supposed to take you to the station."

Zeke pressed his lips together in a mulish expression. "Neither one of us is in any shape to be driving."

Shoni's resolve wavered. She could barely keep her eyes open, but she had a duty to attend to first. "All right, but I have to call Lieutenant Tyler."

She forced herself up and walked outside so she wouldn't disturb Estelle or Lainey. Tyler picked up on the fourth ring.

"Alexander, sir. We, uh, didn't make it to the station. We had a situation come up."

"What kind of situation?" Tyler demanded.

"A kidnapping. A little girl."

"What the hell—"

Shoni rubbed her aching brow. "I'll explain it all later, sir. Right now, I'm too tired to make sense."

"Where are you?"

"Safe in a motel."

Tyler let loose an imaginative run of cussing. Shoni wisely didn't interrupt.

"I want you both at the station bright and early tomorrow—this morning. Do I make myself clear?"

"Loud and clear, sir."

"Damn it, Shoni . . ." He seemed at a loss for words. "Just be careful."

Shoni closed her eyes and nodded. "I will."

She shut her phone and returned to Estelle's motel room.

"Everything okay?" Zeke asked, a hint of worry in his tone.

Shoni stifled a wave of hysterical laughter as she dropped down beside him on the couch. "That remains to be seen. We have to be downtown bright and early."

"A few hours of sleep are better than none." Zeke grinned crookedly. "I've gotten a lot less on SEAL missions."

Although he said it to inject some levity, Shoni couldn't conjure a smile. "At least you knew your enemies."

His own smile faded, and he kissed her brow. "And you know your allies."

Did she? At one time she thought she could count on Tyler, but his friendship with one of the founders of Paladin Security made him suspect. As much as she wanted to believe in Zeke, she couldn't. He'd skipped out on her once, and though she believed him, that he'd done it to protect her, she didn't know if she could ever fully trust him.

But she had to try. Her heart gave her no choice.

Estelle shambled into the living room and plopped into her chair. "She's sleepin' like a baby."

"She's a good girl, Estelle," Shoni said.

The older woman nodded. "I raised my own, then Mishon, and now Lainey. I'm thinkin' I finally got it right."

"It's not your fault Mishon did what she did," Zeke said.

Estelle's dark, work-worn hands twisted in her lap. "Will she be arrested?"

Shoni shrugged. "If Jamar implicates her, she could very well be booked as an accomplice."

The older woman lifted her chin and nodded curtly. "Good. That way she'll be forced to get some help."

Estelle was definitely a tough old bird, but she was tough for all the right reasons.

"You two are stayin' here tonight. That couch pulls out into a bed and you two is gonna use it." Estelle's eyes twinkled. "Don't seem that it'll be much hardship to share."

Shoni smiled self-consciously but Zeke only laughed.

"Thanks," he said.

Estelle waved a hand. "Ain't no problem." After she retrieved an extra blanket for them, she said good night.

Using the sofa's cushions as pillows, Shoni and Zeke settled on the thin mattress and threw the blanket over them. They'd removed their jackets and shoes, and Shoni had taken off her holster and gun.

"Not exactly how I pictured our second night together," Zeke said dryly.

Shoni, lying on her side, her back to Zeke's chest, smiled. "You're lucky there's a second night after that stunt you pulled yesterday morning."

"I suppose," he mumbled, his lips brushing her hair and his warm breath wafting across her neck.

Zeke's arm around her waist, anchoring them together, should've felt confining. Instead, Shoni snuggled closer and laced her fingers through his. Desire meandered through her like a lazy river, unlike the raging currents of the previous night. It was a warm, comfortable feeling with a rightness that should've frightened her, but didn't.

Before that realization could scare her, slumber claimed her.

Chapter Twenty-three

ZEKE bolted upright and fought to breathe.

"Zeke." The name was accompanied by a light press of fingers on his arm.

The remnants of his nightmare slid away. Only it wasn't a nightmare.

Sweat trickled down his brow and he used a wrist to wipe it away. "I know how I lost my memory."

"How?"

It was no longer dark, and the clock on the DVD player read seven twenty. "We both need coffee for this one."

Fifteen minutes later, they sat side by side on the sofa, the bed folded back within it, and cups of steaming coffee in their hands.

"You know about the allegations against some Paladin Security employees," Zeke began, his voice kept low so he wouldn't wake Estelle or Lainey.

She nodded. "Unlawful force against Iraqi civilians."

"It cost Paladin a contract, which they were counting on to pay for more arms and equipment from Markoff."

"They'd already signed a contract with Markoff."

"That's right. And Paladin was desperate to get out of it. Jensen was given the task of finding a way to do that."

"That's why he was meeting Gardner," Shoni said. "But why did you go with him?"

"I didn't figure that out until later. But all along, Jensen's plan was to offer Paladin services in exchange for dissolving the contract."

Shoni's eyes widened with comprehension. "Markoff's death. That was the payment."

Impressed by her intuitive leap, Zeke nodded. "The government contract Markoff was against bidding on was worth a hundred times more than the contract Paladin held with them. Get rid of Markoff's controlling vote, and the bid would go through."

"But even if they bid, it wasn't a sure thing."

"No, but I suspect a company like Markoff has connections within the government." Zeke took a sip of coffee and noticed his hand shook slightly.

Shoni stared down at her cooling coffee, her brows knit with consternation. "What about the other fires? Why were those set?"

"A cover for the real reason. The first fire was used to set the stage. The second, get rid of Markoff. The third, a smokescreen—excuse the pun," he said dryly. "And a chance for Paladin to make a little money."

"Paridot's brother-in-law."

"That's right."

"What about the fourth?"

"The developer is an old friend of Mark Jensen's. They served together."

"I knew there was a connection," Shoni said, her eyes bright. "Did they figure four was the most they could pull off?"

"Around here, yeah. But Jensen was planning to expand.

Paladin Security is floundering. He wanted to make sure it didn't go under."

"What about the other founder, Larry Wren? Does he know what his partner is doing?"

A corner of Zeke's lips lifted in a crooked grin. She obviously did her homework. "Larry was the money man. He didn't get involved in the day-to-day work."

Shoni appeared to be digesting it all. "So how did you find out about all of this?"

Zeke stood and topped their cups with fresh coffee. He sat back down, his hands wrapped around his cup. "Steve Paridot, Nick Bender, and myself were handpicked by Jensen to do the dirty work."

"Why did he pick you three?"

Zeke glanced down and a slight flush darkened his cheeks. "The three of us had a reputation for taking on the dirty work. When I first joined Paladin, I looked forward to getting into the action. I didn't care what happened to me, not after losing Tiffany and Chelle." He shrugged self-consciously. "I probably went a little crazy. Always ready for a firefight, and the longer the odds, the better."

"So what changed you?"

He stared at the slit of light coming in between the curtains. "I'm not sure. All I know is one day I woke up and realized if Tiff were alive, she wouldn't have recognized me. And I'd probably scare the hell out of my little girl." His vision blurred and he thumbed his eyes, not surprised to find moisture. "But Jensen and everyone else still saw me as Crazy Ass Monroe. And when Jensen described the plan to 'expand' our services, I knew I couldn't let it happen."

"Only they caught on to you," Shoni said softly.

"I knew the police wouldn't take me at my word. I needed proof. I got Sandra, the receptionist at Markoff, to get me printouts of e-mails between Gardner and Jensen. She gave me other information, too. Plus I found papers in

Jensen's office, contracts for the deals he was arranging. I made copies of them."

"So how did you end up on the street with no memory?"

Zeke furrowed his brow. "Steve asked me if I wanted to go to lunch with him and Nick. I said yes, and next thing I know, Nick's got a gun shoved into my side. They were going to shoot me then dump my body in the water. I managed to shove open the door and threw myself out." He took a deep breath and rubbed his jaw with a shaky hand. "Next thing I remember is waking up soaking wet on the wharf in the old warehouse district."

"You probably hit your head when you rolled out of the car and went into the water." Shoni's face paled. "You could've drowned."

"They must've thought I did. I didn't tell them anything, so they must've gone to my house looking for the proof." Zeke shook his head "They didn't find it. The papers are in my safe-deposit box at my bank."

"Why didn't you hand them over to the police? They could've gotten Jensen and Gardner for conspiracy."

"Jensen said he wasn't worried about the police. I assumed he had someone looking out for his interests."

Shoni's face paled. "Lieutenant Tyler. He and Jensen are old military buddies. Just like the developer is an old buddy. A whole network of them."

"Norfolk is full of military people and I'm sure your boss isn't the only ex-military on the force who knows Jensen. It doesn't mean they're all crooked."

Shoni wasn't convinced any more than Zeke. She glanced at the teapot-shaped clock on the wall. "Lieutenant Tyler will be in his office any time now. We can catch him there after we stop by the bank."

They gathered their things quietly. Zeke scribbled a thank you note for Estelle and left it on the table, along with Shoni's cell phone number.

Instead of going straight to the bank, Shoni drove to her

mother's condo. They were almost there when Shoni's cell phone buzzed. "Alexander."

Zeke tuned out the one-sided conversation as he watched the bland concrete scenery skim past. His mind wandered back to his destroyed home. The loss didn't hurt as badly as it might have. He'd lived with far less during those weeks on the street, and though he mourned the loss of his cabin, he was more than grateful for what wasn't lost—Shoni.

She ended the call and turned to Zeke. "That was Raff. He said they're still looking for connections between Paladin and the four fires. He was surprised and a little pissed that Delon had already found one between the developer and Jensen."

Zeke grinned. "Cops must be just as competitive as soldiers."

"And Raff is both—he was an Army Ranger before joining the PD."

At the condo, Zeke was grateful for a shower, but wished he had some clean clothes. He sighed. Just one of many things he'd have to replace in the days ahead.

Shoni, her hair damp, came out of her room wearing fresh clothes. She fastened her holster at the back of her belt and squatted down to adjust the ankle holster of her backup piece.

"When did you get that from your car?" Zeke asked, motioning to the second weapon.

Surprise and guilt flashed in her expression. She smiled, but the gesture appeared forced. "A couple of days ago."

Her vague answer set off his internal alarms.

She brushed past him and nabbed her jacket from a bar stool. "Let's get going. Do you have your safe-deposit key?"

Attributing his uneasiness to his lack of sleep, he dismissed it. He patted his jacket pocket. "Right here."

"Good. I have a feeling this arson case is about to be blown wide open."

The bank was located downtown. Since it was relatively early on a Saturday morning, Shoni was able to park directly in front of the bank. Out of habit, Zeke searched their surroundings. But nobody but he and Shoni knew about the safe deposit box, much less that they were stopping by this morning.

Zeke opened the glass door for Shoni and he followed her inside. Five minutes later, he thanked the bank clerk and joined Shoni in the lobby. He held up the manila envelope. "It's all here. All you need for your case."

Shoni smiled, but the gesture didn't touch her eyes. After her earlier excitement, why wasn't she thrilled to have the evidence needed to close her case?

They walked out of the bank. The morning remained quiet, with only a handful of pedestrians who'd ventured out to buy their overpriced lattes and espressos.

A man wearing a hoodie and jeans walked toward them, his hands jammed in the jacket's large front pocket. As he neared them, Zeke's sixth sense flared. The man's face was hidden by the hood, but Zeke had the impression it wasn't a college kid. Instead, someone older. Someone older, with his hands hidden.

The hooded man walked past them, and Zeke turned his head to follow him. The stranger abruptly turned, drawing a knife from the sweatshirt's pocket.

Zeke grabbed the man's wrist and forced his arm downward. A sharp sting across his thigh made him gasp and nearly sent him to his knees, but he clung to his attacker. Long-ingrained skills took control and he ignored the bleeding gash.

Zeke dug his fingers into the man's wrist, trying to get him to drop the weapon. His attacker was an inch or two shorter but was wider, solid muscle. In a fight where there was some distance between them, Zeke would have the advantage. But up close and personal, and with Zeke's wounds the heavier man had the advantage.

Using both hands, Zeke struggled to get him to drop the knife. But he left himself open, and the man shot his knee up into Zeke's gut, forcing the air from his lungs. As Zeke scrabbled for air, his wounded leg gave way.

A glint of silver arced toward him.

"Zeke. Drop!"

Learned reflexes didn't question the order. His muscles went limp and he fell to the ground.

Two shots rang out and Zeke flinched, but no new pain registered.

The assassin stumbled back, and a growing stain darkened the navy blue hooded sweatshirt. He fell against the side of the car and slid down, like a movie in slow motion. A red smear remained on the side of the car.

"How bad is it?"

He turned his head to see Shoni kneeling beside him, her worried gaze on the blood soaking his leg. "Hurts like a son of a bitch," he replied.

"And here I thought you Navy SEALs were all stoic and strong when it came to tiny little cuts," Shoni said, her voice wet and trembly.

Zeke shook his head. "Don't believe everything you see in the movies."

He started to push himself to a sitting position, and Shoni helped him with a hand on his back.

She glanced at the dead assassin but quickly turned away, her hand to her mouth. "He's the first. . . ."

It had been a long time since Zeke could say the same, but he remembered. He could never forget. He brushed her marblelike cheek with his thumb. "If you hadn't, he would've killed me."

She pressed her cheek into his palm for only a few seconds, as if needing his touch to gather her strength before drawing away. She stepped over Zeke and squatted down, staring at the dead man. Her hands shook as she drew the hoodie back from his face.

"Nick Bender," Zeke said, confirming what he'd suspected. He'd been prepared to have Bender, Paridot, and Jensen arrested, but he hadn't wished their deaths. And nothing could make him forget that at one time, he'd fought side by side with Bender and Paridot. "How did he knew we'd be here?"

Shoni's eyes widened and her face lost even more color. "There's only one other person who knew, and I was the one who told him."

Before Zeke could ask who it was, the police and an ambulance arrived.

As the EMTs took care of his injury, Zeke caught only glimpses of Shoni. She spoke with the police, describing what happened. Her face was drawn, but her eyes were steady and her voice firm. At one point she was on her cell phone and he suspected she was speaking with Tyler.

The EMTs brought out the stretcher to load him into the ambulance.

"No. I don't need a hospital. You said yourself it's not serious," Zeke argued.

"Half an inch deep and four inches long," the husky EMT said. "It needs stitches."

Zeke grinned. "It'll match the one on my arm, which I also didn't go to the hospital for. Just tie it up tight and I'll be fine."

After some more halfhearted arguments, the EMTs did as Zeke said. They had him sign a form saying he declined further assistance, and if he collapsed and died, he couldn't sue them.

The wound throbbed and burned, but he'd been hurt worse and had less care. He'd live. He hobbled over to Shoni, who was startled to see him.

"Shouldn't you be on your way to the hospital?" she asked.

He shrugged boyishly. "Refused to go."

"Seems you and John McClane have quite a bit in common."

"Including our good looks."

Despite her wan complexion, she smiled and rolled her eyes. "Modest, too."

Zeke shrugged, although he was happy to coax a smile from her. He reached into his jacket and pulled the envelope from the inner pocket. He handed it to her. "You'll need this for your case, Detective."

She accepted it, holding it between her hands. "It almost got you killed."

"Almost doesn't count. You have your evidence. Go get'em, tiger."

"We have most of it. There's still one issue that hasn't been resolved yet."

"The leak in the department."

Shoni nodded and gave him a weak smile. "You were right. Tyler wasn't the only ex-military who knew Jensen and the details of the case."

IT was after one o'clock when Shoni and Zeke stepped into the Violent Crimes Unit. There was a domino effect of ceased conversations. Obviously, the police grapevine already buzzed with Shoni's first fatal shooting. Voices started up again, the volume rising to pre-Shoni level.

Zeke gave her hand a reassuring squeeze and Shoni felt some of the tension seep from her muscles. For someone who'd always prided herself on handling things on her own, she appreciated Zeke's solid presence.

Her call to Tyler had confirmed her suspicions, although she took no pleasure in the trap that was being set to snare the leak.

"How're you doing?" Raff asked as they passed his desk.

She glanced down at the concern in his hazel eyes and

wondered how he hid it so well. Taking a deep breath, she baited the trap. "I blew it. We lost all the proof Zeke had against my suspects."

"I'm sorry, Shoni."

"Me, too."

They continued on to Tyler's office.

The scent of some divine coffee intensified as she approached his partially open door.

"Come in," Tyler said.

Her insides quivering, Shoni stepped inside and was reassured by Zeke's limping figure behind her.

"Sit down," Tyler said.

Shoni sank into a chair, then held out a hand to help Zeke lower himself into the other.

"I heard it was just a scratch," Tyler said to Zeke.

"Cut myself worse shaving."

Tyler cracked a grin. "Coffee?"

"You have to ask?" Shoni said with a half smile.

The lieutenant poured them each a cup. "Sumatra Goya. A hearty taste, and if it's roasted just right, there's a chocolate twist to the fruit overtones." He took a sip and smiled. "And this one is just right."

Although her stomach churned and her nerves jangled, Shoni tasted the coffee. She closed her eyes, allowing the flavors to play across her tongue. A slice of heaven before all hell broke loose.

She opened her eyes and caught fond amusement in Zeke's expression, and she was suddenly overwhelmed by gratitude for his calming presence. Shoni set her cup on the desk and reached behind her, pulling the envelope out of her waistband. She handed it to the lieutenant.

"Proof that Mark Jensen, Steve Paridot, and the late Nick Bender of Paladin Security were involved in a conspiracy of murder, attempted murder, insurance fraud, and arson," she said in a steady voice.

Tyler accepted the envelope and opened it. He glanced

through the papers and his expression grew stormy. "I've known Mark for years. I never would've believed he was capable of any of this." Tyler dropped the papers on his desk and swiveled slightly to gaze out the window. "He asked about the arson case a couple of weeks ago. I thought it was odd, since he knew how I felt about ongoing investigations. But he didn't pursue it, so it didn't even occur to me that he might be involved. Or that he would recruit one of my own detectives—another ex-military friend—to feed him information." Tyler looked like he didn't know whether to be angry or disillusioned.

"For all my jokes about his fashion taste, Raff had to get the money for those fancy suits someplace. I just never thought he might be dirty."

"Nobody did." Shoni nodded and took sip of her coffee. The phone suddenly rang, fracturing the silence. Shoni stood and moved to the window, stared up at the blue sky.

Tyler hung up the phone. "We got him." His voice didn't sound victorious, only old and tired.

A tear rolled down Shoni's cheek. Two comforting hands settled on her shoulders and she leaned back into Zeke's strength.

"Raff almost got you killed," she said to Zeke.

"And you. Don't forget about the bomb."

Another tear followed the first, and she dashed it away. She turned to Tyler. "What will happen to him?"

"That's up to IAD. But he'll probably be facing criminal charges." Tyler took a deep breath. "Delon's going to need a new partner. Interested in a full-time partner?"

Shoni drew back her shoulders. "I have to be cleared of the shooting first. Then I'll have to find out if I still have a job in Homicide."

Tyler glared at her. "It was a righteous shooting. And if anybody tries to steal you from my unit, they'll have a helluva fight on their hands."

"Thanks, Lieutenant. I'll have to think about it." She

smiled, and some of her sorrow lifted. "I'm not sure my eyes will survive Delon's shirts."

Tyler chuckled.

"I'm going to take your advice and take some time off once this case is wrapped up." Shoni glanced back at Zeke, and his roguish smile brought heat to her cheeks. "Zeke and I have some talking to do."

Tyler snorted, but couldn't hide the twinkle in his eyes. "Right. Talking. Finish your coffee, then get Monroe home. I'll get the arrest warrants issued for Jensen and Paridot, and have them picked up and booked." His expression turned grim. "I'm delivering Jensen's personally."

"I'm sorry."

"Don't be. The law isn't tailored to individuals. Friends, enemies, rich, poor." He paused. "Co-workers. It doesn't matter."

Shoni reached across the desk and laid her hand on Tyler's. "Thank you."

"Yeah, well, you can thank me by coming over for Thanksgiving dinner next week. Helen won't accept no for an answer." He glanced at Zeke. "You come, too, Monroe. We can swap war stories."

Zeke chuckled. "Yes, sir. I'd like that."

Zeke settled his hand on Shoni's waist and guided her out of Tyler's office. As they passed Raff's empty desk, Shoni kept her gaze straight ahead.

Chapter Twenty-four

Zeke didn't raise an eyebrow when Shoni drove them straight to her mother's condo. It was the place where it had all started, and it would be where it either ended or began anew. Besides, his place was smoking rubble.

"Sit down," she ordered once they were inside.

He didn't argue.

"Take off your pants."

That *did* cause an eyebrow to arch upward. "Finally."

Her face reddened. "Even if the spirit was willing, I suspect the flesh isn't up to it."

"Why don't we find out?"

She propped her hands on her slender hips and her eyes sparked. Despite himself, Zeke felt a jolt of lust. Cop. Woman. Lover. Sometimes as infuriating as hell; other times, as seductive as heaven.

He latched onto her hips, his hands settling over hers and his fingers curving around to her backside. She stumbled toward him, avoiding his injured leg, and used his shoulders to catch her balance.

"You're crazy, Zeke Monroe," she said, her eyes glittering.

"Better crazy than boring."

"No argument there." She leaned forward, her lips finding his.

Zeke deepened the kiss, sweeping his tongue into her mouth. He shifted his hands and cupped her ass, bringing her hips flush against his half-hard groin. The past twenty-four hours had sent enough adrenaline through him to wrestle an elephant, and he had a surefire way to put that adrenaline to a much better use.

Continuing to swirl his tongue in her sweet dampness, he used one hand to unzip her jeans. He slid his fingers between her trousers and silky panties, and rubbed her soft mound. She moaned deep in her throat and increased the pressure of her mouth on his.

The scent of her desire brought him to full hardness. He pushed aside her panties and dipped a finger into her hot heat. She bucked against his injured leg, and the pain put a serious crimp in his libido.

Panting and red-faced, Shoni retreated and zipped up. "Sorry, sorry."

Zeke laughed even as his wounded leg throbbed. "Don't be. I just overwhelmed you with my charms."

Shoni's amused smile softened and she studied him with a tender gaze. "You and John McClane."

"Which one?"

"John McClane first, then Zeke." She crossed her arms beneath her breasts. "John was a man stripped of everything but the basics. He's strong, protective, loving. Zeke is that same man but molded by his job, his family, and tragedy. I could have fallen in love with either of them, but together . . ." She lifted her chin. "I do love you. Both of you."

Zeke's breath stuttered in his throat. "That sounds pretty crazy."

Hurt filled her eyes and she turned to walk away. He

caught her wrist and felt the rapid beat of her pulse. "But it makes sense, in a crazy sort of way." He swept his thumb across the velvety soft skin on her wrist. "John McClane didn't trust you, but he sure as hell wanted you."

"And Zeke?" Her voice was a bare whisper, her body poised to flee.

His lips curled upward. "Zeke decided to trust you. The loving part came easy after that." He cupped her nape and drew her close. A sliver of green surrounded her large pupils. "Both John and I love you, too."

She giggled, her warm breath fanning his lips. "You do realize we're both a little crazy."

He smiled, breathing in her essence. "Don't you mean all three of us?"

Shoni laughed and threw her arms around him. Zeke didn't know who kissed who first, but he was more than willing to participate.

SHONI listened to Zeke's steady breathing beside her. For the past ten days, they'd been living at the condo instead of Shoni's tiny apartment. Once Zeke's cabin was rebuilt, they would move out there. Zeke had confided that maybe the loss of the cabin had been a blessing. This time, instead of filling it with what Tiffany had wanted, the furniture would be something Shoni and Zeke picked out together.

Just as Tyler had predicted, the death of Nick Bender was ruled a justified shooting. It bothered her that she'd killed a man, and between Zeke and the police counselor, she'd worked through most of her guilt. She had agreed to work with Delon, who had taken Raff's betrayal hard. When Delon had returned after taking a few days off, his colorful attire had been toned down. Surprisingly, Shoni missed the flash of his bright shirts in the bullpen.

Her arson case was closed. Jensen and Paridot were pleading guilty and trying to get the best deal they could.

Paladin Security locked its doors two days after the arrests. Raff admitted to accepting payoffs from Jensen, a former military associate, in exchange for information about the case and Zeke. It seemed Raff's creditors were pounding on his door after too many years of living beyond his means. Jamar was facing life imprisonment and was trying to strike a deal with the DA before his two thugs did. Last she heard, Jamar was losing the race. He wouldn't be bothering Lainey again. Mishon was also in jail, facing accessory and drug charges. As Estelle had said, Mishon would get the help she needed, but at a high price.

Only one piece of unfinished business remained.

Shoni rolled her head toward the clock. Ten forty-five. She and Zeke had ended up in bed after dinner and she'd managed to exhaust him. She shifted to her side to gaze down at him. His long eyelashes brushed his cheeks and his whiskers were dark against his skin. The shaggy hair had been trimmed to his collar, exposing his nape, which she found extremely sexy. She could barely make out his dimples and reached out to trace one, but stopped an angel's breath from his skin.

Her mother had been right. Soul mates were real, and sometimes a person was fortunate enough in their lifetime to find theirs.

Shoni eased out of the bed and carried her clothes into the living room, where she dressed. She left her badge and Glock in the locked box in a kitchen drawer. Those held no place in what she had to do.

Pausing by her bedroom door, she gazed at Zeke's face, limned by the moonlight. Her heart expanded painfully in her chest.

"I'm sorry," she whispered.

She carried her shoes into the hallway and tugged them on. As she passed the security desk in the lobby, she nodded at the guard, whom she didn't recognize. She retrieved the metal box from the trunk of her Camry and slid it under the front seat.

LIGHT spilled out of the parted curtains of the living room window, just as she expected. Durkett often stayed up late drinking after his wife and son went to bed. It gave her the opening she needed to get to him without being seen.

She leaned down and brought the metal box out from under the seat. Opening the lid, she stared down at the anonymous handgun. The dull steel both beckoned and repelled her. Her fingers shook as she picked it up, its weight feeling awkward and unbalanced in her hand. She ignored the sense of wrongness and willed herself to get out of the car, but her muscles refused to obey her.

Killing Durkett wasn't like shooting Bender. This would be cold-blooded murder.

No, it's justice. Durkett killed her mother while driving drunk. His pattern of drinking almost ensured he'd hit someone else someday. She was saving an innocent life by ridding the world of him.

Killing him won't bring back your mother.

Her father's voice?

No, it couldn't be. But even he couldn't stop her. Nothing mattered but avenging her mother's death.

She shoved open her door and jumped out, the nondescript gun in her hand.

What about Zeke? If you're caught, you'll lose him.

Her mother's voice this time.

Shoni pressed her hands to her head. "I have to do this. It's justice."

"No, it's not."

Shoni spun around to find Zeke standing ten feet away. She blinked. Was he just another apparition her conscience conjured? He didn't disappear.

"What are you doing here?" she demanded.

"I followed you."

Anger surged through her. "You had no right."

He took a limping step toward her. "If I don't, then who does?" he asked gently.

She retreated. Nobody was to know, especially Zeke. "You aren't supposed to be here."

He lifted his outspread arms. "But I am. So now what?"

Shoni's heart pounded and she couldn't get enough air into her laboring lungs. This was to be *her* secret. "He killed Mom and the courts can't touch him. It's up to me."

"Killing him won't bring back your mother."

Her mouth gaped. Those were the same words her father "spoke" to her.

"You know what it's like to kill another human being," Zeke continued. "And you did that to save my life. But if you kill this man, it'll be murder, pure and simple."

"It's justice."

Zeke shook his head. "It's revenge." He took two more steps toward her and his blue eyes pierced her. "You're a damned good cop, Shoni. You help people like Estelle and Lainey. And John McClane. If you murder that man, you're going to prison for the rest of your life. You won't be able to help anyone ever again. Is that what you want? Is that what your father would want?" He paused and his eyes glistened under the streetlights. "If you do this, I'll lose you. Even if you don't get caught, I'll know. You"—his voice fractured—"You won't be the woman I love."

Shoni stared at him, at the face she'd come to know as well as her own. Anguish and desperation sharpened his features. She turned toward the house that sheltered the person who took her mother away from her. Then she glanced down at the cheap gun in her hand. It would be so easy. Squeeze the trigger, watch him die.

But it wasn't only Durkett she'd be killing. It would be

herself . . . and Zeke. A tear slid down her cheek and her arm dropped to her side. The gun slipped from her fingers to the street.

Zeke limped forward, leaned over, and picked up the weapon. He folded her in his arms and she wrapped hers around his waist, burying her face in his chest as silent tears coursed down her cheeks.

I'm proud of you, Shoni.

Her father's words surrounded her, suffused her with love.

Loud voices startled her, and she raised her head to see Durkett's wife coming out the door, their son in her arms and a bag slung over her shoulder. She couldn't understand the words, but the tone was clear.

The woman strapped her son in the child's seat, ignoring Durkett's drunken curses. She got into the driver's seat and backed out of the driveway, rubber squealing on concrete. The car disappeared down the street.

Durkett dropped onto the porch and buried his face in his hands.

"Justice," Zeke said softly.

It would have to be enough.

Shoni swallowed the lump in her throat and raised her head to find Zeke's loving gaze on her. "Let's go home."

Zeke nodded and ushered her to his SUV. "We'll get your car tomorrow."

Zeke helped her into the passenger seat and snapped her seat belt in place. He got in the driver's side and remained silent as he drove.

"Would you have let me shoot him?" Shoni asked, fearful of the answer but more afraid not to ask.

Zeke glanced at her and reached across to thread his fingers through hers. "No. But I wouldn't have stopped you to save him." He paused. "I would've done it to save you."

Shoni blinked. Her throat was thick and aching, but she smiled. "My protector."

"Always." He lifted her hand to his lips and brushed a kiss across her knuckles.

Tears blurred her vision and she turned her gaze to the night sky. A shooting star, followed closely by another.

And Shoni swore she heard her parents' loving laughter.